Devious Magic

Stella Mayweather Series

USA TODAY Bestselling Author
CAMILLA CHAFER

ALSO BY CAMILLA CHAFER

The Complete Stella Mayweather Series

Illicit Magic
Unruly Magic
Devious Magic
Magic Rising
Arcane Magic
Endless Magic

Deadlines Mystery Trilogy

Deadlines
Dead to the World
Dead Ringers

CHAPTER ONE

Something strange was going on, I could tell. With three housemates, all deeply rooted to the supernatural community in some way or another, things were rarely ever quiet in my home. But today my boyfriend, Evan, sat working silently at his laptop and my friend and fellow witch, Kitty, had shut herself in the kitchen for the past hour. As for Étoile, another fellow witch... Étoile disappeared a few days ago as she often did. I suspected the quiet was something to do with my birthday and that they were planning something. I tried to suppress a little smile at my suspicions and let them get on with whatever surprise they were secretly cooking up between them.

Looking up from the college brochure I was reading, I glanced around the room but saw nothing out of the ordinary that would give me a clue. Evan was across the room at his usual spot behind the big table that functioned as his desk. He looked up, flashed me a smile full of pearly white teeth that contrasted beautifully against his olive skin, blew me a kiss, and returned his gaze to the laptop screen.

He ran a business that dealt almost entirely with the supernatural world. The best paying work, he told me, involved catching and delivering supe criminals, like a bounty hunter, only a thousand times more dangerous. His firm was entrusted with delivering important packages and other things that required secrecy and diplomacy as well as the protection from something, or someone. His work was unattractive to any sane person, and, while on the surface that all sounded pretty exciting, Evan was currently hands-off the more physical duties. For the present, he was spared the ones that would take him away from home for days or weeks at a time.

Though my eyes were back on the brochure, I got to the point where I was zoning out, my thoughts full of Evan. I wasn't so full of myself that I thought he stayed purely because he would miss me otherwise, though naturally, I hoped he would. As a latecomer to witchcraft, my innate skills were something that troubled me my whole life. Evan's daily lessons in controlling my magic were vital to me, not only for my personal development but for my protection too. We'd already confronted lethally dangerous witches on numerous occasions and I didn't want to be unprepared ever again. I didn't ask, but I sensed Evan was getting bored without all the action he was accustomed to.

Eavesdropping, I strained to hear my other two housemates. Étoile, a witch like me and my alternate teacher, had announced earlier that she was going to be away for a few days, though she hadn't bothered to say where she was going. Instead, she just dematerialised from existence. "Shimmering," as it was called, was something she was currently teaching me to control. Growing up, I found it frightening and unmanageable. Now I was getting to grips with it, it was pretty exciting. The more I practised, the stronger, and more precise, that part of my magic felt. Magic was firmly part of me now but instead of it controlling me, like it once had, now I commanded it instinctively. While I could only travel short distances at the moment, and found the concentration necessary for shimmering quite tiring, I had ambitions to shimmer much further one day; maybe even to foreign countries. The idea of home, however, was something I kept stuffed firmly at the back of my mind. I missed England, but not enough to return. One day, maybe, but not yet.

I assumed Étoile would come back as unexpectedly as she left but, since I still couldn't hear her at all, I knew she hadn't returned. Not hearing the familiarly faint sounds of her chatting on the phone or moving from room to room in the old, creaky house let me know she was still gone, even though she mentioned celebrating my birthday. She hadn't called in the couple of days she'd been away, which surprised me and I wondered what was going on that she was being so secretive about. I suspected it might have had something to do with her younger sister, Astra, who was very ill and slowly recovering, but I couldn't be sure. I spoke to their other sister, Seren, who was now my boss, as well as my friend, only this morning so I knew Étoile hadn't gone to visit her.

Through the closed kitchen door, my other housemate, Kitty, was listening to music and now making enough noise for everyone as she sang along to it. She banished me from the kitchen straight after breakfast so my ears veritably perked up, looking for clues. As long as she wasn't making potions, I was fine. Like me, Kitty was also a witch and had the unique power to affect the weather which seemed like an odd but very specific skill to me She took great pleasure in creating whatever conditions she chose or preferred. She'd even managed to make it snow over Christmas, much to everyone's delight.

"Have you picked any courses yet?" Evan interjected, suddenly interrupting my thoughts and I turned to him, dropping the brochure onto my lap.

I shook my head. "There's a lot I want to do. Do I take business classes for career development? Or English literature for the fun of it?" I always regretted having to leave school at eighteen, but being a foster child after my parents' deaths, I found it necessary to make a living for myself once I became of age. Now, my life was finally settled after a tumultuous year and I was determined to better myself.

"Why not take both?"

"What if I can't keep up? What if everyone else is really smart?" So many other things in my life loomed in front of me. Alongside the lessons with Evan every day, were those from Étoile, not to mention my part-time job, which took up another three or four hours. At least, I could work flexibly and remotely. As it was, I hardly had any time for study... for now.

Evan held back a laugh. "You'll keep up, and you know you're smart. If you want, you can always transfer credits and go full time to get your degree even faster." He ducked his head back down before I could reply. He suggested more than once that I move to his home in Texas where I could commute to a university more reasonably. All I had to do was

4

say yes, but I couldn't, even though I found it weighing more heavily on my mind.

For the first time in my life, I had a home, my own home, and I was in the honeymoon period of loving every inch of it, not to mention all the new friends I'd made in Wilding. Starting over again scared me a little, despite having Evan. I was being selfish, I knew, because why should my wanting to stay in my home outweigh Evan's need for his? It was time for a compromise that benefited both of us.

"Annalise is walking towards the house." Evan's voice jolted me from my thoughts and I followed the direction of his eyes as my friend, and neighbour, walked along the driveway towards my property. After shuffling my notepad and the brochure into a little pile that I laid on the coffee table, I went to answer the door.

"I've come to invite you to lunch," she said, leaning forward to kiss my cheek. Her blonde curls, streaked with pink, bounced loose. Like always, she smelled of lemon with the faint tinge of earth. She lived across the street from me, in the only other house on this long stretch of road. We'd been friends ever since I arrived, sad, frightened and alone several months earlier. So far, our amity had survived the revelation that she and her brother, Gage, were both werewolves and I was a witch, not to mention, my kissing Gage. As far as friendships went, we were solid. "My treat," she added.

"Sounds lovely. Is Beau coming with us?" I looked behind her for her muscle-bound wall of a boyfriend. An ex-marine and, yes, a werewolf, Beau was her high school sweetheart and lately, they had rekindled their feelings for one another.

"Nah. He's at work."

I looked over my shoulder. "Evan, you want to come?"

"I would love to, but I have a spreadsheet to finish."

"How dull," I quipped.

There was the barest roll of his eyes as he nodded. "Go. Have fun."

"Should we get Kitty?" Annalise asked, just as karaoke Kitty reached a high note and drummed on the counters in accompaniment. We both winced. Kitty found a job in Wilding, our town, as a freelance beauty therapist. She was far better at tweezing and painting nails than she was at singing. We all agreed on that; she practised on us often enough and my nails were currently a fabulous shade of turquoise blue.

Crossing the living room, I was almost to the kitchen when Kitty stuck her head around, her apron-clad body shielded by the door. Her head was blocking my view into the kitchen. There was a streak of flour in her hair. "Hey, Annalise." She waved. "Thank you, but no."

"You didn't even know what I was going to ask."

"To go to lunch, I heard, but I'm... busy."

I craned my head, trying to sneak a look round the door, but Kitty pushed it further closed until her head was smushed between the door and jamb. She puckered her forehead at me.

"Fine." I backed up, defeated. "Smells nice, whatever you're doing in there."

"I'll clean up, promise. You don't have to tell me." Kitty stuck her tongue out, then shut the door with a soft bump. She resumed her singing again.

"Looks like it's just the two of us," I said, grabbing my jacket from the hook. Annalise linked her arm through mine, with a squeeze, and flashed me a perfect smile that belied razor sharp canines. "I'll drive."

Darla's was the first place I set foot into when I arrived in Wilding and now I felt like a regular. I waved to the eponymous Darla, proprietor and good-natured town gossip, as Annalise and I slid into the last remaining booth of the lunch hour. Well known for home-cooked food and prices that didn't make you wince, Darla's was always popular. Right now, I had a craving for her pancakes, which didn't sound like lunch until you saw the stack she served piled high with strawberries and sauce. My stomach gave a little whine in anticipation at the thought.

"So, what are your plans for the weekend?" asked Annalise as she slid off her winter coat. I know I said she was a werewolf but I certainly don't mean she was shedding her fur at the table! Her hair did look fuller and glossier, but it was cold in Wilding and we were bundled up in our winter wear. She looked like she wanted me to ask her what she was doing, more than she wanted to hear my answer, so I kept it brief, "Dinner out with Evan tonight, and no, he won't tell me where, then nothing for the weekend. I have a good book to read. You?"

We had to wait for a moment while Darla ambled over and slid two mugs onto the table, pouring coffee into each. "Staying for lunch?" she asked.

"We sure are," smiled Annalise, picking up a plastic-sleeved menu.

"I'll send you a waitress." Darla popped her gum and moved onto the next table.

Annalise leaned in, her hands wrapped around the mug. "Beau is taking me to an inn by the sea. We're going to drive up tomorrow night and stay there all weekend." I gave the appropriate squeal of glee in response. "This is the first time we've been away together, Stella. He's stayed at my house before, but it's not really the same when Gage is around. And we can't stay at his place too often because of his roommates. He's thinking of getting an apartment of his own." She dropped her voice an octave. "We might move in together."

I knew the appropriate response wasn't *but we won't be neighbours anymore!* So, instead I said, "I'm really happy for you and I hope you have a great trial run this weekend."

"Oh, you think that's what it is? Maybe he won't be so keen after putting up with me for two solid days."

"Are you kidding me? Beau is head over heels."

"Yeah." She giggled. "I hope there's a lot of shagging this weekend, as you Brits say."

"Cheers to that, as we Brits say." I clinked my mug against hers in salute to the fun side of relationships.

"I never thought I'd say it, but I think Beau might be the one. I've been there, done that with the whole marriage thing, and getting divorced from that asshole was the best thing I ever did, so... I never thought I'd feel like this again." Annalise had a faraway smile on her face, like she was in some other place, not sitting opposite me in the bustling diner. "I feel so alive."

"What does Gage think? Will he mind you moving out?"

"No, I don't think so. I guess he'll like having the

house back to himself and it's not like I won't be in and out every day anyway. Plus, he and Beau get on really well. Maybe Gage will finally get a girlfriend if I move out," she mused.

"Oh?"

"I think he's dating someone, but you know Gage, kiss, don't tell."

That hit me unexpectedly hard. Gage and I were getting pretty close once. We dated, kissed and even spent the night in the same bed (alcohol-related and purely platonic... mostly!) On one occasion, we even came very close to having sex, but if we had, it would have been, for me, as much from anger as it was lust. Gage was a handsome man, tall and strong with a jaw covered in near permanent stubble, and thick dark hair. Although I'd always found him attractive, in my heart, I loved Evan. As much as I liked, admired, and yes, even lusted after, Gage... it just wasn't going to happen.

If I were completely honest with myself, some lingering feelings remained but I didn't want to be an indecisive woman who strung along two guys. I made my decision, picked my guy and I was sticking to him. The idea of Gage with someone else, however, still stung. *What was wrong with me?* I shook my head, trying to rattle the thought right out of me and tried to concentrate on what Annalise was saying; something about the inn with its huge fireplaces and the coastal walks they were planning to take.

"I'm going to get the full report when you get back, right?"

Annalise winked, a smile slipping onto her face. "Oh yes."

A perky, redheaded waitress took our orders, her

shoulders hunched, eyes concentrating intently on her notepad as we decided on our order. Her name badge read Aimee. She was new and I thought I'd seen her outside Wilding High a few times.

Wilding was a small town, almost a cliché in that it was the type where everyone grew up knowing everyone else. It put me at a disadvantage when I first arrived but the inhabitants were nothing if not hospitable and welcoming. Most passers-by would never realise that Wilding harboured a fairly big secret: it was home to a sizeable werewolf pack. I still didn't know whether Wilding actively protected their lupine residents, or thought they were some archaic myth. Whatever the case, they resulted in some weird town ordinances such as no pets (no one wanted them accidentally eaten), and few businesses stayed open late whenever the moon was full.

"You know what, hon'? I've got a library book that I need to return. Would you mind if I dropped it off while we're waiting for our lunch? I meant to do it yesterday but clean forgot." Our non-nutritious but pleasing combination of fruit pancakes and French toast would be at least ten more minutes. The library was just down the street, around a ten-minute walk, there and back if Annalise were quick. Our food would probably hit the table the moment she returned.

"No, go right ahead."

Annalise flashed a smile at me, grabbed her purse and coat and left. I watched as she crossed the street, walking hurriedly away, hands in her pockets and head bowed against the cold.

I people-watched while I waited. The thing about small town living was that it was easy to spot newcomers, since they were so obviously out of place, unlike my previous life in London. Here, I could spot out-of-towners as well as tourists who visited our pretty little town. Evan taught me something pretty vital, too. He showed me how to recognise the signature of a supernatural; to know when I was near a witch, daemon, wolf or something else.

Looking around, I tried my hand at spotting supes. I counted two wolves walking together across the street. Jay, whom I'd met previously, (I'd even seen him naked once, but not by design and I tried not to think about it), and his companion, someone I hadn't seen before. I smiled at my skills before glancing away, my eyes coming to rest on a woman sitting on a bench outside the bakery. *Witch.* That surprised me. I didn't know there were any other witches in town. I must have stared a moment or two too long because she looked up, then around her as if she knew she were being observed, before getting up and walking away. It might be nothing, she might just be passing through, but even so, I made a mental note to mention it to Étoile later.

The lunch crowd brought out a mixed bag of people. Suited men and women from the local businesses that hugged Main Street, teenagers from Wilding High with their wolf emblem jackets and scarves, people running errands and mothers holding the hands of little, chatty children.

It all looked so normal but I knew better than most how deceiving appearances could be. Ever since I discovered, in the worst possible way, that people just weren't what they seemed, I'd been more than hesitant to let my guard down for a moment. Sometimes danger seemed to lurk everywhere I looked. The expectation of finding it seemed to be embedded in my psyche now. However, my instincts had gotten a lot better, though that came with a price – being hunted. Witch hunters as well as witches, you name it; I have a target on my back.

I checked my watch. Close to ten minutes had passed.

"Careful now, the plates are warm," said Aimee, sliding my order in front of me, then Annalise's on her side of the table. She set down cutlery wrapped in a napkin and hurried away, notepad out, to wait on a young family who had just entered.

I inhaled the warm, sweet aroma of pancakes, relieved that right now, the only thing being hunted was the strawberry scooting around my plate as it evaded the stabbing tines of my fork. I checked my watch again. Ten full minutes. Annalise should have been back by now and it seemed rude to eat without her, even though my stomach was giving off an ominous rumble. Sighing, I dropped my fork with a clatter and picked up the berry between my thumb and forefinger, biting into it just as I looked up and saw Gage round the corner. He caught my eye, grinned, gave a casual wave and mouthed "Happy birthday!"

I returned his smile just before he barrelled past, bags of dry cleaning slung over his arm, clearly in a hurry to get his chores over with on his only day off. It took every single bit of restraint for me not to turn my head and watch his fine figure retreat. Having never before finding two men attractive and having that interest returned, I didn't really know what to make of my behaviour. Kitty would probably know the right thing to say. I decided I would ask her later.

Catching sight of Annalise's cinnamon French toast, sitting deliciously opposite me, I took another quick look out the window for Annalise, wondering what was holding her up when a shadow fell across my table. Looking up, I expected to see Darla or the pretty, redheaded waitress.

Instead, I viewed a thickset man in a black suit and a shirt so pristinely white, it was like a fresh snowfall. He slid into the booth opposite me, as though I invited him there. I frowned at him, assuming he made a mistake and waited for him to leave. He didn't.

"Good morning, Miss Mayweather," he said after a long pause, resting his wrists on the table and folding his hands together.

I smiled hesitantly at him, in case I knew him while I tried to place his face. It was no good. I couldn't think where I could possibly know him. "Do we know each other?" I asked, thinking I would apologise for my ignorance later after he'd jogged my memory.

"You could say that," he replied. Picking up the menu, he studied it for a moment, then flicked his eyes up at me. "What's good here?"

"Everything," I said, which was true.

He laughed, a short, sharp sound that didn't have a lot of humour in it. "Unfortunately I'm not quite that hungry." He signalled a waitress with a shake of the menu and she walked over quickly, notepad ready. "Coffee," he said to her, his voice easy and melodic. "And... apple pie. Is the apple pie good, Miss Mayweather? It sounds good."

"Sure," I said, now completely distracted from the pancakes I'd already started demolishing. "I don't

13

mean to be rude, but I really can't place you." There was something off about him, something that made my nerves tingle. I couldn't place him at all. His accent was English, in a very proper way that didn't reveal his region, and that was what made him stand out the most. That, and the arrogant way he had taken over my table. This man was a long way from home and I had a bad feeling about him.

"We haven't met formally," the man replied, his attention on me again, coolly assessing me, but not at all annoyed by my question. "But you met some friends of mine, almost a year ago now."

"Oh?" A year ago I'd been on the verge of leaving England, after being chased by a gang of men whom I now knew were murderous witch hunters. They were behind a string of merciless burnings across Europe. The night I left England, I had nearly fallen prey to them and it terrified me.

The man smiled; his teeth a perfect row of white, expensive, dentistry. He could have been a businessman, a lawyer, anything. I was certain I'd never met him.

"Miss Mayweather, you are of interest to my employer," he said, "and my employer would very much like to meet you."

"Are you offering me... a job?" I asked, my brows knitting together as I became purposefully dense.

He laughed. "No, no. My employer has, shall we say, an interest in you. He asked me to approach you, to introduce us to you. His last attempt to make contact with you was unsuccessful and he was most displeased."

"Who is your employer?" I asked.

The man leant back in his seat while Aimee set a

mug down, pouring it to the brim with coffee, then adding a plate of hot apple pie with a little flourish. The man dug his fork in and took a large bite, chewing on it. After a couple of mouthfuls, during which he made appreciative noises, he put his fork down. "First things first, let me introduce myself. My name is Mr. Jones."

"Really?" I blurted out and he laughed, the lines around his eyes creasing. He was probably somewhere in his forties, cheeks slightly puffy, but clean-shaven with dark brown hair, cut very short. I would be hard pressed to describe him later, he was so average.

"Does it matter?"

"Yes. You know my name."

"That I do, Miss Mayweather. That I do." He picked up his fork again, tapping the tines on the plate. "This really is good pie. Am I putting you off your pancakes? I do apologise. Don't let me stop you from enjoying your breakfast."

"What's your first name?" I asked.

He hesitated. "John."

"John Jones?"

He smiled again. It didn't reach his eyes, of course. They remained hard and cold, despite his easy smile. "No, I don't believe it either, but, like I said, it hardly matters. Let's be formal, Miss Mayweather. My employer demands formality."

"Who is your employer?" I asked slowly, my mind racing. I narrowed it down to a couple of unpalatable options. My first thought was the Council, who had returned to my life only a few months ago. It was after I'd gotten caught up in a very strange magical case that drew a lot of witches to Wilding. The

Council were the governing body of witches, a secretive faction of the population. Part organisers, part regulators, they set the rules that witches lived by, and enforced them, imposing sanctions when things went awry, or when a witch turned rogue.

The Council had been in disarray for several months when the last leader was murdered right in front of me. It was that disorganisation which left all the other witches vying for power. Council leadership would be a major coup for whoever got elected, be it legally obtained or by intimidating the competition.

My second thought was the FBI or CIA; some big organisation that might want to harness a witch's power even if they didn't quite believe in it. But that still didn't explain Jones' accent. My final guess was the most unpalatable of them all.

Mr Jones took his time eating another piece of pie before he answered. "My employer is known by many names, but I believe you know him as the head of the Brotherhood."

CHAPTER TWO

My fingers dug into the thick upholstery of the booth bench, my eyes searching for an exit, while I absorbed Mr. Jones' revelation. From the booth's location in the centre of the diner, I realised how isolated I was and my heart sank. Mr. Jones sat between the door and me. A plate glass window with "Darla's Diner" in a thick red font stood between the street and me. To get to the rear exit that opened onto the rear alley would mean somehow traversing the counter before Jones could catch me. Then I would have to dart through the kitchens: all three completely impossible. Much as I hated to admit it, I was trapped.

Mr. Jones barely glanced at me as he forked off a piece of pie, steering it into his mouth. He waved the fork at me as he swallowed. "There's no way out, Miss Mayweather. Besides, we're just having a friendly chat. I'd hate for it to be cut short," he said, his fork already aimed for the last piece.

"Your people tried to kill me," I hissed, lowering my voice. The enticing aroma of my pancakes suddenly smelled cloyingly, sickeningly sweet.

Mr. Jones shook his head, his eyes rolling just a fraction. "Not I. That's a job for the minions." Pushing his empty plate away, he reached for his mug and sipped the coffee, while riveting his cold eyes on me the whole time. "Do pay attention, Miss Mayweather, you can't leave until we've finished our chat."

He was wrong. I could. I could shimmer out of there, even though I knew I wasn't supposed to do it publicly. All I had to do was lean down, out of sight, so no one else noticed, and disappear. It didn't matter if this Mr. Jones saw. He already knew who I was, so it stood to reason that he had some idea as to what I could do. In thirty seconds, I could be safe, away from his mild-mannered threats.

"I know what you're thinking and I advise you against it," Jones warned.

Playing the innocent, I asked, "Advise me against what?"

He leant forward, closing the span of table between us. He hissed the word as if it were distasteful. "Disappearing."

"Why shouldn't I?"

"Because I'll kill every person in this place, Miss Mayweather, and that blood will be on your hands." Mr. Jones arched his eyebrows as he leaned back against the red leather, one hand stroking it as if to remind me that the same colour could splatter every surface, if he so chose.

I glanced around the diner, at the row of people who sat eating at the counter, talking amongst themselves; then at the table behind me where the family with the two little children, sucking their juice through straws sat giggling. Their little legs were kicking gleefully back and forth. As far as arguments went, he had a good one, and I wasn't prepared to test it. I wasn't even going to ask him how he could kill so many people without someone stopping him. It seemed wiser just to accept that he could, rather than encourage him into a demonstration. Instead, I just nodded, appearing somewhat defeated. "I thought that was for the minions." Perhaps mocking him wasn't the best idea, but it slipped out.

"Don't look so cross. It doesn't suit your pretty face."

His hand rested on the coffee cup and my already nervous magic began to spiral. I channelled it into the coffee until it reached boiling point, with little bubbles teasing the surface. Jones, staring at me the whole time with his vacant eyes, put it to his lips and sipped, only to shudder when it scalded him.

"Cheap trick, Miss Mayweather," he murmured, licking his lips, then dabbing them with a napkin. I didn't feel bad, not one bit; I hoped it blistered his tongue.

I waited, expecting him to do something to chastise me but Jones just sat there, staring, and panic rose inside me. My magic bubbled, unbidden once again, to the surface and I felt it tickling my skin as I struggled to restrain it for the sake of every person who could be injured from the fallout.

Jones watched my inner conflict, his eyes boring into me as I tried to match his immovable demeanour despite the magic inside me looking for an outlet. I focused on my training, on neutralising my power. Whatever he had planned, I didn't want to be a part of it but I was trapped. As time ticked past and I waited, I knew I needed to be ready to defend myself and anyone else I could.

Most of all, I knew I needed help before Annalise came back, stumbling onto us, As soon as she slid in next to me, she would completely block my exit and put herself within arm's reach of Jones. Like hell would I put my friend in any danger of the witch hunter sitting in front of me. Especially if there were even the remotest possibility that he knew what she was.

On autopilot, I called silently, wordlessly yelling to my closest ally. Gage. I only wished he could hear me, as well as the desperation in my soundless plea. Mr. Jones waited, watching his coffee cup. I wished frantically that Gage would come back so I could get his attention somehow, so he could rescue me from the Brotherhood's foot soldier. Jones' gaze remained solid, his eyes threatening in a way that was so subtle, only I could see it. He was waiting to see what I would do.

Thoughts spiralled through my head, but there was only one obvious route I could take. If I couldn't escape, I would have to play along for a while, draw him out, and find out what the witch hunters wanted. So I did nothing. "What do you want?" I asked, simply.

"That's the right question, Miss Mayweather." Jones' thin lips curled at the edges into a smile but his body didn't relax one bit. "My employer extends an invitation. He would like to meet with you at his home in England. He doesn't travel much. The house is called Hawkscroft and is located in Yorkshire. Perhaps you've been there?"

I shook my head, no, saying, "I can't." I left

England almost a year ago, when my friend, Étoile, rescued me from the Brotherhood. They chased me out, and I stayed out. I even had the idiotic notion that the Brotherhood couldn't find me, even though the occasional news of a murder could be attributed to them on this side of the Atlantic. They had been strangely, ominously, quiet of late, not that I'd been complacent in any way. I couldn't afford to be.

Mr. Jones arched an eyebrow at me again, his voice cajoling this time, "I'm sure you can. We've gone to a lot of trouble to find you."

"How did you find me?" I asked.

"Let's just say... a little birdie whispered your address in my employer's ear."

Fear rippled through me, first as raging hot anger, then clamouring cold. I'd been warned that the concentration of power created by the witches who came to Wilding months ago would bring unwelcome attention. I couldn't fathom, however, who would be cruel enough to pass my address onto the Brotherhood. As far as I knew, only witches and wolves attended our gathering. Oh, and a ghost, I remembered. But she had been forcibly returned to where she belonged and thereby prevented from causing more damage. I glanced at Mr. Jones, hoping some trace on his face would declare his revelation as a lie. I saw nothing. Nothing to indicate if it were true and nothing to say it was false.

He pulled an envelope from his inside suit pocket and pushed it towards me where it rested in the middle of the table. Then he tapped it with his index finger. "Inside this envelope is a plane ticket and funds to cover any unexpected complications you might encounter. We will arrange for a driver to collect you from the airport and take you to Hawkscroft. You will stay as my employer's guest."

"Why does he want to meet me?"

"That's not for me to know."

With one finger, I pushed the envelope back. "I'm not coming."

I almost laughed when Mr. Jones pushed it towards me again; it seemed so comical. "I don't think you understand, Miss Mayweather. It's not so much an invitation, as a... summons. You will attend."

"And if I don't?"

Mr. Jones looked around the diner, taking in the familiar faces of my adopted hometown's residents. "Consequences," he said in a low voice. "There will be consequences. I suggest you don't test my employer. He's not... pleasant when crossed."

"You can't hurt me," I retorted. He could, though. I knew that. But this employer of his was perhaps the only reason I'd survived this conversation so far. I could feel the fear slicing through my bones as he laid his cold gaze on me. In my head, I yelled for Gage again, the fear emanating from me even as I sat still, tense enough to stop the shaking that followed in its tracks. Of all the people who could help me, Gage was the closest. I knew he would defend me, or at least, offer some kind of backup. That might make this man think twice about threatening me not to mention all the people in the diner. Even without his wolf heritage, Gage was a tall, imposing man, someone to be reckoned with.

"No?" Mr. Jones leant back in his seat, seemingly amused. "Are we negotiating? Or are we in denial?"

I kept my voice low. "Tell your employer that I don't care to meet him or have anything to do with the Brotherhood. I want to be left alone."

"Oh, Miss Mayweather." Mr. Jones shook his head, doing his best to look sad. "You and I both know that's never going to happen." Standing up, he dabbed his mouth with a napkin, which he then laid over his plate. "Before I forget, happy birthday! I do apologise for not bringing a gift, but I hope you'll think of me when you cut your cake."

"Go to hell."

The corners of his mouth flickered. "What makes you think we're not already there?" He dropped enough bills on the table to cover his breakfast and mine and walked out. At the door, he turned and smiled, giving me a little salute. I thought about giving him a little salute of my own, but I resisted the urge.

I was frozen with fear for a moment at Mr. Jones' summons and the damn envelope resting on the table in front of me. It was strange how menacing I found it, how repulsive it was to see my name written across the front in flowing black ink, all curls and flourishes. Before I could really think about it, I slipped out of the booth and raced outside.

For a moment, I stood on the sidewalk, right at the junction where I could see the whole intersection; but the man had gone, almost like he melted away, and was never here. A moment later, I felt strong hands grabbing me and I barely stifled the shriek rising in my throat as they spun me around.

Gage's eyes searched mine as he held onto me, his hands clamped over my upper arms. "What happened?" he huffed, breathless, like he'd been running hard. "I heard you. I heard you in my head, calling me. What's wrong?"

"I... I was calling you. He was here, he was..." I

gasped back a relieved, but frightened sob, looking wildly around me, expecting the man to come back at any moment.

"Who, Stella?" Gage gripped me harder. "Did someone hurt you? Tell me!"

My hair fell over my face as I shook my head. I brushed it back roughly with my hands, tucking the stray strands behind my ears. "The Brotherhood," I gasped, at last, continuing to turn in a circle, scanning the landscape for Mr. Jones. "The Brotherhood was here. He sat at my table and he..." The tears were running freely down my cheeks now and Gage pulled me into his chest. He held me close to him, vaporising my fear with his safe embrace. I could hear his heartbeat in my ear where my head was pressed against him. Circling my arms around him, I let him hold me. As I hugged him, I felt so grateful for the comfort of someone safe and familiar. I tried not to think about the last time he had his arms wrapped around me, and how that had been so very different to the comfort he offered me now.

"You're okay," he whispered, stroking my hair as I stiffened, momentarily feeling awkward in his arms. Gradually, he seemed to realise that, and reluctantly let me go, His hands were still wrapped around mine as he stared down at me. "I won't let anyone hurt you. You're safe, sweetheart, you're safe now," he promised.

We stood there, side by side, hand in hand, for what felt like forever until Darla came outside carrying my jacket, the envelope and a small brown bag containing a box with Annalise's uneaten lunch. Reluctantly, or with relief – I couldn't tell – I detached my fingers from Gage's to take them from her, muttering, "Thanks."

"You okay, sugar?" Darla asked, her forehead puckering into a frown.

I nodded, not trusting myself to speak.

"That man bothering you?" she persisted.

I nodded, again.

"Hmm, well, don't be a scaredy-cat. You call me over if he bothers you again," said Darla. "You need a coffee to go? Warm you up?"

"I'm taking her home," said Gage, slipping his arm around my shoulders, and giving me a reassuring squeeze. This time, it was less tender and more like being clamped by a vice.

"I've got my car," I protested. "I can't just leave it here. Plus, I'm waiting for Annalise." I could just see her now, walking hurriedly towards us, her pace picking up when she saw Gage. She waved happily.

"Leave your keys with me. I'll make sure it gets to your house," offered Darla. "Look at you, shivering. You don't look like you're in any condition to drive."

"She's right, Stella. Annalise can drive your car home. I was leaving anyway and it's not like you're out of my way. Just let me take you home."

"Lucky you," I thought I heard Darla say under her breath as she turned away, heading back to her diner. Annalise took her place a moment later, searching my face then Gage's, her happy demeanour faltering.

"I got caught up. Sorry. What happened?" she asked, looking puzzled.

Five minutes later, Annalise had the whole story, my keys and her lunch bag, and I was being bundled into Gage's car. I was glad he wasn't riding his motorcycle today because I wasn't sure I could concentrate enough on balancing.

"You ever done that before?" Gage asked, taking his eyes off the road for a moment to look me over. He hadn't said anything for a few minutes after settling me into the passenger seat of his car. I was quiet, trying to remember everything so I could retell it later to Evan and our housemates. "That mind-transmitting thing?"

I shook my head. "No. I was just as surprised as you. I didn't think you'd even hear me."

"Loud and clear. Took me a minute to realise I wasn't just hearing things, but, you know, actually *hearing* things."

"Sorry about that. I really don't know how I did it. I panicked and I'd just seen you so I... shouted."

"No problem." Gage took his hand off the wheel to pat my leg. "I'm probably receptive to it because of my blood anyway."

"Do werewolves mind read?" I shuffled in my seat to face him, curious. Neither Gage nor Annalise talked much about the other part of their lives, though they had no problem with me seeing them in wolf form now. All my knowledge about werewolves came from myths or Evan and Étoile, so it was all second hand.

"Only in a limited sort of way when we're in our wolf form. But most definitely, never with anyone out of the pack. Even then, it's more a feeling than an actual conversation." He thought for a moment. "We should try it again. It might turn out to be useful."

"I guess."

"There's one thing I want to know."

"What's that?"

He braked for the stop sign and, after glancing in

the mirror to see if Annalise was still behind us in my car – she was – he looked at me. His face had taken on a guarded look that I recognized when he was about to ask something that he wasn't sure I wanted to answer. "Why did you call for me, and not Evan?"

I chewed my lip. "Because you were closer?" I said, my voice rising into question, not quite believing myself. That had been just part of it; it hadn't occurred to me to call Evan, or even Annalise who must have been just as close to the diner.

"Evan would have been there in seconds, wherever he was, if he'd heard you."

"Right." I swallowed. Gage had been in my mind because I'd just seen him. I knew he was in town, and he was closer to the diner, I told myself. Nothing more. *Absolutely nothing more.*

Several times over the past few weeks, I had to remind myself not to think about Gage in a way that would leave me feeling compromised. I didn't want to be the woman with one guy, one great guy I loved, knowing and enjoying him all the while another man carried a torch for me. I made a commitment to myself not to string Gage along, even if there were a definite spark there, once. I wasn't going to be indecisive, flitting from one to the other, nor encouraging, when there was really nothing to offer. Gage was dating other people and that was a good thing. Gage was my friend. That was it. And if I could convince myself to believe that, I could make anyone.

Thankfully he changed the subject. "You won't be able to come this way for a couple of weeks," he told me, pointing to a large works notice sign as he made the turn. "The county is getting those trees cut back, so this road will be closed. I'll show you a map of another route later. It's slightly longer, which is why Annalise and I, as well as everyone else, always use this route."

"That would be helpful. Thank you."

"No problem. I'm glad you called me, for whatever reason. You know I'll come, any time you call."

Not trusting myself to speak, unsure of whether Gage was talking about now... or something else, I just nodded. He continued to look at me, silently, like he was unsure of the situation as well. Then, after a minute, he sighed, ignoring me the rest of the way home.

We parked across the street at Gage's house then walked over the desolate road. Despite it being early afternoon, there was something curiously quiet about my house. Annalise hit a red light so she was a couple of minutes behind us and just pulling into my driveway. She drew the car alongside Evan's larger rental car that he preferred to having his own car shipped. I walked towards the porch steps, Gage no more than a pace behind me.

I paused on the bottom step, waving a hand to Annalise as she parked, and turned to Gage, asking. "Wilding isn't safe anymore, is it?"

"I don't know, Stella. It's as safe as anywhere, I guess."

"I don't know what to do." My voice was barely louder than a whisper. He warned me something otherworldly would be attracted to the sudden and fleetingly strong power in the area. It was caused by the hasty and unexpected concentration of agitated witches months before, but I knew we all privately hoped that nothing would disturb our peace. I hoped we agreed that the Brotherhood had to be the worst of our threats but I didn't ask because ignorance could be bliss for a few precious minutes.

"You don't have to make any decisions."

My shoulders slumped, dejection pulling at me. "So long as I am the one making the decisions."

Gage looked at me for a long moment, then nodded. "That's the spirit, don't get pushed around."

With a sigh, I ascended the last few steps, reached for the front door of my house and pushed it open. I stepped inside to an explosion of streamers and hoots that made me retreat in surprise, only to bump into Gage.

Right in front of me stood Kitty, holding a cake and trying hard not to bounce up and down in her excitement. Étoile stood next to her, clapping her hands. Beau was there too, popping little streamer ribbons, and Evan, my lovely Evan, was lighting the candles that had blown out, using fire from his fingertips. He looked up and smiled at me.

"Happy birthday, Stella!" Kitty yelled as Beau sent ribbons streaming towards me. "Smile, dude! It's a birthday party!"

Gage stepped in closer behind me, giving me a little push forward, his big frame filling the doorway. Annalise nudged past him to stand by my side. "We've got a problem," Gage said ominously.

Just like that, the mood fell flatter than an English pancake and I knew I'd remember my twenty-fifth birthday for all the wrong reasons.

CHAPTER THREE

"Tell me again," insisted Evan, his hand comfortingly wrapped around mine. We had parked ourselves in the living room, the seven of us dotted between the two sofas and the armchair, except Beau, who preferred pacing. The chocolate cake sat on the coffee table between all of us, looking a little lonely. Wisps of smoke trailed from the slim, coloured candles. I hadn't even made a wish.

I rattled off the Cliff Notes version. "He just sat at the table and told me his name was John Jones, though it obviously wasn't really his name," I explained again. I felt like I was talking in circles as they all watched me. "He said his employer wanted to talk to me. His employer is the leader of the Brotherhood. Anyway, he gave me the envelope, holding a plane ticket and money and said if I didn't come, there would be consequences."

"Obviously you're not going," said Evan with a shake of his head.

"Obviously." I rolled my eyes. Sure, it wasn't an

attractive habit, but the mood called for it.

"I'm not sure Wilding is safe anymore," Evan said as he looked from me to Gage, who remained expressionless. Gage sat in the armchair and his long legs were stretched out in front of him. "The Brotherhood know you're here. Georgia Thomas does, too, and other witches. We should move you." He caught my sharp look at that, rephrasing, "We should *think* about moving you somewhere safer."

I contemplated that. I'd been hiding from the Brotherhood for over a year and now they had finally found me. Georgia Thomas was another matter. As a witch, she saw herself as the next leader of the Council. For several months, she'd been drumming up, or, rather, scaring up support across the country. When she didn't succeed through charm, she threatened. We locked horns when I foiled her foray into necromancy. She was attempting to bring back dead witches who were loyal to her and would support her cause. Though we were also certain she was capable of murder, there wasn't much we could do without proof. So, for now, Georgia remained free. Since our clash, she never returned to my house but I didn't know how long that would last; or when she'd get it into her head that it was time for payback.

"What's the point?" I asked, dragging my attention back to the current source of my distress. "I ran away from my country to get away from them and I didn't stop running until I got here. Wilding was the only place where I'd found peace. Besides, who's to say if I ran somewhere else, they wouldn't find me there, too? And the next time and the next?" I fingered my hands through my hair, knotting it back as I concentrated on the problems the Brotherhood's sudden arrival had spawned.

Although Wilding might be my home and my closest connection to my long-dead parents, it was irrelevant in the grand scheme of things. I slumped back on the sofa, stretching my arms up and legs out. My sweater rode up to bare a strip of taut stomach, and I suddenly realised Gage was watching me with more than a little interest. I stopped stretching, narrowed my eyes and shot him a look. He grinned and his chest heaved once, like he was trying to restrain a laugh.

"She's right," agreed Étoile, with a nod. "Running is no life for a witch."

Speaking of witches. "I saw a witch in Wilding today."

"Oh? Did she approach you?" Étoile asked.

I shook my head. "No, I just saw her from a distance."

"She sure picked the wrong day to be in Wilding. It's probably nothing." Étoile didn't seem too interested in the news.

"So what do we do?" I asked, looking around the room. Annalise had pulled Evan's desk chair over; Beau stood behind her, his hands resting on the back. Kitty and Étoile were opposite me on the other sofa, looking thoughtful. Evan sat rigidly next to me. I could feel his anger with even the slightest movement of his body, though his hand was gentle around mine.

"We could hunt the bastard down and eat him," Gage huffed, breaking the silence as he looked around. "Unless there are any other suggestions?"

"That would involve finding him," I pointed out. As far as I knew, the wolves only hunted wild animals, so I hoped he was making a joke.

"We might still catch a scent. It's only been a few hours. We can see if this 'Jones' is still in the area and if there are any others with him," Annalise looked across to Gage and he nodded thoughtfully as she continued indignantly, "And, no, since you didn't ask, we won't be eating him. I can't believe any of you would even think that."

Kitty pulled a face at me and I suppressed a nervous giggle.

"Sounds like a good plan," said Étoile, which was received by nods of approval that repeated around the room. "What do we do with this 'Jones' guy when we find him?"

"Kill him," said Evan.

"Evan! What is with you guys? Is your answer to everything 'kill'?" I looked from Evan to Gage. I killed someone once, in self defence, and it was something that weighed heavily on my heart, even though I knew it was the only thing I could do.

They looked at each other and nodded, in agreement, for once. Evan shrugged. "It's not like they haven't tried to kill you. They're serial killers, Stella, psychopaths. They don't negotiate and they won't ever stop pursuing you."

"Aren't you even curious about why they want Stella?" piped Kitty.

Evan raised his eyebrows. "If they're all dead, it won't matter."

"That's the problem though, isn't it? Jones is just a lackey. The Brotherhood, the ones who really pull the strings, might be at this Hawkscroft place. It doesn't matter who you kill here, there will be more and more and they'll just keep on coming." My voice was taking on a note of hysteria and I had to close my eyes for a moment to block everything out. When I opened them again, I felt calmer. I got up and walked around the sofa to the window overlooking the porch. I found myself pacing, trying to work out the fear and anger I was reliving at the thought of their relentless pursuit.

What did I ever do to the Brotherhood? What was so wrong with my living peacefully? They were nothing more than racial supremacists, except they didn't care a bit about the colour of my skin. They just wanted to rid the world of magic. That's what painted a bull's eye on my back, and every other person in this room. So far, the Brotherhood had only targeted witches, but I wondered now if they knew what else lived among us. If they knew, they probably wouldn't rest until we were all eradicated.

"She's got a point," said Beau, no longer pacing, his hands resting on Annalise's shoulders.

"Fine. We'll find him first and see what's going on. What date is that plane ticket for?" Evan held out his hand so I fished it out of my jacket pocket, pulling the ticket out of the envelope to peer at the print.

"Two days from now," I said, handing it to him. I pulled a sheaf of crisp notes out, flicking through them. "There's at least a thousand pounds here," I said, looking up, before passing the notes over to Evan. He quickly glanced at them before stuffing them back into the envelope, along with the ticket. Then he handed the whole lot back to me.

"It makes sense that they would hang around until at least then, to make sure Stella got on that plane," suggested Kitty.

"They've got to know that I'm not going to get on it." Nothing about it made sense. They had to know I wouldn't return to England willingly using their ticket, ensuring their tracking my every move. Why would I? They'd already marked me for death; it wasn't like I would present myself to them out of mere curiosity. There was no way I'd go alone, at risk of being ambushed at any moment.

"I'll call some of the pack and we'll see if we can follow his scent. I didn't see this Jones guy, but maybe I can get a scent off Stella and work from there."

"Sniff her jacket, wolf," Evan said, glancing up, his voice a warning hum.

"What did you think I was going to sniff, daemon?" Gage fired back, holding back a laugh as he held out his hand. Shrugging out of my jacket, I handed it to him and he sniffed it, then passed it to Annalise who pressed it to her nose, inhaling, before passing it on to Beau. "It's faint," said Gage. "But we'll try. Annalise, Beau, you're with me. We'll go see what we can find."

"Call me when you get something?" I asked both of them.

"Sure thing. It's not a strong scent, but it should be enough." Annalise knocked me on the shoulder playfully after giving me a quick hug. "Save me some cake."

I looked at the thick chocolate frosting on the cake Kitty had clearly been baking all morning and pulled a face. It looked delicious. "Only if you hurry."

"Gage, let's go. I've got a slice of cake with my name on it." Annalise banged out the door, with Gage and Beau shadowing her. I watched them go, talking to each other, until they were out of sight. A moment later, I saw Gage's car pull out onto the road and point towards Wilding.

"They'll be okay," said Kitty, coming to stand beside me. "Gotta lotta faith in those puppies." Kitty, my newest housemate and oldest friend, had met my neighbours for the first time a few months before. She drove out to my house after a long convalescence in hospital. It wasn't a regular hospital, but some kind of magical unit hidden in deepest Oklahoma, of all places. Her injuries had been sustained during a battle with a rogue witch, the same one who killed the last Council leader, and the woman I'd been forced to terminate. It took Kitty a long time to recover.

I was glad to have her back, and if I weren't mistaken, there were a couple of members of Gage's pack who were pretty taken with her, too. She hadn't exactly been lucky in love, so I was pleased for her. She wasn't the only one who had gotten herself a wolf following. Étoile also had a rather enthusiastic admirer amongst the pack. So long as they didn't territorially cock a leg on my porch, I was cool with it.

"Are there any kinds of spells we can do?" I asked as I glanced back over my shoulder to include Étoile in the question.

"Not my speciality. Now, if David were here, that would be a possibility," replied Étoile, reminding us that David, and his girlfriend Seren, had gone home months earlier. David was Kitty's and my spell craft teacher while we were ensconced in a safe house, far from the Brotherhood's reach. Kitty had never really taken to spells but I did. Under David's tutelage I learned the rudiments of practising spells and the necessary ingredients for success.

I could weave simple spells now, like the wards that surrounded my house, protecting us from anyone who would do us harm. Anything more complicated, however, was beyond my capabilities.

When it came to magic, I was of the blood variety. Magic swam freely through my veins and was always an intrinsic part of my existence, just like my heart or brain. Although I once viewed my magic as a curse, now I could rein it properly, I couldn't imagine being without it. It would be like losing one of my senses: debilitating but not deadly.

Glancing at the mantelpiece where I had a small clutter of photos, my eyes rested on the white envelope I stored there for safekeeping. It was a wedding invitation for David and Seren's wedding in late summer and I was really looking forward to it. Étoile, as Seren's sister, was going to be maid of honour.

"Magic sucks," I muttered.

"What about the spell book?" Kitty started tentatively, shrinking a little when three pairs of eyes turned on her. "The one you showed me."

The spell book was on loan to me but it was a weird, temperamental thing. I'd almost finished reading it when it disappeared. A few days ago, I took a call from the family it belonged to saying it had reappeared at their house; they thanked me for its return.

"Not an option," I said, knowing Kitty would know what that meant. She muttered something rude about the book under her breath, possibly because it had always eluded her grasp.

"Never mind. Some cards came while you were out." Kitty went to pick up a small stack from the little console table we had by the door. It was constantly cluttered with keys, mail and coins.

I took the stack with a "thanks" and started to slice them open while my mind provided a bunch of scenarios for what the Brotherhood were planning. I felt uneasy having them in my town, my hometown, but it wasn't like I could march over there and demand they leave. They were all about the waiting game. It felt strange to be taking a lesson from their notebook; I would have to be patient too.

The first envelope I opened held a card from Seren and David. It was covered in pretty little flowers that floated off the card and hung in the air before dropping back to the card again like confetti. It was unexpected and very, very sweet.

There was a card from my old friend Marc Bartholomew, too, which was a surprise. I hadn't expected him to remember, much less, send a card. The last time we'd seen each other had been a horrible experience, though neither of our faults. I imagined neither one of us wanted to remember that. On a positive note, it was also the same time Marc got his magic back, after a lifetime of being illicitly bound.

A piece of folded paper tucked inside the card slipped out and I unfolded it. It was a note from Marc, brief, like he wasn't one for letter writing. It just said he was looking forward to seeing me at the summit and getting a chance to talk. He said he missed me and hoped we were all well. He didn't mention his magic at all, nor what he was doing now. I flipped over the envelope. The postmark was smudged but, all the same, I wondered if he had gone home. All in all, it was a short and sweet note that gave me a smile. My smile, however, faltered slightly when my eyes flicked back to "summit." I frowned.

What was that about?

Both cards went on the mantelpiece amongst my framed photographs, Marc's note too, along with a silly musical card from Kitty and Étoile. A shiny blue one with 'Happy Birthday' in big letters from Evan and dozens of kisses inside made Kitty coo and me blush.

Turning the third envelope over in my hand, I frowned. It was more business-like than the others, in a soft manila shade with my name in neat type. Maybe it was a bill. *What a pain.* I opened it anyway and withdrew the card inside, flipping it open. It wasn't a birthday card, or a bill. It was a summons.

"What is it?" asked Kitty.

Without looking up, I replied, "I've been invited to attend the Council summit."

"Why?"

I scanned the neat type. "They are ready to elect a new leader. Did you know about this, Étoile?"

Étoile nodded. "I got my invite too."

"I don't think you should go," interjected Evan, before she could say anymore. His forehead knitted into a frown as he came over to stand by me, reading the invitation over my shoulder. When it came to witches, my boyfriend had mixed feelings. He loved me and tolerated Étoile, although he now counted her as a friend. He seemed to like Kitty well enough, and included my warlock friend, David Langstrom, among his friends, but that was as far as it went. It was mostly a trust thing. Evan was daemon, not exactly your average witch's best friend, and certainly formidable to have as an enemy.

Such prejudices meant nothing to me. I loved Evan unreservedly. I knew he loved me too, and it wasn't just that he told me every day but I could see it in the sacrifices he made to stay with me. Although he travelled home to Texas regularly to confer with his employees face-to-face, I knew he was getting agitated about being so hands-off in his business. I was starting to worry that my desire to stay in Wilding wasn't going to be good for us, long term.

One day soon, I was going to have to make a decision, or offer some kind of compromise. I couldn't continue to let Evan do all the running for me. I wasn't being fair, and I knew it. The thought of it made me feel awful, but there were more pressing things at hand, as usual.

"It's a summit. Étoile's going." I knew I sounded petulant, but it slipped out anyway. I didn't have many dealings with the witch community but I got the gossip drip-fed to me by Étoile and Seren, and even Kitty, if the dirt were particularly juicy. I'd always been hesitant to get further involved, especially while the Council was in such disorder from lack of leadership. Maybe it would have been different if I'd grown up knowing I was a witch, and understanding the subtle nuances and hierarchy of the community. Instead, I'd been launched into it, full pelt, a year ago. While I was taking to magic well, I didn't think the magical community was taking to me quite as favourably.

"Étoile is stronger than you and she's been around this all her life. It could get dangerous," Evan sensibly pointed out. "Some of the witches have been getting out of line lately. You've seen that."

"If I don't get with the magic programme, I'm never going to learn." I threw back even though I was still undecided. "Plus, how dangerous can it get?"

"Georgia Thomas will be there." Étoile looked a little pale.

"Oh." *That* dangerous. Well, that made things a little different. "Who's with me for cake?" I asked, pinning a smile on my face.

~

Settling into the desk chair in the little office Evan helped me set up in the sun room (or not-a-lot-of-sunroom as we currently called it), I switched on my laptop. I leaned back on the cushioned seat while I waited for it to power up.

A month ago, Seren and David had surprised me by calling up and offering me a job. Turns out, they'd had more than enough of being pushed and pulled around by the Council too, and decided to open up a small shop and online business together. They were primarily targeting the witch community, who often found it hard to source the kinds of herbs and ingredients they needed for spellcraft.

Seren and David's set-up was simple: a small shop that sold herbs, homemade potions, gifts and other mystical new age items like candles and crystals that catered to the foot crowd, the non-magical patrons. They set up a warehouse in the back, where they stored the herbs they sourced and then shipped to customers, along with anything else the witch community requested.

Once business started picking up, they realised they couldn't keep up with the administration, as well as the shop maintenance and product sourcing so they hired me to deal with the admin.

For a few hours a day, I answered customer queries or passed on emails to Seren or David if they were too complicated for me to answer. I arranged the orders for processing, as well as kept track of their website and stock levels. It wasn't the most mentally taxing work I'd ever done, but they paid me a reasonable rate and were pretty flexible with my hours, so it worked out well. Most of all, I just loved the feeling of being productive again, as well as earning my own money. It would help pay for college, once I'd picked some classes.

My job, combined with my daily runs, often with Evan or a wolf at my side, ensured I was feeling fitter than ever, although my magic lessons might have had something to do with that too. I certainly felt more in tune with my inner witch. The strange things I once caused were very rare now, so rare, I never had to worry about them. My magic came to me easily now that I understood I wasn't merely controlling it; I was allowing it to be part of me.

To drown out the little voice in my head that wanted to know everything about the Brotherhood (*right now!*), I concentrated on answering the small overnight flurry of emails. Seren and David's business was doing well and they were attracting witches from all over America, as well as further afield. Just last week, I'd seen orders from Canada, Australia and even Italy. I always kept an eye out for any orders from England, but, so far, saw nothing.

I made my way through the orders quickly, compiling them all before I emailed the documents to David's inbox for packing and shipping. So far, they were doing everything between the three of us but, if business improved, I hoped they would hire someone else to help them out. That job done, I checked the website to make sure all the text and images were showing up properly. After adding some new images and copy for the latest products they were stocking, I made sure the day's books were in order, finally.

Though I worked remotely, we'd agreed that every few weeks or so I would make the journey up north to their shop and audit their files to keep them in order. They may be witches, but the IRS still wanted to see decent records and that was my very human responsibility.

I was looking forward to going, even if it meant leaving Evan behind for a couple of days. Since he'd arrived in Wilding, we'd spent every day together and I was happily used to him being in such close proximity. Sometimes, however, it was an adjustment to share my daily life with another person, not to mention Étoile and Kitty, too.

Next to me, the cordless house phone trilled, jolting me out of my thoughts. I picked it up on the third ring.

"Happy birthday!" Seren's voice filled my ear. "I only have one question, why are you working? And don't say you're not. I can see you online."

"Just making sure I keep up. I want to win employee of the week."

Seren laughed. "Honey, you're employee of the week, every week. Now stop! I don't want you to do another thing. Oh, David, wants to say something."

"Happy birthday, Stella," David's voice came on the line. "Did you like our card?"

"Yes, it was beautiful. Thank you."

"You're welcome, and stop working. Boss' orders."

"Yes, boss."

A knock sounded on the door just as I hung up and Étoile stuck her head around. We hadn't had a chance to talk privately since she left abruptly a week ago. In typical Étoile fashion, she hadn't been totally clear. "Hey. How are things?"

"Okay," I said, thinking that said nothing and everything. "Where have you been?"

"New York."

"Oh." I hadn't expected her to answer, as she'd been so cagey when she left, but it surprised me that she had been in the city that was her other home. Étoile told me once that she had an apartment there, though I'd never been, and she had previously worked in finance in the city before the Council and her family took over her life. "What were you doing there?"

"I'll tell you about it another time." That was Étoile all over: strictly need to know.

"Sure."

Étoile pulled the door closed and leant against the frame, her arms folded. "The Brotherhood being here is bad news, Stella. Even if you don't go to England, and I really recommend that you don't, they can come back any time. They can leave people here to watch over you, maybe even infiltrate your life a little bit at a time and you won't even know it. And it's not just you, Stella, they're a risk to Kitty, to me, to Seren and David. They could use you to get to any one of us."

"I know," I said, feeling a little sick because it had already occurred to me. "I know."

"Evan will go to the ends of the earth to guard you and ensure your safety, but what about when he's not around?" she asked. "The wolves have also extended their protection, but will it last if they start getting picked off? I mean, no disrespect to Gage, Annalise or any of the pack, but none of us can guarantee their loyalty in the face of death."

"Isn't this what all the lessons have been about?" I asked. "So I can protect myself? So I'm not a burden on any of you?"

"Oh, Stella, you're not a burden. Please don't think that you are. I just want to keep you safe."

"And think about leaving?"

"Temporarily," she said. "We could go to New York, or you could go to Texas with Evan. Just for a little while, just long enough that they don't look for you here anymore."

"I'll think about it."

"Good. In the meantime...."

"You don't have to say it. I won't be going anywhere alone."

"Keep Evan with you at all times, or Gage. Either of them would be a match for the Brotherhood. I'm glad I came home when I did." I think Étoile was as surprised as I was when I heard her call my house "home," but I let it slide. She'd only brush it off anyway. Nevertheless, I was glad she felt comfortable here. She'd been my mentor as long as she'd been my friend and I didn't like to think of what she might have sacrificed to stay with me. What she and Evan both sacrificed.

Perhaps that made me selfish, but it wasn't like I had many friends when growing up. I'd actually been pretty lonely and, for the most part, I thoroughly enjoyed having a houseful now. My heart panged at the thought of losing them all, or of us splitting up again.

Étoile gave me a little wave and stepped back through the door, sliding it closed behind her.

Turning back to my laptop, I ran through the few

emails that had come through while Étoile and I were talking. Then I emailed Seren and David, filling them in on anything they needed to know before I closed that window, calling it a day on work.

Opening a new window, I scrolled through my watch list. Since I'd gotten my laptop and had the world at my fingertips, I'd been keeping a cursory eye on the Brotherhood's news appearances. No one seemed to know who really ran the organisation, but they had a surprising amount of supporters. There were message boards and websites dedicated to their cause: denouncing witches, speculating on who might be one. There were a few Hollywood actors, singers and politicians with bizarre claims of witchcraft attached to them. Apparently, dark magic was the source of their success, said one conspiracy website which ran a gallery of images of suspected witches.

On the other side, there were a lot of people who thought the Brotherhood were deranged. They also believed there was no such thing as magic and called the whole thing crazy. Like many things, both sides had a portion of the truth, but they were too diametrically opposed to even consider piecing together the jigsaw in unison.

The media was just as bad. Witches and serial killers made great stories and there was much speculation and comparison drawn from the witch-hunts of several hundred years ago. People had even written scholarly papers for science journals claiming or disproving evidence in support of their theories.

Today was mostly the same old, same old: ranting conspiracy theorists, badly spelled urgings from people hiding behind nicknames, and some sicker posts about what some would like to do to female witches. I grimaced and scrolled post those quickly before I lost my lunch.

I moved on to one of the more moderate websites that focused more on the discussion of whether magic existed or not. A lot of conspiracy theorists abounded here too, but at least, it was a lot tamer than the other websites.

I read for ten minutes before a comment, buried deep in a rant about Hollywood covens – dear Lord – caught my eye and I leaned in closer to read it again. It read: *I gotta ask, how are these people funded? It must take a lot of work to hunt down witches so it's not like they have full time jobs or whatever. And if it is all true, it's still murder, right? Why aren't these people being prosecuted?*

"Very good questions," I said to the screen. I just wish I had the answers. For one thing, I wanted to know how they were funded. Did the Brotherhood have financiers or sponsors? If so, those people had to be sick individuals or more closely entwined with magic than any of us had even fathomed.

Secondly, the murders had garnered a lot of press coverage, mostly in Europe where they were more numerous. I could browse the newspapers online so, every once in a while, I searched through them, but the reports had become more infrequent during the past few months and dwindled to almost nothing, as no new murders arose.

Despite the extensive coverage throughout Europe, no arrests had ever been made, no suspects brought in for questioning. That led me to thinking other unpalatable thoughts. Did the police from every country where a murder had taken place really discover so little that they had no suspects? Or were they willing to turn a blind eye? If the latter were true, someone high up must hate witches so much they were prepared to allow people to hunt them. Perhaps I was just reading too many conspiracies. Despite that, when I closed the browser, I shivered.

For a moment, I had the mouse pointer hover over the "shut down" button; but then I pushed it up and opened my documents folder so I could bring up my latest notes. I'd been keeping track of questions that puzzled me, as well as notes, and any nuggets of information, which reminded me... the address on the Brotherhood's summons had been Hawkscroft, Yorkshire. No street address. Only very large houses in England didn't require a street address.

Calling up a fresh browser window, I tapped the house name into the search box and hit "enter." A moment later, a Wikipedia entry popped up so I opened the page, scanning my eyes over it. There wasn't much information, just some notes about the house's architecture, when it was built and that it had always been owned by the same family but failed to give their names. The picture showed a large, imposing house set back behind sprawling lawns.

I added a few notes to my file, including the web address for the house's entry, saved it and then started the power down process.

"Work all okay?" asked Kitty, putting down her magazine when I walked into the living room a few minutes later.

I struggled to keep my face even. "Yeah, no problems at all. Where's Étoile?"

"Kitchen." As I started walking away, I heard Kitty call, "If she has her fingers in the frosting, tell her she has to wait until everyone's had a piece."

Étoile was actually making tea in the teakettle she

gave me for Christmas along with a tin full of tea bags. There was everything from black "builder's" to herbal varieties. When I asked her again what she had been doing in New York, she muttered something about witchy business and clamped her mouth shut. I sighed inwardly.

"Just spit it out, Étoile."

Étoile had made it obvious that she wanted to protect me, but I wasn't sure that was what I wanted anymore. So far, protecting me seemed to put me in as much danger as keeping me out of it! Her lessons in magic taught me how to defend myself and my telekinesis was improving considerably, but I still didn't know much of the goings on of the witch community and I had a feeling I really should.

"It's complicated," she said, after a long moment of staring at the countertops. "I really wish I could tell you, Stella, but you'll find out soon enough."

"It's to do with the Council, isn't it?" I pressed.

Politically, things were getting heated. They functioned as a quasi-Council for months until a new leader could be elected. Without a powerful director, the Council had little or no power. They were also swiftly losing respect, so calling the summit was probably a smart thing to do on their part.

So far, the biggest, scariest and only contender was Georgia Thomas. I knew she was still canvassing for support as the new head of the Council and few wanted to risk standing against her. That was an uncomfortable enough thought in itself. But throw in what would happen to the community if she got more power, and it was a bitter pill to swallow. Sure, there needed to be a regime change, but not one that had the potential for a dictatorship. What those ramifications meant for me, I didn't know; but I couldn't imagine it would be painless. I embarrassed and humiliated her and she wouldn't forget that easily.

Whichever way I turned, danger loomed.

CHAPTER FOUR

At dusk, Gage, Annalise and Beau returned, the three of them looking grim.

"You're not going to tell us anything good, are you?" I said, handing them each a plate with a thick slice of cake to make up for whatever they were about to disclose. Kitty was already munching her way through her second slice.

Slumping into the armchair that he favoured, Gage told us, "We followed them to the Blue Moon Motel, just off the interstate, a few miles north of Wilding."

Annalise and Beau both nodded, with Beau saying, "There are only two of them so far as we could tell. We left a couple of the pack to watch over them tonight."

"What were they doing?" I asked, sucking the last bit of cake off my fork. I couldn't have been any less graceful if I tried.

Annalise shrugged out of her jacket and folded it across her lap, before taking a bite of cake, and savouring it for a moment. "Not much, as far as we could tell. Just ordinary stuff like making phone calls, watching cable, and eating take-out. No torturing or killing witches that I could see."

"I suppose it would be kind of noisy to do that," I mused. "Did they look like they were staying for a long time?" I tried to picture the motel. I'd passed it a couple of times and it was a neat box of a building that was always nicely painted and bedecked with colourful plants. I suspected if i got close, I'd probably find out they were plastic.

"We couldn't get inside the room, but the man at the desk said they were paid up until after the weekend."

"So they are waiting to see if I leave?"

"Guess so," said Gage. Catching my eye, he slowly licked a dab of frosting from his top lip and winked at me. Suppressing a smile at his audacity, I looked over at Evan who sat very still. His hands were balling into fists, until he saw me watching and unclenched them. I swear, sometimes Gage deliberately tried to wind him up. "Jay and Kristen will watch over them tonight. Annalise and Michelle will take over in the morning. We'll have eyes on them twenty-four hours a day," Gage promised, looking from Kitty and me to Étoile. "I don't mean to insult the witches here, but I think it's best if you stayed away. They know Stella is here, but we don't know what kind of intel they have on anyone else."

"I guess our dinner plans are off," I said to Evan with a sinking feeling. I'd been looking forward to our evening out for the past few days. Not that we didn't go out, of course, but just the two of us would have been special.

When Evan smiled, it was just for me. "I can make us something here," he suggested.

"Blecchh," said Kitty. "I'm going to my room."

"I'm coming with you," Étoile added. I wondered if her lack of plans had something to do with Jay having scored the Brotherhood night shift. They'd been on a few dates, which surprised me because he didn't look like her type. And that was without adding werewolf to the mix. He may have been rough and ready, but he was good looking with light brown hair and a quick smile as well as buckets of charm. They seemed to enjoy each other's company and I got the impression Jay would be quite happy to see her on a more regular basis. Any attempts to draw Étoile out on that led to blank looks.

"I can take a hint." Annalise nudged Beau. "Let's go to my house. Gage, are you coming? Don't you have a date to get ready for?" She winked at him.

"Uh, no, not tonight. I'll be at the Loup. Thanks for the cake." Gage put his plate on the table. Despite the cold, he was in short shirtsleeves and a khaki padded vest. Like Evan, Gage ran a little warmer than most people. While the cold got to my bones, it didn't seem to bother them as much. "Before I go, we, Annalise and me, that is, got you a birthday present."

"You did?" I lit up at that.

"Yeah, we thought it was perfect for you." Annalise produced a small square red gift box from behind her back, leaning forward to pass it to me.

I unwound the glittery black ribbon and pulled the lid off the box. On the velvet cushion lay a necklace, a delicate strand of silver links with something long and thin hanging from it. I looked closer to see what it was. *Oh, very funny.* I held up the broomstick pendant and laughed. "I love it, thank you."

"Gage designed it and a friend of ours made it. She exhibits at the same fairs I take my stuff to," Annalise explained as Gage gave an off-hand sort of nod. She operated a one-woman craft shop from her home, making beautifully intricate blankets, and other small soft handiwork. I'd been helping her make a website, something that she'd finally caved and agreed to. "Here, let me help you put it on."

My company ended up staying for another hour, the conversation moving quickly from the Brotherhood to the coming weekend. It seemed everyone had plans... and, maybe, just maybe, no one wanted to be alone. I had to admit, being in a group of supes made me feel a lot more relaxed than I would have been otherwise; especially knowing the Brotherhood were just a few miles away.

Kitty made her excuses first, claiming she needed an early night. For the past few months, she'd put in a bunch of hours at the local college and earned her qualifications. She'd been working so hard to get her fledgling beauty business up and running that she'd been enduring a lot of early mornings and late nights. She'd already explained her plans for the weekend, which involved hiring some local high school students to stand in as models and let her style their hair and makeup. She hired a local photographer to take some pictures so Kitty could set up a portfolio to jumpstart her beauty business.

Before she arrived at the same safe house where we originally met, she had plans to go to beauty school. Now she planned to run a mobile business, travelling around as she saw to brides, prom girls and anyone else who needed a new look. She'd practiced on me so often, I got used to having consistently perfect nails. Recently, Kitty confided her dream about styling in Hollywood, but, so far, it was baby steps.

Étoile remained tight-lipped about New York. Something seemed to be worrying her intensely. I wanted to ask her what weighed so heavily on her mind, but not in front of everyone else. After a while, she made her excuses and I heard her bedroom door shut softly.

Really, I think both of them just wanted to get out of the way. Originally, when Étoile then Kitty moved in, I enjoyed having a constant house full. The endless comings and goings, someone to talk to, friends visiting. Most of all, I liked the ambience. Sometimes, however, like now when I wanted to be with Evan, it seemed that the house was too full.

Gage, Annalise and Beau left together in a flurry of hugs with the door banging shut behind them. I cleared the plates quickly, Evan helping to carry them into the kitchen.

"So, we're finally alone." Evan wrapped his arms around me, resting his head on my shoulder as I soaked the plates.

"Guess so." I hid a smile. Switching off the faucet, I shook my dripping hands over the sink. Evan slid his hands under mine, holding them up. Heat rose from him, instantly drying my hands. "Thanks for holding back on the flames," I teased.

"Special daemon trick. You want your present now?"

"You got me one?"

"Close your eyes." As I closed my eyes, he scooped me into his arms. Judging from the direction he was walking, we were headed for my bedroom. *Oh, hello.* Shutting the door behind us, he set me on my feet, warning me to keep my eyes closed.

"Seeing as our dinner was put off tonight, I thought I'd bring it to us."

Opening my eyes, I saw a picnic rug laid across my bedroom floor. There were plates and little bowls of tasty looking things to eat. The rug was dotted with tea lights that lit one by one as I looked upon them.

"Look up."

Above us, my ceiling appeared to have disappeared, replaced with a velvet canopy of midnight blue, punctuated by golden stars. I gasped as a shooting star sped across the scene. "How did you do that?"

"Magic." Evan looked pleased with himself. "A picnic under the stars is nice, right? And seeing as it isn't exactly warm enough to be outside..."

"It's lovely," I breathed, watching the stars twinkle. I didn't care how he did it, it was beautiful. "Really lovely. Thank you so much."

"I did get you a gift too. I was waiting until we were alone to give it to you."

"Is it a sex gift?" I asked, covering my mouth with mock shock, "because you've given me plenty of those."

Evan chuckled. "No, it isn't." He crossed to the nightstand on his side of the bed – it still seemed strange to think of his side and mine – and opened the drawer, rummaging inside. While he did that, I sat on the blanket, crossing my legs under me.

I'd been spoiled with presents already today. Along with Annalise and Gage's necklace, Étoile gave me a sizeable gift voucher to an online store I liked and Kitty bought me a gift basket from Sephora.

When Evan turned round, he had a slim package in his hands. He settled down next to me, leaning against the footboard of the bed, and passed it to me. "What is it?" I asked.

"Open it."

I opened the box, and found another container. I opened three more, each a different colour and texture before I got to the final, small, square box. Opening it, I gasped. The ring inside was beautiful. Platinum set with little jewels, each a different colour. It was unlike anything I had ever seen before. "I don't know what to say."

"It's an eternity ring." Evan took it from the box and picked up my hand, sliding it over the middle finger of my right hand. I held it up, admiring the way it caught the light. "The jewels are very old but the setting is new. Do you like it?"

"I think it's the most beautiful thing I've ever seen."

Evan's face lit up. "It has special properties which I'll tell you about another time."

"Sounds intriguing." I leant over and kissed him, brushing my lips across his. Pulling me into his arms, he returned the kiss with a depth and passion that left me breathless. Suddenly, I didn't feel so hungry.

My heart was racing slightly. Distinctly carnal thoughts rose to the forefront of my mind as I reached for him, my arms wrapping around his neck. I knelt in front of him and leant into his kiss. It seemed to last forever as he pulled me in deeper, our tongues finding each other happily.

"Bed?" Evan asked, breaking away for a moment, his hands still wrapped in my hair.

"Floor," I replied, one hand on his chest, pushing him backwards. He tipped me with him, kissing me again, and then his hands were moving, over my shoulder and back, and to my front where he played with my shirt buttons, popping each one.

"I like it when you wear shirts," he said, against my throat, which he was peppering with kisses.

"You could just magic it off."

"Sometimes I just enjoy undressing you."

I shuffled on top of him, feeling his growing hardness budding against my leg. "Duly noted."

"Being with you makes me very happy," he told me.

I wriggled so I was sitting up, astride his thighs, and smiled down at him. He had unsnapped the last button and was tweaking my shirt apart, running his hands up my stomach to rest over my satin bra. I took a moment to be glad I was wearing nice underwear before focusing on what I was going to say. "I'm glad that makes you happy, but what about everything else?"

"What do you mean?" He slid my shirt down my shoulders and tossed it in the vague direction of the laundry hamper. It missed woefully.

"I mean are you otherwise happy? I know living here isn't what you want."

"Are we going to have this discussion now?" Evan looked disappointed, but being the truly focused daemon he was, he reached up and unsnapped the front hook of my bra, teasing back the cups, smiling then.

"Yes, because we haven't been alone all day and it's been on my mind."

He thought for a moment and I watched the

strong structure of his chest rising and falling. Sturdy and masculine, he was truly an exceptionally enjoyable sight, clothed or unclothed. He said, "I do find myself missing home and the life I had before. I was very active, worked very hard and travelled a lot. Now I find I am not adjusting to the administration of the business quite as well without being as active. My employees have grown, but I never get the chance to be as hands-on as I would like. My name is my business and I am not doing as much as I should. I'm going to need to travel more often and that worries me."

"Why does it worry you?"

"Because you attract danger and I want to protect you. I can't do that if I'm somewhere else."

"Isn't that partly what all the lessons for? So I can protect myself?" I asked, just like I'd asked Étoile earlier.

Evan nodded. "We're almost at the end of our lessons now. I can't teach you much more, neither can Étoile. Most of what we do now is practice anyway, to push your boundaries. The only other things to learn are about the histories of our different races, and you can read books on that. You don't need me to give you history lessons."

"I know. So... I don't want a babysitter, Evan. And I don't want you miserable either."

"I'm not miserable." He shook his hand as if to emphasise his point. His hands had somehow covered my breasts as we talked and he was playing with my nipples, running them between thumb and forefinger. He sighed. "I'm not sure Wilding is the place I want to be forever."

"I know." A small pang of guilt struck me. Of

course, I knew that, but now it was out in the open, it couldn't be ignored. I felt an enormous surge of gratitude for everything he'd done for me, for all the times he'd come to my aid. But he was right; it was time for me to stand on my own two feet. "We'll have to find a happy compromise," I offered, wondering what that could be.

"Can we do that after sex?" He looked hopeful. His hands dropped to my waist, and he pulled me up his body slightly. Okay, he didn't need to point out the absolute obvious.

I laughed. "Mmm," I murmured, pushing thoughts of the future aside. Our happy compromise could start, right now, with something we both wanted. I ran my hands down his chest, pausing at his waistband to unsnap the button, levering the denim open. "Can you do something about these clothes now?"

As I said it, I felt our clothes melt away until we were nothing but skin against skin. A rush of heat spiralled through my body. Lifting slightly, I rubbed myself against him, enjoying the look on his face as he hardened, pushing back against me. He lay back on the rug – suddenly empty too – and held my hips, encouraging me. Pushing up on my knees, I positioned myself over him, bearing down until I could feel him entering me. I gripped his upper arms and took him within me, a sigh escaping my lips.

I set the pace, his hips rising and falling to meet mine, then pulling me down so he could kiss me again, our tongues mating as our bodies conjoined. The feel of him filling me, over and over, was bliss incarnate. I loved the soft groans that escaped him, the feel of his torso pressed against mine, one hand cupping the back of my head while the other pressed against the small of my back.

Just as I felt my climax rising, warmth spiralling from my core, he grasped me with both hands and, in one swift move, I was on my back looking up, beyond his handsome face to the starry canopy he'd conjured above. Dragging my eyes away from the spectacle, I fixed on him. His eyes had taken on the purple-black hue they always did when we made love. I called them his horny eyes and, while he didn't disagree, I wondered if it meant something more to him. If there were anything I needed an owner's manual on, it was daemons.

My fingers dug into the sculpted muscles of his back as my orgasm ripped through me. My lashes could barely obscure the stars I saw shooting across the sky, one after the other, like fireworks. Under that sky, his hands folded under my hips to arch me up to him, Evan pushed one final time, and then melted over me, his lips nuzzling at my neck. "Happy birthday," he whispered.

"I wish it was my birthday every day." I was attempting to hold back a giggle. My face was flushed and I was riding a freight train full of endorphins. "I like the thing you did with the shooting stars."

Evan craned his head to glance over his shoulder. The last star shot across the canopy and exploded into a little burst of fireworks that seemed to drizzle earthwards, the glittery droplets disintegrating as they reached the floor. "That wasn't me," he said, turning back to me with a smile. "That was you."

"Oh," I whispered. "Cool."

In another room, music clicked on. I frowned up at Evan, dropping my voice to a whisper. "Were we too loud?"

"No." He looked in the direction of the music. "Though maybe we can discuss living alone? I have a yen to have you in front of the fire in the living room."

I raised my eyebrows, a smile curling on my lips. "I'll add both to the agenda."

~

Gage, along with Annalise and Beau, came by in the morning to report. Pack members Jay and Kristin kept watch on Jones and the other Brotherhood minion throughout the night. Gage put his phone on speaker so when they called in with their news, we could all listen.

They didn't have much to report. It seemed the Brotherhood men currently holed up at the motel were quiet and hadn't left their room all night. However, they had been seen making several calls before the drapes were drawn. Even wolf ears couldn't hear far enough across the parking lot and through walls to know who they were calling and why.

I yawned, slapping a hand over my mouth as Jay and Kristin signed off. Despite the very pleasurable end to my birthday, I'd had an uneasy night. Knowing that the Brotherhood were so close by, and almost certainly knew where I lived was an uncomfortable thought. I half expected them to arrive in the dark, torches blazing, and attack my house. In reality, hopefully, nothing they could do would work – magic protected my house and a daemon slept in it. But it didn't stop me from worrying.

Evan pressed a cup of hot coffee into my hand and sat next to me, asking Gage questions about what vehicle the men were driving and did they discover anything about the second man. Sipping my coffee, I saw the plane ticket Jones handed me, the same one that I placed on the mantelpiece last night and ignored until now. In the back of my mind, I saw the date and time counting down, like a flip board, or a bomb about to go off.

I had some time to think about it this morning, when I woke up much earlier than Evan. I doubted that Jones expected me to be on that plane; but it seemed an awful long way to come on what currently amounted to a fool's errand. It wasn't just that I had no intention of going to Hawkscroft, but that I had no intention of ever willingly meeting another Brotherhood member, much less their leader. Not even the idea of being on home shores placated, or attracted, me. There were a lot of things I missed about England – the chocolate, the familiarity, sometimes even the more mundane parts of my previous life. But the Brotherhood, along with the weather, I could definitely do without.

Now, playing on my mind too was both Evan and Étoile's separate suggestions that Wilding wasn't safe. Leaving wasn't something I wanted to think about. Realistically, I knew I could, and easily. I could work remotely from wherever I was, and I'd only been in Wilding for a matter of months, not long enough to put down deep roots, but enough to know that I had found true friends. The idea of starting over again wasn't all that appealing, even if I knew I wouldn't be completely alone.

Étoile's behaviour was puzzling me too. She'd already made several phone calls this morning, but each time, she'd been extra careful not to be overheard.

Just prior to the wolf's pack arrival, Kitty mentioned that Étoile had also been trying to force a vision, to see if she could glean any information from a glimpse into the future. It wasn't an easy job to do, especially when she was so far from her sisters and their mutual power boost. A little part of the old me slipped through, thinking it was crazy to even think in terms of that. Sometimes the witch life was a real mindblower.

"Maybe we should pre-empt them?" I said after I swallowed the last bite of bagel that Kitty had toasted and offered around. I spread it with a thick layer of cream cheese that was sticking my mouth together. "Go to them, force them to tell us what they know."

"They might not know anything," pointed out Étoile. "And pushing them might have the opposite effect."

"Such as?" I asked.

"There might be more of them here. It's unlikely they'd send two unprotected humans to confront a witch, especially if they suspect you have help."

"I guess."

"The best thing to do is make sure you always have someone with you," added Étoile, reiterating yesterday's agreement. "We'll make it difficult for them to approach you again."

I hated to point out the obvious. Having someone watch my back was reassuring, but it certainly wasn't tenable. We all had jobs, none that involved babysitting me. "For how long? This can't go on indefinitely."

"Maybe you should rethink what we discussed? It might be time to leave Wilding for a while." Evan's voice was low and concerned, and not at all full of snide satisfaction. I knew from the previous night that he wanted to go home, but I knew he wouldn't force me. We agreed to discuss our future living arrangements, though now really wasn't the time. There was too much weighing on my mind. Sighing lightly so as not to offend him, I sipped my coffee again and avoided his eyes. Much as I didn't want to admit it, he probably did have a point. Texas might be safer, but I'd be on the move again and I wanted to fight for my corner. I had to stop running some day or I could be running my whole life.

"Then at least, make sure you're not alone," Evan added. He and Gage exchanged looks. They might not exactly have formed a friendship, but there was an uneasy truce when it came to me. Although it seemed to run more along the lines of "be nice when Stella is around," all bets were off when I wasn't looking. I wasn't an idiot. I could tell they had their issues, and unfortunately, they all centred on me.

When I first arrived in Wilding alone, not knowing what happened to Evan, Gage and I flirted with the beginnings of a relationship. However, all that had gone out of my mind the moment I knew Evan was staying. I had yet to confess to kissing Gage when Evan once stormed off in anger, not long after returning to my life. It had been a weak moment for me, one I did my best to forget, but I knew things could be infinitely worse if I confessed. I wasn't used to keeping secrets and this was one that gave me some trouble, until I refused to think about it anymore.

A truce was a start.

"I'm going to head out and relieve Jay and Kris."

Annalise got to her feet and took her plate and mug, carrying them towards the kitchen. "Michelle's probably already waiting for me."

"Just leave them by the sink, I'll do them in a while," I called after her.

She stopped, looked back at me and frowned. I made a big thing out of being house-proud – it was hard not to, now that I had so much space of my own. "You sure?"

"No problem, go fight evil." I grinned.

As alpha male, Gage was taking the organisation of the stakeout very seriously, which gave me some reassurance. Annalise was scheduled to take on the next watch alongside a pretty, redheaded wolf called Michelle Dunphy who was a couple of years older than I and a relatively new member of their pack. I knew Annalise's eagerness to leave early this morning was less about getting to their rendezvous on time and more about getting some extra alone time with Beau, who was due at work. He called the early evening Brotherhood-watch shift. I hoped to hell this was not going to spoil their weekend plans.

They slipped outside, hand in hand, walking towards Beau's truck. For a moment, I envied Annalise. She not only had a great brother, but also lived in her hometown surrounded by her childhood friends. I admired her joyous nature, her ability to make everyone feel welcome. Most of all, I envied her freedom. Few people would mess with Annalise and risk the wrath of the pack.

Before I'd arrived to Wilding, the pack had free rein to run wild out in this neck of the woods. They even had a private meeting house, the Loup Garou, that was a mile or so away, at the other end of

Shadow Wood Lane. They were forced to lie low when I arrived, until they discovered I was something other than human. Only then, did they reveal themselves to me. Now they were a regular fixture in the woods and I often saw them in both their human and wolf forms. Out of respect, I stayed away while they transitioned, since it was a very personal thing and they always ended up naked. Occasionally, I'd see one of them through the change, as some didn't seem to care. It was a strange thing to watch bones slide and lock into new positions, claws grow or retract, muzzles become noses and so on.

"Is there anything I can help the pack with?" I asked Gage. I hated feeling useless while the pack came to my aid again. A few months ago, they chased off the large gathering of witches who arrived uninvited to my house. While a few of the witches were intent on causing trouble, the rest were spectators. They were mainly interested in seeing if any battle lines were being drawn, all part of the Council's leadership challenge. I proved myself to them and that I was a force to be reckoned with, the wolf pack right beside me. No one was quite sure what the repercussions would be, but, so far, things had been quiet on that front. The inevitable power surge, however, brought other unforeseen problems we didn't want in Wilding.

"Not a thing. Like I said, we've got the Brotherhood on twenty-four hour watch and that's all under control. So long as we know where you are, and where they are, and that it's not the same place, we're good."

"I really appreciate it."

"I'll say it again, not a problem. Happy to help."

Gage stood, tugging on a light jacket as some concession to the late winter air. "I have to get to work though. You've got my number. Call if you need anything."

"Sure." I left Gage to walk himself out.

After Kitty and I washed and dried the dishes, and Evan excused himself to work, Étoile insisted on carrying on with our magic lessons as normal. Despite Kitty's big gap in her studies while she'd been in the hospital, her magic was coming through thick and fast. Her weather specialism afforded her a very strong connection to the earth. It seemed like she could create any climatic conditions she chose. On a small scale, she was terrific. On a larger scale, she wavered a little but I'd seen her create tropical sunshine, and then make snow fall in the same location.

Kitty was instructed by Étoile to practise making and directing mist, coiling it like candyfloss around her hand. Meanwhile, she had me practise my telekinesis. Throughout my life I'd made things happen and sometimes, it had really scared me. Then, almost a year ago, under Evan's tutelage, I deliberately used it to make an inanimate object move.

Now, I found tapping into my magic much more easily. I simply had to focus on the object in question and will it. No longer did things slide across tables. I could make them float to me, land in my hand, or alight wherever I chose.

Currently Étoile had me calling specific objects from different rooms, mundane things and things she planted, which involved a lot more concentration, something I found scarce while I was worrying about the Brotherhood's next moves.

After an hour of moving objects around the house, I felt exhausted and I was just resting my head on the kitchen table when I heard Evan's footsteps approaching. I looked up, smiling, as he stuck his head around the door.

"I'm going out," he said succinctly. "I'll be gone a couple of hours."

"Where to?" I stifled a yawn.

"Errands," he said, and was gone before I could ask what sort of errands. As far as I knew, Evan had people who ran around and did things for him. In regards to his business, he was currently outsourcing most of his daily work to various employees – whom I'd yet to meet – leaving him free to manage the overall business. Apart from occasionally mailing packages, I'd never seen him run any kind of errand. A little part of me was suspicious that he had discovered something about the Brotherhood that he was choosing not to share. All at once, I felt bad at that. I'd gotten used to sharing everything with Evan. The same little part of me that wondered if I were making a mistake by not being more acquiescent to his desire to go home, also wondered what parts of his life he kept from me.

His business was operated only on a fairly secretive basis, and Evan told me that sometimes he thought it was best I didn't know. He didn't say in case it put me in danger, but that's what I inferred. Maybe that should have made me more worried than it did, but it didn't. He didn't interfere with my job, so I didn't interfere with his.

Remembering I had a question that I wanted to ask him, I stepped through to the living room. The lingering heat told me Evan had already gone, shimmering out of the house. He could be anywhere by now.

"I have to go pick up a package," Kitty said. She sat on the arm of the chair as she pulled on her boots.

"I have a couple of errands to run too." Étoile looked from me to Kitty, wrinkling her nose in thought.

"Anything I can do for you?" Kitty offered.

"No, but thanks anyway." She stared at me and I found myself pulling back.

"It can't wait though. I need to pick up a few things before I make my trip on Monday. We'll all have to go together."

"What trip?" I asked. It was the first I'd heard of it.

"Just a quick visit to the city. Nothing important," she replied breezily.

"I'll be okay in the house by myself. I can call Evan if anything happens."

Étoile contemplated that for a moment. "I'd rather not risk it. You're under our protection, missy. Let's go."

We piled into Kitty's car and she drove us into town. I followed them around like a naughty puppy while they went about their business before we separated, with Kitty shooting off to the post office. It was only when we passed the pharmacy that I felt like I'd been hit by a truck.

Evan and I hadn't used any protection the previous night. *Shit! Shit! Shit! Shit!* I didn't know what to think about that. We'd never gotten so carried away to the point of not using anything before and it made my stomach lurch. I was twenty-five and, although that made me reasonably old enough to be a mother, it wasn't anything I'd ever thought about. Could a witch and a daemon even procreate together? I guessed so because we'd always used protection before.

"You look like you've just seen a ghost," said Étoile, glancing over her handwritten list. "What's up?"

"Nothing." I shook my head. It wasn't something I could discuss with her, not until I'd spoken to Evan, anyway. Come to think of it, I wasn't sure how I felt about having a conversation like this with him either. This ventured into serious with a capital "S" category and there were a whole lot of other things in that category that needed to be broached too.

"Oh, shoot," muttered Étoile, looking in her bag. "I forget to pick up my dry cleaning and they have my favourite coat and my black pantsuit. Crap. We're going to have run back to pick it up."

"Ugh," I groaned, looking all the way down the street then back to Darla's, less than twenty yards away. Coffee sounded way better than traipsing after Étoile. I jabbed a finger at the diner. "I'm going to wait in there. I can see Kristin at the counter."

Étoile looked around for Kitty again, sweeping the street, probably weighing up the chances of anything awful happening to me. There weren't a lot of people around now that lunch hour had passed but still enough for any kind of attack to be unlikely. "Fine, but go straight in and don't..."

I raised my eyebrows. "I am going to talk to people."

"Fine. Text Kitty and have her pick us up outside. I'll be back in ten minutes." She looked at me and I stared back. "Go in," she urged, flapping her hands at me like a mother with a hesitant child.

"Fine." I stomped away and pushed the diner door open, blankly smiling at whomever was in front of me. Kristin waved and turned back to the woman she was talking to. They looked so deep in conversation that I didn't like to interrupt. I wasn't sure how long I could take being babysat. I hoped the Brotherhood would go home soon and leave me alone so I could get back to leading my normal life. *Normal. Hah.*

I ordered a coffee to go and sat on the stool at the window, looking onto the street. Pulling out my phone, I tapped a message to Kitty, telling her where to meet me, then, as I slipped it back into my bag, I saw Kitty's car barrelling down Main. I grabbed my coffee, popped a plastic lid on it, picked up my bag and jogged outside, reaching the sidewalk just as the car screeched to a stop in front of me. The window unwound and I leaned down to look in.

"Get in," shouted Kitty, reaching over to pop the lock.

"What's wrong?" I asked.

"We got a sighting in town. The Brotherhood are on the move."

"Where to?"

"They're headed east, towards a private airstrip near Deliverance." Deliverance was our nearest big town, just marginally too small to be a city, and I recalled seeing the airstrip off the highway. It was used mostly by a flying school, but, every so often, visiting dignitaries would use it too.

"That's good, right? They're going?" I climbed in, barely having time to lock the seatbelt in place before Kitty had hit the gas, peeling out of there.

"No," Kitty shook her head, taking her eyes off the road for a moment to look at me, fear etched all over her face. "They've got Étoile."

CHAPTER FIVE

My mouth dropped open in horror. Étoile and I may have only parted company a matter of minutes ago, but now I thought about it, I turned my back and walked straight into the coffee shop. Everyone had been so concerned about me, it hadn't even occurred to us to seriously think someone else could be the target. "How the hell did they do that?" I gasped.

"I was just getting into the car when I saw them grab her off the street so I took down the registration and called the pack, before I came to get you. They spotted the van leaving town and they figured that's where they were headed."

"How do they know they were going to the airstrip?" I puzzled. There had to be a dozen places going east, including a train station and several warehouses, as well as the Blue Moon Motel they were staying in.

Kitty sped through the light just as it changed to red and pointed the car east, in pursuit. "We'll stop them, okay. You don't have to worry about a thing."

"I'm more worried about what Étoile will do." Étoile would be the last person I'd try and kidnap. Any witch hunter who had done their research would know that she was powerful, far more so than Kitty or I. Kidnapping Étoile would be an incredibly stupid move. Of course, I could be wrong by giving the Brotherhood the benefit of thinking they were smart and well researched, but all indications showed that they bided their time, waiting until they had the right victim. I once thought they were smash, grab and burn, but I knew now they were well orchestrated, well funded and somehow protected from the law.

"Just relax, okay? We'll get there in ten minutes. We can save her."

"Shouldn't we call for back up?"

"The wolves will meet us there. They're already ahead of us."

"Which ones?"

"I don't know. The big one, the leader, spotted the van."

"Their leader?"

My bag started to vibrate and I unzipped it, rooting around inside to find my phone. Finally I saw it glowing next to my wallet. I reached in and turned it over, stopping before pulling out. The screen was bright and in bold letters, I saw the last name I expected to see calling me. I hesitated, looking at it.

"Everything okay?" asked Kitty, looking sideways at me.

"Uh, yeah. Fine!" I tried a small smile. I probably squeaked that out, my voice a little too high as I struggled to contain my sudden panic. Taking a deep breath, I frantically scrambled to remember everything Evan taught me, while keeping my expression blank. Something was awfully wrong. Gage was at work in Deliverance and would be until at least six. Kitty knew that, and she would have known his name too.

Slowly, I shifted my vision so my eyes were slightly out of focus, then inhaled deeply. Just the scent alone told me whoever was in the driver's seat was not Kitty, despite having the same face and clothing.

Circling my head just like boxers do whenever they need to ease a crick or an ache, I rested my vision on the shape-shifter impersonating my friend. I could see the vague outline of a person, a woman underneath the shell. Whoever she was, she was good at concealing herself because I couldn't get an impression of exactly what she looked like. I could only be sure that she wasn't who she was supposed to be.

I must have looked at her too oddly, or for too long because her hand shot out and grabbed my neck, strong fingers pressing against my carotid. Despite the intense pressure from her fingers, she didn't lose her shape, or waver at all. I clawed at her, trying to pry her fingers from choking me. She held on tight with one hand, while the other steered. Breathing was painful and I knew if I didn't do something soon, the air would squeeze out of my lungs. She'd either choke me unconscious or kill me.

With one hand still pulling at her fingers, I squeezed the lid off my coffee with my free hand and threw it in her face. Apart from a scream of anger as the hot liquid hit her, she barely decreased the pressure on my throat.

I scrabbled around my seat for a weapon of some

kind but all I found was a map book tucked into the pocket on the passenger side door. I latched onto it and slammed it at her head, hitting hard once, twice, distracting her long enough that I could yank at her fingers. With a sickening crack, I heard one snap. She screamed and let go of the wheel, punching wildly at me with both fists.

I slunk down into my seat, pushing my bag onto the floor. Swivelling, I raised my legs, pulling my knees back as far as I could and kicked her firmly in the solar plexus.

Pulling back again while she was winded, I landed another blow under her chin, her head rocking back. Her grip slackened and her eyes rolled back into her head, her eyelids drooping.

It took me a second to realise that her foot was jammed on the gas pedal and we were hurtling forward, accelerating as the speed marker slid around the dial on the dashboard. The shape-shifter started to slide forwards, and the wheel lurched to the left sending the car speeding across both lanes, aiming towards the ditch.

I leaned down, grabbed my bag and shimmered out of there, reappearing on the side of road, a hundred yards or so away just as the car careened into the ditch, its hood crumpling and popping open. I had half expected an explosion. For a moment, I just stood there waiting, but nothing happened except for a plume of steam rising from the engine.

Kitty was going to be so pissed.

Delving into my bag, I pulled out my phone and hit the redial button, breathing in relief as the real Kitty answered.

"Stella, oh my gosh! I went to Darla's looking for

you but they said you got into a car. Where are you? Are you okay? Where did you go?" Her questions came in a rush.

"I thought I was in a car with you," I said, trying to hold back the tears of relief I suddenly felt. Kitty was okay. I was alive.

"My car's been stolen."

"I know. It's totalled. A shape-shifter was pretending to be you and I got in. She said Étoile had been kidnapped." I felt so stupid. I should have checked, but between the lack of sleep and the anxiety, I just didn't think. I saw what I expected to see, and hadn't questioned it.

"I'm with Étoile now. She, we, want to know where you are." Kitty's voice was full of concern.

"I'm a few minutes east of town, on the way towards Deliverance."

"We're coming to get you."

"Music to my..." I must have heard something that registered before I had a chance to properly process it, because I turned around just then, just in time to duck as a fist swung for my face. The shape-shifter still wore an assimilation of Kitty's body, but there was a long cut on her forehead where it must have hit the wheel when the car landed in the ditch. Her nose looked broken. "Kitty's" curls were plastered to her head with blood that flowed from the gash on her forehead but she just kept on moving, swinging for me wildly while I danced out of her way.

I dropped the phone as she took her first swing and I could hear Kitty and Étoile screaming. I didn't need to hear the words, I got the gist: *get out of there.*

Kitty number two caught a clump of my hair, pulling me forward as she swung a punch in an upper cut that would connect with my jaw. Unfortunately for her, I'd just focused on the real Kitty and Étoile, and my desire to be with them, and started to shimmer.

When I opened my eyes, I breathed out in relief. My friends were standing in front of me. Kitty looked momentarily horrified, then turned away, her hand over her mouth as she bowed her head. Étoile managed to close her mouth long enough to step around me, reach over and tug at something in my hair. "Don't look," she said, her face grim.

When you're told not to look at something, the automatic response is to look at it. I turned around, saw what Étoile held and my stomach heaved. I was afraid of this. When I shimmered, the shape-shifter grabbed my hair and, as I vanished, I took her arm with me. The problem was... the rest of her remained behind.

Fortunately, Étoile and Kitty hadn't waited in front of the diner, where they would reasonably have expected me to be. Instead, they rounded the corner into an alleyway that was partially shielded by dumpsters from any passing traffic. The three of us stood in a triangle and Étoile dropped the severed arm in the middle of us where it lay on the ground.

Étoile stooped down and examined it briefly, seemingly not finding anything too odd about it other than it not being attached to its former body. She took a reusable plastic bag from her purse and gingerly dropped the arm into it. A moment later, it was gone, bag, arm and all.

"Where'd it go?" I asked.

"You don't want to know."

"I do."

"Your refrigerator," she said, pulling an apologetic face as she continued, "to preserve it until we can get it sent away to be analysed. Evan can probably do that."

"You are so buying me a new fridge." I didn't add *and everything in it*. I hoped that would be a given. I wondered if she put it in the meat store. Yuck. I was going vegetarian.

Holding out my hand, I called my bag and phone to me from where I'd dropped them on the road and, a moment later, they were in my hands. Aside from a few scuffs, my phone had fared okay from me dropping it on the tarmac. I hit the speed dial for Evan's number. He answered after a couple of rings.

"What's up?" He sounded frazzled and I wondered what I was disturbing.

"Long story short," I started, taking a deep breath. "I nearly got kidnapped and now there's a dismembered arm in my fridge."

"Okaaaay," he drawled, absorbing that. He was silent for a moment, then, "Where is the rest of the body?"

I gave him the rough location, continuing, "It was a shape-shifter and I shimmered when it, she, pulled my hair."

"Is the shifter dead?"

"I don't know."

"I'll send someone to retrieve it, and deal with the arm. Where are you now? Are you safe?"

"I'm with Kitty and Étoile."

His voice dropped a notch. "Are you sure it's them?"

"Positive."

"Good. Stay with them. Why you aren't at the

house, where it's safe, I don't know, but I'll see you there soon. Go straight home, okay." It wasn't a question; it was an order, one I was inclined to take. "I'll be there in less than ten minutes, just as soon as I wrap up here," Evan promised. "You can tell me the full story then."

"Okay." As I hung up, I twisted to look over my shoulder. I should have realised a dismembered arm wouldn't be a nice clean cut. There was a nasty smear of blood down my jacket and what looked suspiciously like some kind of sinewy human material. I would probably have to burn my jacket. Seeing as I couldn't exactly walk around with that kind of gore dripping from me, I shrugged it off and wrapped my jacket in a ball; all the while hoping my breakfast would not revisit me. I calculated how far I had shimmered. Probably a few miles... and remotely retrieved my things too. *Pretty good.* A wave of fatigue hit me. "How are we going to get home? I'm not up to another long shimmer."

"And I can't carry you both." Étoile looked thoughtful as we followed her out of the alley. Her face lit into a smile and she started to wave. I turned and saw Annalise crossing the street towards us, probably wondering why we were lingering in an alley.

"What's happening?" she asked brightly as we stepped out to meet her.

"You so don't want an answer to that," muttered Kitty, earning a frown from Étoile.

I shook my head. "I'll explain later. Did you finish your shift?"

"Sure did. The Brotherhood packed up and left. The next shift are following them and they just called in to say they're heading towards Deliverance. We've called around and there's a plane scheduled to leave from that private airstrip. It's bound for England, so we figured that's too much of a coincidence for Jones and his cronies not to be on it." Annalise looked to her companion, Michelle, who was nodding in agreement causing her red ponytailed hair to bob along with her. "Michelle and I are just heading back to my place. We grabbed some sandwiches before we have to report in."

I raised my eyebrows at Étoile, who was looking thoughtful. What Annalise told us was both good and bad news. Good that the Brotherhood were going, at last; bad that, if the shifter had succeeded, I might have been on that plane too. Like many things about the Brotherhood, what I couldn't understand was why they would use a shape-shifter to ensnare me and how they knew about them at all. The Brotherhood hated all things magic. A shape-shifter should be right at the top of their hate crimes list, or at least in the number two spot, if they hadn't yet added werewolves and daemons. "Can we catch a ride with you?" I asked, remembering that Kitty's car was in a ditch.

"Sure. What happened to yours?"

"We took Kitty's car and it's totalled."

Annalise pulled a face. "Sounds like your explaining will take the whole trip."

Annalise was parked a block away so we walked there. Michelle called shotgun and, seeing as she was taller than any of us, no one complained. Reaching the car, she slid in and opened a paperback novel to read. Étoile, Kitty and I shuffled into the back and I gave a brief rundown of my run-in with the shifter as Annalise pulled out into the traffic. The roads were light this time of day and she made short work of navigating the car out of town.

"Where are we going?" I asked, suddenly realising that we weren't taking the fastest route home. I altered my vision quickly, my heart thumping. Yeah, twice in one day would be too much action for me. Annalise was definitely Annalise.

"There's a road crew that started clipping trees about a half hour ago so we're taking the back route. It's scenic, meaning longer," she added for our out-of-towner benefit. I remembered Gage's explanation about the impending road works. "But we'll be home in no time," Annalise concluded.

"What's Evan going to do with the arm?" Michelle asked, turning to look back at us. She folded the paperback away as I spilled my story, thoughtfully contemplating what I said for the last few minutes.

"I don't know. Maybe find out who it belonged to, with DNA or something? If he can find out who it is, maybe, he can find out why they were trying to kidnap me," I surmised.

"I would not want to be on the wrong side of your daemon, if that happens." Michelle shivered. Annalise had the heat turned up full so I wasn't sure if it were just for effect.

I knew daemons had a bad reputation but I still didn't like to think of Evan as violent. He'd never showed that side of himself to me, so I was content to live in my little bubble of safety. Perhaps I was wrong?

Still, Michelle chattered on. "A few years ago, when I swore allegiance to a pack in Chicago, before I knew they were no good, he came to retrieve the pack beta who owed a big fine to a casino in Nevada. Anyway, the casino was demon-owned and they wanted their money back fast, so they hired Evan. You should have seen him. He took on a good number of the pack, left a bunch of broken bones and still got the beta. I've never seen anyone fight like that." She sounded awed, impressed.

"Are you sure that was Evan?" All the times he talked to me about his business, he made it sound like it was stealth, not might, that got him through.

"Sure. Evan Hunter. I could not forget him. He did that weird flame thing from his hands and he fights like a... well, uh, a demon." Michelle grinned, waggling fingers in the air. "I left the pack a few weeks after that. Turns out, they were a bunch of crooks. Don't know what happened to the beta, but I heard he still has a limp. Lucky that's all he got, if you ask me. I cannot tell you how happy I am being with Gage. I mean, with Gage's pack," she corrected herself, but not before Annalise turned her head slightly, raising her eyebrows. Michelle unexpectedly blushed. That's when it hit me. Michelle was the girl Gage was dating, the potential new girlfriend. Somehow I hadn't expected to know the woman he was interested in; but it struck me how silly that assumption was. This was a close-knit town; they were both werewolves, not to mention single and good looking. Why wouldn't they be drawn to each other?

I swallowed back the uncertainty of both Michelle's description of Evan and her dating life. "Right," I muttered. Luckily, before I could say something stupid, or defensive, something that would show exactly how little I knew about my own boyfriend, or that I was surprised about her and Gage, the car started making spluttering noises and slowed down.

With a groan, Annalise swung the wheel over and brought the car to a stop on the side of the road, her fingers searching for the lever to pop the hood. "I'll just be a minute," she said, climbing out. Michelle got out next and I shook away the brief twinge of jealousy seeing her tall, willowy body. What did it matter to me if Gage had a girlfriend? Nothing. It shouldn't matter a darned thing. The two of them pulled up the hood and peered inside. After a moment, Michelle stepped onto the road, looking for something, then kneeling, to look under the car. After a moment, she got up and walked back around to Annalise. I could hear them talking. Then Annalise stuck her head back inside the car, looking worried.

"What is it?" asked Kitty. "Did the car overheat?"

"Nope. There's a trail of gas all along the road. Something's happened to the fuel pump, we think," replied Annalise.

Michelle stood by the open passenger door. "It's no accident. Someone jammed a screwdriver or something into the fuel line."

"Sabotage?" said Étoile, opening the back door, swinging her legs out. She fished her phone out of her pocket. She tapped a message and pressed "send." "I let Evan know what happened so he doesn't worry if we're late," she told us, peering at the screen. "Oh, reception isn't great here."

"It's too open for us to just wait out here, given the circumstances," said Michelle, turning to look up and down the road. "And not many other people are going to drive out this way."

"Should we head back to town?" I asked. Kitty and I had gotten out of the car and we were standing in a huddle on the tarmac.

"Nah. If we cut through the woods, we'll come out through the woods at the back of my house," said Annalise, pointing to the trees. "It's not far."

"You sure?"

"I've spent a lot of years running these words, honey. Course, I'm sure."

Michelle nodded. "I'd rather do that than wait here to see if whoever fucked up the fuel line comes along to see how we're doing."

We contemplated that for a moment. "Let's go," said Étoile, deciding for us. "Grab your stuff."

"I'm going to go wolf, just in case," announced Michelle, stepping out of the way, just as I slid out. She peeled off her shirt, jeans and boots and tossed them onto the passenger seat. I turned away politely, not before wondering if Gage would appreciate the view, and walked around to the other side of the car where a grassy strip separated us from the trees. A moment later, a reddish brown wolf circled the car and paused next to us. With a yip, she sprang forwards, quickly lost to the woods.

"Lead the way," Étoile said to Annalise, then turning to Kitty and me, "Stay together." Only a few minutes' walk took us into the denser trees. The cool, blue sky came close to being obscured by a thick, leafy canopy as the spring leaves were starting fill in. I could smell earth and the faintest scent of animal. Annalise was inhaling deeply, her keen wolf nose far more likely to pick up something than our human senses.

"Men have been here recently," she said, looking around. "Very recently, but I couldn't tell you who. This is private land so maybe it's the owner. There's no border between his property and ours." We pressed on, the trees parting ahead into a clearing.

I knew there was something wrong as soon as we stepped into the clearing. A quick glance towards Étoile and Kitty confirmed my suspicions. They felt it too. It was the quiet that got me first. We should hear birds, insects, small animals, but they were gone. Even the light breeze was absent.

Turning in a small circle, I looked through the clearing to the woods surrounding us. Annalise sniffed again. In a low voice she said, "Something's not right. The scent is stronger, more recent here. I don't like this. Let's call Gage. Maybe he knows who's been using the woods."

I tugged my phone out of the bag and squinted at the screen. The bars had all gone. "No coverage."

"Me neither," added Kitty.

Annalise breathed deeply through her nose, exhaling cold air that clouded in front of us. "I'm going wolf," she decided. "I'll be faster than you two-feet folk. I'll head back to the car, change, and call Beau or Jay and get them to meet us. Maybe we should have just waited? I'm sorry, this was a bad idea. I just thought it would be quicker than waiting in the open. I'll do a circuit of the area and come find you. You want me to call Evan too?"

"He said he'd be back in a few minutes, so I guess so. He isn't far away."

"No problem. Grab my clothes, okay?"

"Hey, Annalise, should we keep moving?" Étoile asked, tapping her arm to get her attention before she undressed.

"Uh, stay in the clearing, just in case, until I come back. It's probably nothing," Annalise said, perhaps a touch to hopefully.

"Sure."

Annalise stripped deftly and her change was fast and assured. The pale wolf shot into the woods and she was quickly lost from view. I scooped up her clothes and boots and tried to make them into a neat parcel to carry, along with my own jacket. We poked around for a while in the clearing before standing and looking at each other.

"I don't see anything," I said, feeling relieved. "I mean, it's quiet but I don't see any footprints or litter or anything that says someone has been waiting here. Maybe the owner had a hunting party or something?" I had no idea how these things worked, but that was the best I could come up with for why Annalise smelled a scent she hadn't expected.

"I'm glad we don't do any of the naked witches in the woods stuff," I said. "I don't think I could get comfortable with that."

"You should meet my mom," replied Étoile.

We waited, poking around the clearing, not wanting to move any further away. "Annalise has been gone too long. Let's start making our way back. Maybe she got someone to patch up the car," said Étoile, grabbing both Kitty and me by the hands and tugging so that we started to follow our own tracks across the clearing. "No point waiting around here if Annalise and Michelle are waiting by the car."

We followed swiftly, pausing at the edge of the clearing when Étoile touched my arm then put a finger to her lips, silencing us both. "Shh! I hear something."

I tried to focus on my surroundings, searching for whatever it was Étoile could hear. Then I heard it. A shuffling sort of sound in the undergrowth, then a whistling as something sailed past us to land in the dry grass off to our left.

Fire erupted in front of us, spreading quickly in lines to the right and left, cutting us off from the path. I smelled gasoline. With horror, I realised it was poured onto the grass before we'd arrived, ready to be lit. Étoile and I stepped one way, and as a wall of fire sliced past us, I saw with terror that Kitty had lurched in a different direction. I could hear her screaming our names as the fire cut us off. In the distance, a wolf howled, a shrill, aggrieved sound.

Wheeling around, I could see Kitty, just as the flames grew upwards. She was cut off from two sides. On the third and far side, I got the briefest glimpse of a man standing near the tree line before that edge caught fire too, trapping her in a triangle.

Kitty screamed my name and I felt something shift in the air, the cold turning into something more substantial. The air felt wet. Kitty was trying to make it rain, but, though the air was getting heavier, nothing happened.

"They've made some kind of protective circle," Étoile hissed, holding my hand as we stepped back, away from the hungry licks of the fire. "I think I can shimmer us out of here, but I don't know if I can get back for Kitty."

"Can we get through the flames at least? Maybe if all three of us are together we can power off each other?"

"The fire's intense, but you're right, we should..." Étoile didn't get a chance to finish what she was going to say. I had the strangest feeling of my ears beginning to pop, then an intense blast of heat before the world went dark.

A moment later, and everything was gone, the woods and the fire... and Kitty. Instead, we were in what looked like a hallway of a house. I stood on large black tiles, a set of wooden double doors behind me. Looking around, I took in white walls and a small amount of nice furniture; a console table with a pair of lamps, a single upholstered chair. We were standing in the hallway of someone's house, a very impressive space with a double level that reached up to a soaring ceiling. The height was emphasised by a staircase, upstairs a glass balustrade spanned the hallway's width. Behind me was another door, closed. It was darkly glamourous in a masculine sort of way.

I still had Annalise's bundle and my jacket under my arm and Étoile was sliding her hand out of mine.

Evan was next to us, rolling his shoulders.

I blinked, adjusting my eyes. They stung from the smoke. "What just happened?" I asked, my heart pounding.

"You couldn't get out, but I could get in and out. The magic protecting that circle was for witches only. Like a loophole."

"Where's Kitty?"

He paused for a moment. "I couldn't get you all."

I felt like screaming at him. Instead, I dropped Annalise's bundle and battered my fists against his chest for all the good it did me. "You left her there to die?" I choked through tears that sprang to my eyes as the force of Kitty's anguished cries sounded in my ears. It was a good job I was in control of my emotions these days. Things could have been a lot worse if my magic took over. The long, modern chandelier in the hallway didn't deserve to shatter.

"Hell, no!" Evan looked appalled. "I got Étoile's message about the car being sabotaged just as I was checking out the arm. I'd already decided to come get you once I saw the message but the arm sealed it. Then, Annalise called Beau, and he called me, told me to get my ass over to you all, seeing as I could get there faster. He was worried someone might have followed you. We got there just as the fire started and split up. I got you two, they went for Kitty. No problem."

"Are you sure?" I patted my pockets for my phone, found it and started scrawling my call list until I found Kitty's number. I got her voicemail and left a panicked message, telling her to *call me, right now.* "How come you got to us so quickly?"

Evan ran his hands over my arms and stared down at me. "Beau was already driving and it took me about thirty seconds, since you weren't far." He released me with a sigh, and started walking further into the building beckoning for us to follow. I took a moment to look around.

"What did Annalise say when she called? Where is she? Hey, where are we anyway?" I asked, following him after a glance at Étoile. She shrugged and shook her head.

Evan looked back at us and gave me a cautious sort of smile as if he weren't quite sure that I would like what he was going to say. "My house," he answered.

CHAPTER SIX

"Your house?" I repeated, realisation dawning on me as I followed him along the broad hallway. Nothing cluttered the space and it smelled faintly of lemon cleaning solution, like someone had mopped the tiles recently. My voice was slightly incredulous as I clarified, "In Texas?" In all the time we'd been dating, well, if you call moving in together dating, I'd never been to his house although we often talked about it. It was a case of one thing or the other that stopped us from making the trip together: work, lessons... evil.

Evan didn't pause to answer, just saying, "That's the one."

My phone rang then, showing Kitty's number and I stopped, bringing the phone to my ear. "I'm fine," she panted on the line. "Well, except for some minor burns on my arms. Beau helped me, and a couple of the guys. Gage just picked us up and we're heading back to his place. They're sending a tow truck for Annalise's car."

"Oh, thank God. I'm so glad you're okay, except

for the burns, obviously." I didn't like to ponder on luck, but it seemed more than serendipitous that the wolves had arrived at just the right time.

"They'll heal, though I smell like a really nasty barbecue. We aren't going to be able to grill for a while. Where are you anyway? Evan got you both, right?"

"Yeah. We're at his house."

"In Texas!" Kitty squeaked. "I thought he'd take you to *your* house, not across the damn country. You need to get back here, like now."

"What's going on? Is Annalise mad that I've still got her clothes?" Not only that, I had her boots too and it was cold. At least Michelle had the good sense to toss hers in the car.

"No, it's not that. Well, she probably will be but... We were just a distraction, honey." Kitty rushed on, hardly taking pause to breathe, "The Brotherhood got Annalise. They must have known they were being watched. Gage said Jones and the other guy were followed as far as the plane. But this ambush definitely smacks of Brotherhood, so we missed something, somehow. Maybe they just got lucky and decided to snatch Annalise because she was on her own, and we were with you."

A familiar feeling of guilt crept over me and I had to put my hand against the pristine white wall to steady myself. "Are you sure they have her?"

"Yeah, the keys were still in the ignition and the guys caught a couple of scents. They think Annalise got grabbed as soon as the fire started, cutting us off from the road. They knew we wouldn't let them get you, honey." Kitty paused then said, softly, "There was a lot of blood on the door. She fought back."

I choked back the sob rising in my throat. There was no telling what they would do to Annalise now. "What about Michelle?"

"We found her out cold next to the car. I think she came to help Annalise and someone hit her over the head. Jay took her to the hospital. Listen, there was a letter left on the windscreen addressed to you."

"Open it." Evan and Étoile both stepped closer, waiting.

I fiddled with the phone, hitting "speaker" before holding it out in my palm. There was a sound of tearing and then rustling like Kitty was juggling the phone as well as the envelope. Over all that, I heard the hum of the engine and the occasional word from Gage, talking to someone. "It's just a short note," she said after a long moment. "It says, 'Got your wolf friend. Accept the invitation or she bites it.' Do you think that was a bad pun? There's another plane ticket, too. First class. It's for tonight."

My stomach plummeted. "I've got to go," I whispered.

"Yeah, you should talk this over with Evan and Étoile."

"No, I mean, I've got to go. To England."

Kitty made a little clicking noise with her tongue. "I don't think that's a good idea."

"I don't have a choice. I can't let them hurt Annalise."

I heard an angry growl in the background, then the low hum of a car engine cutting out while a door opened. Someone was muttering the things they would do if Annalise got hurt. It sounded like her boyfriend, Beau. Considering how big he was, and his military service, I was glad he was on our side, but my heart wept for him.

"What does Étoile think?"

"Étoile thinks we're in deep shit," said Étoile, leaning in.

"What she said," I added. "Listen, I'm coming back. I'll meet you at my house. We'll make a plan as soon as I get there."

"Hurry, Stella." Kitty clicked off and I slid the phone back in my pocket.

"They've got Annalise," I whispered, even though they already knew that.

"Shit." Evan ran a hand through his short hair, looking perturbed.

Something occurred to me. "That witch I saw today in Wilding. I didn't recognise her. Do you think she could have anything to do with this?"

"Maybe," Étoile said. "But it's unlikely. What would a witch have to do with any of this?"

"She could make a car break down at exactly the right place." I've been thinking about that, how the gas trailed out just at the spot where the Brotherhood were waiting. It was a huge coincidence that we broke down where we did, if not.

"Hold on," said Evan. "We're talking about a conspiracy between witches and the Brotherhood, two factions that hate each other."

"There's a whole lot wrong with this situation." Another thought occurred to me. "Jones said someone told him where I was. What if this is Georgia Thomas' way of getting back at me?"

"Shit," cussed Evan.

"Yeah, we got that far. I have to go back." The mileage between Evan's house and mine was almost impossible to gauge. All I knew was it was further than I had ever travelled before. No one knew for sure how shimmering worked, but, thanks to my bonded connection to my house, I was pretty sure I could transport myself back there if my need was strong enough. Neither Étoile nor Evan would have any problems following. Both of them had long distance experience while I was strictly a short-hop wonder. This morning, I was thrilled to do a few miles. Now I was planning something that would make a shimmering marathon look like a hop around my living room.

Evan shook his head. "No, you don't. You go back there, they know exactly where you are and they can come for you anytime. We don't know how many are in the area or where they are. It's too dangerous. Look what happened to Annalise! That could have been you!" he finished sharply.

"I can't stay! They're taking Annalise to England and I have to go after her. It's me they want, not her."

"Let the wolves look after one of their own. They'll get her back."

"And risk their lives because of me? Annalise's life? What kind of friend would I be if I didn't help?"

"The kind of friend who didn't get herself killed on a wild goose chase to another country on the pretext that her friend might be alive. Stella, I didn't want to say this, but Annalise might be dead already. They could be putting her in a shallow grave somewhere near Wilding and you're chasing nothing."

I fought back tears. "I can't do nothing!"

"You aren't doing nothing. You're staying alive, and staying safe until we work out how we can get rid of the Brotherhood, once and for all. This isn't just about you, Stella, this is about every witch, every supernatural creature on this earth. Think about it, Stella." Evan slammed a palm against the wall, his fingers spreading across the plaster as he leant there. His questions came thick and fast. "What happens if we're revealed to the world? You think regular people will want to live alongside us? You think they won't want to harness what we can do or punish us because we have what they don't? Or maybe the Brotherhood will be the fucking heroes who get to hunt us without any danger of being prosecuted because they're just performing a public service. We have to be smart about this."

I froze, my eyes flicking over to Étoile as I waited for her support. Annalise was her friend, too. She held up her hands in surrender. "I think he's right. We need to keep you safe and hidden until we can eliminate the threat, not send you right into it. And we need to be absolutely sure that they have Annalise before we do anything at all."

I stood my ground. "If she's alive, the longer we wait, the less time she has."

"There are a lot of ifs here, Stella," Étoile warned but she didn't sound her usual confident self at all.

Following Evan along the hall, we arrived into what looked like a living room. It was sparsely furnished with black sofas set at right angles on two walls. A sleek glass coffee table that seemed to be suspended over metal legs spanned a broad geometric-print rug and dark wood cabinets; very elegant and so completely opposite to my house, it hit me like a punch in the gut. I didn't even know Evan's taste when it came to décor. It seemed like such an inconsequential thing to think about as I looked around. Everything looked so glossy and expensive that I almost wanted to apologise for my home which, though fresh after new coats of paint, still had that work-in-progress vibe.

"You'd sacrifice Annalise for a few unanswered questions?" I asked, wondering if I could squeeze any more guilt on. I felt nasty doing it, but I felt even worse for Annalise. I wondered if she were conscious, or drugged, on the plane or, like Evan said, waiting to be found in a shallow grave. I hoped she wasn't afraid. I had to close my eyes for a moment as the room seemed to spin about me.

Étoile's mouth set in a grim line as she echoed the unpalatable. "Like Evan said, she might already be dead."

"She's not dead until I see a body."

"You might be dead before you even get that far!" Evan yelled unexpectedly. "They've tried to kill you twice now, Stella. They don't care about letting you get far enough to even see Annalise, never mind rescue her. If you rush in, I'm afraid... I'm afraid for you, Stella."

I gulped. Fear from a daemon was not something I ever expected to see and it shocked me to my core, like nothing else could. "I still have to try," I said in a small voice as I concentrated on home and shimmered.

I vanished, but I didn't get far. Hitting a solid surface, I materialised again. I had a moment of brief, terrified distress when I eyed the white plaster ceiling, only inches from my face before plummeting to the floor with a scream... But I didn't hit the floor. Instead, I hung there, level with the sofa, suspended. My arms and legs drifted lower while my body felt like it was resting on a plank.

"Put me down," I said slowly through gritted teeth, breathing hard. A second later, and I was resting flat on my back on the rug, slightly stunned. I was still in Evan's house. "What happened?"

Evan stooped next to me and offered his hand so I could sit up. I was too furious to feel embarrassed but I felt my cheeks redden anyway. "You can't use magic here," he explained. "The house is protected."

"I can't stay. I need to go."

"You need to be protected. Let me protect you. Please, Stella." He stayed on his knees next to me, my hand in his, his eyes matching his worried expression. He searched my face, looking for some hint that I would do what he asked.

I hated to disappoint him. "I need to help my friends."

"Kitty's safe, I promise. We can't do anything for Annalise, just yet."

"Why can't I use my magic here?" I asked again, realising that Evan had been the one to break my fall, levitating me so that I wouldn't hurt myself. It occurred to me that the fall could have broken my back, or my skull.

"Witch magic doesn't work here. This is a daemon-owned house and I had to take precautions."

"From me?"

"No, not from you." He almost smiled then. "The protections were put in place long before I knew you. Just like you have wards around your house protecting you from harm, I have wards on this one. But here it's daemon-made magic, not witch, and it guards against lots of things. It's essential in my line of work."

"You expect to be attacked?"

"No, but I don't intend to be unprotected the day some fool tries. The wards are too complicated to take down but I can assure you your magic is still there, just suppressed." Evan stood up, holding out his other hand to me. I took it, and he pulled me to my feet.

"Are you okay with that, Étoile?" I asked, turning to my friend. She pulled an unhappy face and just shrugged, again. I sighed. "Fine, no witchy magic here."

"You need to meet someone. Micah!" A moment after Evan yelled, another man joined us, walking quickly along the hallway and sliding to a halt when he saw us. He was shorter than Evan by a few inches, slim and not quite as powerfully built but something about him said deadly to me. He had short hair with long sideburns, very neatly trimmed with lines cut in as they reached his cheeks, then trimmed into edges that pointed to his jaw, but no moustache or goatee. His skin was a beautiful chocolate. He was wearing a sleek black suit with a white shirt and purple striped tie. My senses told me he was demon, a purebred. My human senses told me he was on alert.

"Witches?" he spat as he looked at us with undisguised revulsion, like we just announced we trampled something gross into the house.

"Guests," clarified Evan, moving to stand in front of us. "You know about my girlfriend, Stella, already. And this is Étoile Winterstorm, whom you might know. This is my assistant, Micah."

"Is this the one I've been cleaning up after?" he asked, relaxing slightly as he nodded at me, ignoring Étoile.

I looked up to Evan. "What does he mean?"

100

Micah answered me before Evan could. "I believe I picked up a body earlier that you dismembered."

"It was an accident!" I protested but Micah looked sceptical, which I supposed was reasonable. There couldn't be that many accidental dismemberments after all; I hoped not, anyway. I added pointedly, "She was trying to kill me."

Micah ignored that, inclining his head towards Evan, asking something in a low voice, almost a stage whisper. I was starting to get the impression he was teasing us, more than threatening, though his sense of humour left a lot to be desired. Perhaps it was a demon thing? Evan's daemon humour seemed to run a lot closer to my idea of funny. "May I kill them?" he persisted.

"Me calling them 'guests' might be a clue of what my answer is going to be," replied Evan, then, "Just to be clear, that's a no."

Micah persisted, his eyes flashing hopefully as he asked, "Are they prisoners?"

"Now you're being deliberately obtuse." Evan squared up to him, arms folded, eyebrows raised and Micah gave a little shrug, like he was giving up.

"And you're absolutely sure I can't kill them?"

"I like him," said Étoile softly, leaning into me while keeping her eyes on him. "Very polite."

"He's asking Evan if he can kill us," I hissed back, also keeping my eyes fixed on Micah, suddenly unsure again. If my magic didn't work here, we would either have to hope Evan had a firm handle on the situation, or run. I favoured the first option.

"Like I said, very polite, for a demon anyway. Many would just kill a witch without a second thought."

I raised my eyebrows. "I don't think that's grounds for liking him, Étoile."

"I do."

"Fine," said Micah, interrupting us. "Welcome, Stella and Étoile." With an audible sigh, the demon wheeled on his heel and clacked away down the hall, exiting to a door off the right. Étoile shrugged her shoulders, gave me a smile and trotted after him, probably determined to make the horrible demon her friend. *Good luck with that.*

"Don't be mad at me, Stella." Evan took a step closer and I held up my hand in the universal signal for stop.

"How do you expect me not to be? You saw an opportunity and you yanked me right out of there, across the country!"

"You know it wasn't like that. I want you to be safe and this was the first place I thought of. Besides I already had Micah pick up the shifter and we've been talking."

"Yeah, I bet he wanted to extend the invitation personally."

"Once you get to know him, he's okay."

"You forgot to add 'for a demon'." I stomped away in the opposite direction from the odious Micah, pausing as I reached the long windows on the other side of the room. It looked out onto a neat expanse of lawn, and a brick-paved patio. There was a doorway off to the left that was closed. The opposite wall was occupied by a broad entertainment unit and a big, flat-screen television. I didn't know whether to stand still, or stomp out of the room. I couldn't just stride off to the hallway. The only thing stopping me from moving at all was not knowing if the doorway led to a closet. That would make stomping out look pretty stupid.

"What do you think of my house?" Evan's voice was soft as he came to a stop next to me, standing so close that our arms were almost touching. "I'll show you around."

"Might as well, seeing as I'm your prisoner." I threw Micah's term at him. I knew I sounded bitter, angry even, and I was, even though I understood Evan wanted me to be safe. I just didn't get how I could possibly feel okay with being safe when my friend wasn't. All the possibilities were floating through my mind: dead, tortured, scared, not one was palatable. I couldn't even begin to fathom what would happen to her if they took her to England.

I smoothed my hair back, stopping when I reached a matted section. Drawing my hand away, I could make out the faintest shade of red. Blood. That was enough. My stomach lurched as the horrible day caught up to me in a sudden rush of fear, revulsion and inadequacy. "Bathroom," I forced out, my eyelids drooping as my stomach convulsed again, forcing me to retch.

Evan half carried, half propelled me out to the hall, then into the downstairs bath. I dropped to my knees and retched again, gripping the toilet seat, then emptied my stomach while Evan held my hair back, stroking it.

After a few minutes, during which I was very still, and trying not to cry or throw up again, I sat back against the tiled wall, while Evan flipped the lid and flushed. He didn't say a word and I just sat there, more embarrassed than I could possibly say, with a horrible acrid feeling in my mouth, and a worse one in my heart.

Evan stepped around me. I heard running water then a cup was pushed into my hand. "Drink this," said Evan, pressing it upwards to my lips. "Little sips." When I'd drunk a couple of mouthfuls, I started to struggle to my feet and he helped me up, his hands gently firm on my hips.

"Toothpaste?" I croaked, leaning against the sink. My skin felt clammy and I was sure I was a fetching shade of puce.

Evan scrabbled in the drawer of the vanity and came up with a new tube of toothpaste and a brush in a translucent green plastic. We probably matched. I stripped off the cardboard packaging, squirted on some paste and brushed my teeth quickly, dropping them both by the side of the sink after I finished. I'd be a better houseguest, I promised myself.

"Let's get you settled on the couch." Evan kept one arm around me as I walked gingerly towards the living room. I didn't think I was going to be sick again, but the thought of it was bad enough and I was grateful that Evan kept his movements gentle.

The whole day had been a nightmare and, on top of feeling frightened for Annalise, I felt wretched. My muscles ached, my throat felt hoarse and I had a shape-shifter's dried blood in my hair.

"I need to change my clothes," I said. I needed a shower too.

Evan hesitated for a moment. "What do you want to wear?"

"Jeans and a t-shirt, please. Comfy clothing."

"Done." I half expected him to click his fingers, but the only indication I got that my clothes were disappearing then being replaced was a brief whisper of cool air. Instantly, I was in clean, comfortable clothing and feeling absolutely shattered. At least, Evan had the good sense to put me in yoga pants and a long sleeved cotton t-shirt. Normally, given the option, he liked me in a dress.

"Can you do something about my hair too? There's blood in it."

"No problem."

Lowering myself to the sofa, I struggled for something to say, something that wouldn't be angry or show me up any further. My boyfriend held my hair back. I felt my cheeks heat and my eyes well with tears again.

Evan settled us on the couch. "Hey, don't cry. It'll be okay."

"You don't know that." Guilt weighed so heavily on me, I was sure I'd gained a few extra pounds.

"No, I don't," he conceded, his arm tightening around me as I rested my head on his shoulder. I slipped my arm across his waist, willing to put aside my anger for a moment in return for the comforting presence of his body. "But I'll do everything I can to find out what happened and, if Annalise is alive, I promise you, we'll get her back."

"I need to find her. This wouldn't have happened if it weren't for me."

"You don't know that. Annalise knows what a werewolf's life is like. She's run into danger in her life and she's survived. If she's alive, she'll fight."

"That's what I'm afraid of. The Brotherhood think nothing of killing women; they'll think nothing of killing Annalise if she gets in the way." No matter what I said it all came back to one thing: if they hadn't gotten rid of her already.

"If she's alive, they won't kill her, especially if they think using her as bait will get you."

Evan made a good point. I scrambled to calculate how long she might have. "So, assuming she's alive, and assuming they're watching the airport, they'll keep her alive at least until they know whether I got on the plane or not."

"They most likely will assume you won't get on the plane, but they'll be sure that you get there. That should add another couple of days."

"Three days," I said. "Seventy-two hours, maybe. Great."

"Try not to think about it. Will you be okay here for a while? I need to go to my office and talk to Micah. It's just off the hall, so I won't be far. I'll call Gage too; see if they've found anything yet or gotten any leads yet."

I nodded just to show that I heard him, and I'd be okay though I didn't want to think too closely about what he meant by "found anything." I didn't want to be on my own but there were things more important than I.

"Just shout if you need anything, and go wherever you like. The kitchen is through that door if you want anything to eat or drink. I'll send Étoile back if you want?"

"Not if she's more useful to you."

"Then I'll keep her until she starts turning Micah dangerous." Evan tried a smile, and I made a weak effort at returning it. He hugged me a little tighter, dropping a kiss onto the top of my head. "And try not to be mad at me until we know everything. I didn't mean to bring you here against your will. I really was just trying to bring you to the safest place I could think of in those few seconds."

I was glad he didn't add *don't worry* because really, what else could I do?

After settling my head on the arm of the couch, I listened long after the door of Evan's office – at least, that's what I assumed it was – clicked shut. A sense of weariness swept over me suddenly and I yawned. It had been an incredibly long day, filled with lots of strange things. I'd been attacked, shimmered, attacked again, then swept halfway across the country.

My skin still tingled slightly from the method Evan used to transport. Daemons and witches were different beings, though we both looked human. We could do similar things, but we did them in different ways and he understood my strengths far more than I understood his. I much preferred my method of shimmering, but Evan's was far more powerful and precise. He only shimmered with me when I'd have been in danger otherwise.

What felt like minutes later, I jerked awake. Étoile was sitting opposite me, tapping away on a laptop.

"How long have I been asleep?" I asked, looking around groggily as I rubbed my eyes. Then it hit me. Annalise could still be out there somewhere and I had been fast asleep on a comfy sofa in a safe, warm, house. I couldn't have felt like a bigger traitor.

Étoile looked up. "Just a couple of hours."

Shuffling, I swung my feet to the ground so I was sitting upright. "Any news?"

Étoile clicked another couple of keys then closed the laptop, leaving it across her knees as she folded her hands on top. "Gage's pack swept several miles around the area where Annalise was kidnapped and they didn't find anything... in the way of bodies, that is. They caught her scent and tracked her to the airstrip where it vanished. In light of that, we think she's definitely on that plane."

I didn't need to say it out loud but I did anyway. "So they've definitely taken her to England."

"Looks that way. It will be several more hours before they arrive." Étoile's tone seemed apologetic. Nothing much shook her, but her voice was low and she seemed upset. "I tried to get a vision, but nothing came."

"We have to go to England, Étoile," I leaned forward, beseeching her. "If the Brotherhood captured Annalise in wolf form and knows what she is, there's no telling what they'll do to her. The note said she'd bite it. That can't just be a lame ass joke!"

"What are you going to do when you get there? Hmm, Stella? Are you going to *reason* with the Brotherhood? Are you going to ask them politely to let Annalise go, and you too? Or maybe offer yourself as an exchange?" Étoile shook her head and her words were harsh. "If they know what Annalise is, you can be sure they'll never let her go. She'll just be something else they can hunt and kill."

"So you expect me to sit here and do nothing?"

"That's exactly what I expect you to do, Stella. Let us get a plan together, then we'll do something. But if we go to Hawkscroft unprepared, we're all dead."

CHAPTER SEVEN

We were at an impasse. There was no point arguing with Étoile, not when she spoke in that stern tone. Plus I had to face facts. Positives first: Now we knew where Annalise was, we were almost positive that she was alive and would stay that way at least for the hours she was on the plane. After that, there was a strong chance they'd continue to keep her alive if only to lure me to Hawkscroft. On the negative side, my brain reminded me all too dolefully, I was in Texas, nowhere near where I needed to be. I didn't have a plan and it wasn't just the Brotherhood against me. My boyfriend and friends didn't want me to go to the aid of Annalise either. For the first time, in a very long time, I felt horribly alone. Even worse, I felt afraid and incapable.

Given my current mood, and clearly not up to an argument, none that I was going to win anyway, I surrendered. After a few minutes of silence, Étoile went back to whatever she was doing on the laptop and I went in search of Evan.

Following a couple of false starts in which I opened the door on the bathroom, then a closet, I knocked on the door nearest the front door and Evan called, "Come." He had been sitting behind a desk, but he stood and smiled when I came in. However, he seemed a little wary of whatever I might say.

"Hi," I said. "I'm awake." Well, duh, he could see that. What I meant was *tell me you have a plan, please*.

"How are you feeling?"

"Okay."

"Good. Micah interrogated the shape-shifter while you were sleeping."

"Do I want to know what that means?" I tried hard not to shiver, especially once I spotted Micah sitting in the chair closest to me. He scrutinised me with cold eyes.

"No," said Evan, at the same time that Micah said, "The shifter is very, very angry. Fortunately, the arm can be reattached."

I suppressed an immediate urge to say sorry. Perhaps I was oversimplifying things, but the shifter was attempting to kill me and I was only trying to escape. The loss of a limb versus my loss of life? Well, at least one of those could be sewn back on if it were lost. I couldn't say I felt much sympathy for the shifter.

"We haven't ascertained who the shifter was under the employ of... yet." Micah made the last word sound horribly ominous. "But you can be assured the prisoner is now..."

"Don't say 'armless.' It's not funny." To emphasise my point, I rolled my eyes. Micah grinned. It wasn't pleasant.

"The prisoner is no longer a threat," he finished.

"The job was to get you to the airstrip and hand you over."

"The same place they took Annalise?"

"Yes."

"So it was the Brotherhood."

Evan nodded again.

I looked around the room while I mulled that over. Like the living room, it was sparse. A broad oak desk and a big, expensive-looking, leather chair behind it. Evan stood, resting his arms on the back of it as he leaned in. Two more chairs in front, one of which was occupied by Micah. A row of bookcases covered the wall behind Evan, stuffed with books and a few ancient looking objects. A tall plant filled a large basket in one corner and the window looked to the rear, over a small courtyard. This was a man who definitely did not do mall shopping.

"The shifter didn't know who the employer was. She was subbed out," explained Evan.

I dropped into the chair adjacent to Micah's and absorbed that for a moment while Evan and Micah conferred about something the shape-shifter said. I wasn't going to waste time wondering why they had a contract to find me and deliver me for money. What struck me was that it sounded uncomfortably like the way Evan once described his job. He even showed me how he could change bodies and appear as though he were a different person. At the same time, he showed me how to recognise the true being underneath. That was what confirmed the shifter's identity, and probably saved me. I wasn't sure how I felt about Evan doing things like the mysterious shifter sent to kidnap me.

Looking at him, I wasn't even sure I wanted to

ask. For a little while longer, I wanted to stay in my cosy little bubble where I had a boyfriend who loved and protected me, and never participated in frightening, and quite possibly illegal, things in the name of business.

Perhaps I was being stupid. Perhaps I was just waking up and the world would never be the way I wanted it to be. It was full of scary, hostile beings and I had to learn faster, or learn the hard way. I seemed to be having a strange little epiphany. Right now though, I'd have to leave the soul searching for later. There were more important things to tackle.

"Does that mean the Brotherhood know what about shifters?" I asked, wondering if they'd discovered Annalise's secret yet.

"Maybe, maybe not." Evan moved around the table to sit on his desk, one leg still on the floor. "They could have hired an agency who works with freelancers like this shifter. The middleman may never pass on who's working for them, and the client would never ask."

"Do you know the agency?"

"A rival of mine. They touch work I won't do. I prefer to keep my business above the law. Kidnapping law-abiding women isn't a service advertised in my catalogue."

"Glad to hear it." I paused, then readied myself to say what I knew would be fruitless. "I need to get to England."

"We've been through this. It's too dangerous. You aren't at full power and you can't take on the Brotherhood alone. You'd be risking too much."

"But I..."

"No, Stella. This is not up for discussion." When I

opened my mouth to protest, Evan held up a hand, silencing me. "I mean it, Stella. It's too risky. I can't allow you to go."

I raised my eyebrows. "Allow me?" I repeated incredulously. *Who did he think he was to give or deny me permission to do anything?*

We glared at each other, in a deadlock. Evan had explained enough to me that I knew roughly what we were dealing with, but he seemed clueless about what would happen at Hawkscroft. It was that cluelessness that made it difficult to formulate a plan. "Can't your employees do something?" I tried not to look at Micah, because I doubted he wanted to be told what to do anymore than I did. "They're experienced in stake-outs and catching bad guys, aren't they?"

"Everyone is working their asses off keeping the business running for me, so I can be with you." Evan closed his eyes briefly like he realised what he'd just said, and how it sounded.

It stung, mostly because we had an audience and I could think of a whole bunch of people I'd rather argue in front of than Micah. As we stared at each other, I tried to think of a way to convey that I never asked Evan to step in and teach me, not at the beginning, when I was a neophyte. I also never demanded that he stay, even though I saw his growing restlessness, but I came up with nothing. Having it spelled out in plain words was another uncomfortable truth I wasn't sure I wanted to hear, but it did remind me we would be having a conversation about this very soon.

"I didn't realise it had been so hard on you," I replied stiffly, breaking the uncomfortable stretch of silence. Micah politely stared out the window, as if he were imagining he wasn't there.

Evan ran a hand over his jaw, his lips pressed together in a stiff line. "I didn't mean it like that," he said softly.

"No, it's fine, I understand." I stood up, smoothing imaginary creases out of my yoga pants. "I'll leave you to get on with your work." I was at the door, when Evan called my name tenderly. I turned, my hand on the doorknob, half expecting an apology, but instead he said, "I was going to order pizza. I didn't have time to arrange for the kitchen to be stocked."

"Yum," said Micah, snapping back into the present.

I looked at him in surprise. "You eat pizza?"

"I normally eat small, sweet animals like bunnies but the fur is a bitch." He bared his teeth at me, pausing for a moment so I could get a good look at the sharp, pointed ridges, then winked. "Of course, I eat pizza. Who doesn't?"

Shaking my head, I looked back at Evan. "Fine." I didn't wait for a reply; I just shut the door behind me, my heart heavy.

As I pulled the door closed, I heard Micah say, "Nice ring your little witch is wearing."

"Quiet!" snapped Evan. I stood on the other side of the door for a moment, frowning while I worked the ring in a circle around my finger with my thumb. The pretty jewels – rubies, emeralds, and sapphires – sparkled up at me. Evan told me that it had interesting properties; clearly it was something that Micah recognised, even if I didn't. I didn't want to barge back in and demand an answer, partly because my cross demeanour wouldn't win me any favours, and partly because I didn't want to be embarrassed in front of Micah by asking something he clearly thought I knew, even if Evan hadn't thought an explanation were important. To be fair, he had mentioned special properties; I just hadn't followed up on what.

I alternated between furious and worried through dinner, which arrived, steaming hot, thirty minutes after our conversation. We spread the boxes across the kitchen counter, and passed plates and napkins around the four of us. I kept my answers to a monotonous "yes" and "no" as we ate, too tired and cross to engage in the conversation. Instead, I listened as Evan and Étoile relayed what they learned individually – not much – and tried not to look at Micah who was evidently enjoying the pizza. Finally he brushed his hands together over his plate, nodded at Evan and snapped out of the room, a brief rush of heat the only thing he left behind.

"I thought magic didn't work here."

"Witch's," Evan pointed out. "Micah and I both use magic here."

It seemed futile to argue that I was no threat, not when Evan was clearly suspicious of me, watching my every move just in case I leapt up and made a run for it. Funnily enough, the idea hadn't even occurred to me until then. Now that it had, I couldn't help wondering what would happen if I did just open the door and try to leave. Would there be a magical barrier preventing me? Would alarms go off?

Finally, when my eyelids were drooping, and I was slumping ever lower in my dining chair, I still wasn't quite on speaking terms with Evan. He said goodnight to Étoile, picked me up and carried me all the way upstairs to his bedroom.

"I'm sorry I didn't get to give you the tour earlier. I expected your first visit to my home, to be very different from this." He walked through an open doorway, kicking the door shut with his foot.

Like everything about Evan, his bedroom was understated in an elegantly masculine sort of way. Big bed in a glossy dark walnut, set off by white sheets and pale grey walls. He deposited me on the edge of the bed and the nightstand lamps came on automatically, casting a soft glow around the room as the long drapes shut themselves. Kneeling, he started to help me with my socks.

"I can manage, thank you," I said tartly and, after a moment, he let my foot go and rocked back on his heels.

"Don't sulk."

"I'm not sulking." Well, I was, a little, but most of all, I was sick with worry about what was happening. I was terrified for Annalise because I knew that death wasn't always the worst thing that could happen to a person. It was everything that preceded death that was the big problem. Most of all, the tremendous guilt of being safe and protected when my friend wasn't made me feel traitorous.

I wondered about Kitty and how she was treating the burns and whether Michelle was out of hospital. I thought about Gage and how worried he must be about Annalise, and Michelle, too. Then Beau, because he loved Annalise too and it must be killing him that he wasn't there to protect her.

Evan, never one to give up, tried again. "Don't be mad at me then."

"How can I not be mad at you? You've taken

away my magic and won't let me leave."

"I haven't taken it away. It just doesn't work here. This house is protected by daemon magic and I can't strip it just because of you, or Étoile. She gets that."

"Goody for her," I mumbled.

"It's to protect us all."

"I don't mean you harm."

"You sure about that right now?"

That teased a smile out of me. Looking briefly relieved, Evan got up and stretched, moving round the side of the bed. I swivelled, drawing my legs up onto the bed, and watched him shuck his shirt and jeans, tossing them on an ancient-looking leather chair. Even through my anger, I could still appreciate what a fine figure he had.

"I don't have anything to sleep in."

"Oh, well." Evan flicked an eyebrow, a smile slipping onto his lips.

"Mind out of the gutter. I'm too worried to think about having sex."

"Might take your mind off it?"

Rolling my eyes, the frustration briefly at bay, I muttered, "Down boy." Yawning widely, I slapped a hand over my mouth. "Sorry. Long day. I don't mean to be mad at you," I said, by way of an apology. I really didn't mean to be mad at him. It was the situation that made me angry. In my heart, I knew Evan just wanted what was best for me, in the same way as Beau would always do what was best for Annalise.

I did a sort of sit-down-wriggle to get out of my clothes, fished my phone from my pocket and laid it on the nightstand, then pushed back the covers to slide under. Evan joined me a moment later, pulling me into him so he could wrap his arms around me and press me into his warm body... Oh! *His warm, naked body.* For a moment, I wished I could forget everything but him.

"I don't want to just wait around while everyone else charges off to find Annalise. She's my friend and she's missing because of me," I said, snuggling against him.

"Can't you understand that I don't want you to get hurt?" Evan's mouth was near my ear, his voice soft and low, anguished. "It's not about not *letting* you do something. This is more than that. The Brotherhood might not have powers like you or I, but they're brutal and vicious and they would think nothing about killing you."

"Then why invite me? Why not just kill me in Wilding?"

I felt Evan shrug, his muscles brushing my back. "To get you on their turf where they feel safer and therefore, more powerful," he said, his voice carrying just a note of question.

I squirmed onto my back, turning again to face him. "Why me, anyway? If they want a powerful witch, why not go for Étoile, or anyone else?"

"Maybe that's just it. Maybe they don't think you're that powerful. Maybe they underestimate what you can do."

"Hmm." I mulled that over. "I could use that to my advantage."

"If you were there, which you're not," Evan reminded me, unhelpfully.

"I still don't get it. They must want me more for something than just what I am. Otherwise, why go to the bother of inviting me, making their presence known, and then kidnapping my friend? If she's been taken to England alive, like it appears to be, well, that's a lot of trouble, time and money spent to get me there."

"Who knows? The Brotherhood aren't known for being rational. They've killed countless people and they're not about to turn friendly now. Use your brain, Stella. They want you dead and they're just playing a game with you because you're the one that got away. Maybe there's a bonus on your head." Evan sighed, rolling onto his back. He didn't have to make that any clearer. The Council told me that I was the last of the English witches, the last of the blood witches whose veins ran with magic. "Stay here," Evan urged. "I'll keep you safe and we'll send others to look for Annalise and bring her back. I'll call in some favours. I promise."

I could have laboured the point and insisted that I go, but Evan was as stubborn as I and I was too tired to press anymore tonight.

"How'd you get the scars on your back?" I asked, after we'd been quiet for a moment. I noticed them the first time we slept together and never asked about. It didn't seem polite. At first, I didn't think Evan heard me and I was just going to ask again when I heard him draw a deep breath.

"My father," he said finally. "He's a full blooded demon. They were punishment for misdeeds when I was younger, before my mother died."

"That's horrible."

"Yes, it is." Another long pause then, "He can hurt you just by looking at you. It's one of his special talents."

"Where is he now?"

119

"Far away."

"Can you do that, hurt people just by looking at them?"

"Yes, but not as powerfully and I don't choose to."

"What about Micah? He's a full-blooded demon, right?"

"Yep, but not as powerful as I, even though I'm daemon, a half-blood. My father's family are very, very powerful and it passed through to me, but I have more of my mother's humanity. Micah, on the other hand, is from a lesser line but he's bright and able, and he finds humans very interesting."

"I wouldn't have guessed," I huffed. Micah hadn't given me the impression that he found anything worth his interest. I suppose I falsely assumed that most of his time was taken up trimming his impeccable facial hair. "You ever see them?"

"My father's family? Not if I can help it."

We lay in silence a little longer, then I edged closer, closing the space between us, and Evan wrapped his other arm around me again. I lay my head on his chest, smiling when he kissed the top of my head. Gradually, the kisses moved to my lips, growing deeper as I felt the tug of sleep slip away and turn into desire for something far better. My exasperation pushed aside for now, I drank him in, his familiarity, his warmth, his desire and, when his hands ran experimentally down my sides, then up and over my breasts, I didn't push him away. Instead, I pressed my body against his, encouraging, welcoming, my leg sliding over his until he fit perfectly against me, every contour of his body finding solace in mine until, finally, we were part of each other.

Part of me knew already what I was planning to do, and how much it would hurt Evan. I knew I would go to England, even if I didn't quite know how, and I knew it would probably put me in harm's way. But leaving my friend to an unbearable fate while we took our sweet time coming up with a plan wasn't the sort of thing I could, in all good conscience, do.

Brushing the thought away, I arched against Evan's body, holding him closer. My arms curled under his arms so that my palms lay flat against his back, my fingers digging into his flesh. I wanted to bury myself in the bliss of loving him, knowing that I might lose him.

"I love you, Stella." Evan's voice was a whisper against my ear, barely audible. I wrapped my legs around his back and kissed him hard, hungrily, as he continued to move, our rhythm growing faster until our gasps and moans were muffled in each other's mouths.

"I love you too, Evan," I whispered as we held each other, not wanting to break apart.

I slept fitfully that night, my dreams vivid and active. I saw wolves' eyes shining in the dark, an imposing house in the shadows. As if it were really happening, I felt myself running through a forest, branches catching at my clothes, the cloying scent of wet leaves and earth; then I was falling, falling far into the darkness.

Once, when I reached out for Evan, I thought I saw fire but I wasn't sure if it were a dream or a vision of things to come. Finally, in the early hours of the morning, long after the house fell silent, I felt a hand press against my forehead just as everything went dark.

CHAPTER EIGHT

In the morning, no one woke up with a stunningly brilliant plan of how to get Annalise out of trouble, destroy the Brotherhood or create peace amongst witches. We did, however, manage to make three cheese omelettes with minimal fuss. Sitting around the big kitchen island, we ate, talking quietly. It seemed that no one wanted to be the first to say Annalise's name. It was like by uttering her name, we would break a spell or something, and there would be no turning back.

Micah didn't join us until mid-way through breakfast, and, when he arrived, he was looking sharp again in a navy blue suit complete with a patterned silk tie and matching cufflinks.

"Don't you all look maudlin," he said, by way of a greeting.

"Do you do casual Friday?" countered Étoile.

Micah looked at her like she'd asked if he read bedtime stories to children before he kissed them goodnight. "No," he said, succinctly, taking in her wool pants and peacock blue silk top as she perched on one of the tall stools. "Do you?"

"Perish the thought, demon."

"You have news to report?" asked Evan, dropping his knife and fork onto his plate and pushing it away, eyeing them with wearied amusement.

"The shape-shifter doesn't know anything beyond what I discovered yesterday." Micah reached for the coffee pot, saw it was empty and sighed. He rooted around in the overhead cabinet for filters and grounds and set about making a fresh pot, muttering something that sounded horrendously rude. When he was finished, he took a seat at the table. "I tried several methods." Micah smiled disconcertingly at me. I shuddered to think what that meant.

"Did she return to her form?" I asked.

"Yes, though she is somewhat lopsided now."

"Take her back to wherever she came from, and return the arm so it can be reattached," instructed Evan. "Plant the idea that she won't seek revenge against Stella."

"Now?" Micah looked wistfully at the coffee pot as it began to perk. I bet he was wishing he had trade union enforceable breaks.

"Yes, now."

"Do you want me to serve her employer while I'm out?"

"No, I'll take this higher up."

I wasn't sure what to make of this exchange, so I just listened. When Micah left, flashing out in a burst of heat, I asked, "What did he mean?"

"About?"

"Serving the shifter's employer?"

"The employer should have notified me that they had taken a fee to hunt someone under my protection."

"How would they know I was under your protection?" I asked, sliding off the stool and crossing to the fridge to pull out the bottle of orange juice. Somehow, a few groceries had made it into the kitchen, but I wasn't sure who was responsible. I was fairly certain Micah didn't do shopping and Evan never left.

"Home delivery," said Étoile. "Broadcasting loud and clear today, Stella."

"Um, sorry?" I said, my voice rising an octave to show I was not feeling particularly apologetic as I made an effort to close my mind. As I poured a glass of juice, I prompted, "Evan?"

"We have a registry." He held a hand out. Across the kitchen, a glass lifted from an open shelf and floated towards him, landing neatly on the table in front of him. With a smile, he pushed it towards me so I filled his glass too.

"Who's we? And who can search this registry?"

"In our community, we have to enforce some regulations or it gets chaotic and we risk exposure to humans. So, we have some cross-supernatural bureaus that take care of affairs. My business falls under one of these headings. As a daemon, I can put certain persons under my protection. In theory, it not only protects them from harm, but also tells anyone tempted to defy the protection order, to whom they will owe restitution. That is, if they're not smart enough to leave the job alone. The registry would have been searched. Witches have a similar thing with their houses." We both looked at Étoile and she nodded in confirmation.

Houses were made of families of witches; and anyone claiming kinship could reasonably be offered protection as well as be expected to provide it, in conjunction with their sister and brother witches. As a witch with no family, I had no house as such, but the Winterstorms offered to take me under their wing when they saw me threatened. Étoile and her sister Seren were my sponsors. Not only did it give me a warm, fuzzy feeling that someone cared, but it also stopped witches like Georgia Thomas from picking on me. Pissing off a whole house of witches was akin to pulling apart a wasps' nest: you just didn't do it and expect to emerge unscathed.

"How long have I been on this registry?"

"A few months." He sighed, expanding, "Since the night Georgia Thomas came to visit."

"The shifter's employer might have searched it before taking the job, and not seen it?" I mused, looking for a plausible explanation as to why anyone would want to risk crossing Evan.

"Perhaps but they should have made regular checks and informed me you were their target. Even so, they owe restitution. Plus, if they cross-referenced your name, they would have seen House of Winterstorm as your backer."

"I'm happy for you to take care of the problem," interjected Étoile.

"Do I get a say in this?"

Evan and Étoile both turned to face me with matching frowns. Evan's voice took on a low authoritative tone, "It's important that we make an issue of this, mostly for your own protection. The registry is worth nothing if it is not enforced."

"Would Georgia Thomas also have been able to access the registry?" I asked.

"Some of it," said Evan. "Why?"

"The Brotherhood aren't the only ones looking for revenge," I suggested. "It could have been her, too. Right?"

"Maybe," said Étoile. "Perhaps Evan could ask for information in return for leniency."

Evan thought about that for a moment, finally nodding. "I'll approach the registry."

"One more thing," I said, "Does being on this registry automatically make me a target?" I wondered how much being a person of interest to one would make me of interest to another. Also: just how bureaucratic were these people? Did they have bureaus for everything? Could one run for elected office, like the witches were proposing at the upcoming summit? It seemed a strange thing to have so many regulations, but I supposed when you have immense power at your disposal, someone, or something, had to prevent it being misused. Like Evan reminded me, revealing the supernatural world could be very bad for all of us. It wasn't like the human race had a dazzling history of acceptance.

Étoile answered, "For witches, no, it's just a way or organisation more than anything. We can trace family trees and familial lines through it. Ours dates back to the seventeenth century."

"For my kind, it doesn't necessarily mean the person is valuable to someone else. We add all kinds of people: employees, family members, lovers, humans who we might offer a favour to, or have done some service for us, and are loyal."

"Oh," I said, not liking the sound of lovers, plural.

"I guess that's okay then."

"I'll make some calls this morning; see what I can find out." Evan cleared the table the old-fashioned, human, way and stacked the dishwasher while I warmed our mugs with the fresh coffee Micah made. He cleared his throat, just as I was spooning sugar into the cups, saying, "Gage called while you were in the shower. He said they haven't had any kind of ransom note, so other than the letter they found on Annalise's car, we haven't had any communication."

"I was expecting they would call to gloat or something. Or at least make her plead so we'd know she was alive." I'd half expected my phone to ring in the night, but in the morning, there was nothing, save a couple of texts from Kitty. The first said Michelle was out of the hospital with a mild concussion and a broken wrist; the second one said that she was going to bed and she'd speak to me in the morning. Curiously, Gage hadn't been the one to call me, but Evan. I made a mental note to send him a message.

"Maybe they know we'll worry more if we don't know anything," mused Étoile. "Let's keep in touch with the pack. Maybe one of them got a call, not Gage. Beau would be a logical choice."

She left the kitchen, leaving Evan and me alone. I had to ask him to summon up some clothes again for me so I was wearing jeans and a top, plain and simple. I don't know where Étoile got her outfit from, so I asked, even though it seemed like a trivial thing.

"She can magic up whatever she likes. I relaxed the house's protection for little things like that. It's like telekinesis, or shimmering. It just takes practice. I'll teach you when this is all over."

"And here I was thinking only you could do it."

He smirked. "I don't mind dressing and undressing you."

"I'm sure you don't." I held back a laugh.

"Let's go sit in the office for a while." Evan took me by the hand. I followed him into his office, dropping into the chair I'd occupied the day before. I don't think he wanted me to be on my own anymore than I did. While he was powering up his computer, I sent a couple of messages on my phone. The first, to Kitty, was simple. *No news here. You okay?*

After a moment, my phone vibrated. *"All quiet. Just called Michelle and she's okay but feeling crappy. When are you coming back?"*

Damn. I told her yesterday I was coming straight home. Then the impact of not being able to use my magic hit me, on top of all the other horrible things that happened. A few years ago, I would have been happy lose my magic and be normal; but now, even though it had only been a few hours, I felt bereft without it.

Not yet. Got some things to do here. I messaged.

"Stay safe sweetie."

"Kitty's okay," I told Evan who looked up from the screen briefly. "So is Michelle."

"Annalise's friend?"

"Yeah. She had a concussion and a broken wrist but the hospital already released her."

"Good." Evan's eyes had already returned to the screen.

I sent a message to Gage next. I had to type and retype it a few times. Given the circumstances, no matter what I wrote, it hardly seemed enough; so I stuck with the facts.

Not heard anything. Trying to come up with a plan.

My phone rang almost immediately, Gage's name flashing on the screen, and I excused myself. With Evan in the office behind me and Étoile talking in the living room, I decided to go upstairs, answering mid-flight.

"Hey."

"Are you okay, Stella? What the hell does he think he's doing, taking you to Texas?" Gage's voice filled my ear. He sounded agitated.

"He's just trying to protect me. I'll be home before you know it."

"Will you?" asked Gage. "I don't think he's ever going to let you come back here."

I closed the door to Evan's bedroom and sat on the bed, pulling up one leg to hug as I rested my chin on my knee. "It's not for long. Wilding is my home, Evan knows that."

Gage sighed, his voice losing some of the anxiety. "I could protect you here."

"I know that."

"I'm sorry. I'm sorry I wasn't there to help you. I should have been. My clients could have waited."

"Shh, it doesn't matter. I'm fine, so don't worry about me. Have you heard from Annalise? Or maybe Beau got a phone call or something?"

"Not a thing, none of us. Beau stayed here last night and the rest of the pack is checking in regularly. I told Evan last night that we lost her scent at the airfield. We scanned the whole area but it disappeared near one of the hangars, so I know they took her. She's always dreamed about going to Europe, you know, but not like this. I'm worried for her."

"Me too."

"What do you know about the Brotherhood?"

"Not much," I confessed. "They target witches and they know about magic. They know it's real and not folklore. When they attacked me, there were a lot of them and they've killed many, many times. Shit, I'm sorry Gage, I can't believe I just said that." I cringed.

"It's okay. I'm not expecting them to be harmless fools."

"Are there any wolf packs in England you can reach out to?" I asked, changing the subject slightly. When I left my native country, I had barely gotten to grips with magic, never mind any other supernatural creature, so I figured Gage had the edge on me there.

"None that I know personally, but I'll reach out through the network and see if I can find a pack who can look out for her or give us some local knowledge. Beau and I have been talking about going to England to this Hawkscroft place. We don't take kindly to people messing with our kind."

"How's Beau?"

"Cut up."

"Tell him we're doing everything we can." I remembered something, then. "I've been doing some research on the Brotherhood. If you go to my house, my laptop is in my desk in the sunroom." I gave him the password and told him where to look on the hard drive for the documents. It wasn't much, but it was something and all I could give him right now.

"Thanks, I'll take a look. Anything is useful for the time being. Call me if you hear anything, and if there is a plan, I want in on it. She's my sister, Stella. I'm not letting those bastards hurt her."

"I wish I had a brother like you." Those wistful little words just slipped out.

"Can't say I love you like a sister."

We were quiet for a moment. "I've got to go," I said, before he said something I shouldn't hear and couldn't respond to.

"Let me know if anything happens." Gage clicked off.

Sitting on Evan's bed, I shuffled position so that I sat cross-legged, the phone cradled in my lap. I realised neither one of us had mentioned Michelle. Did he expect me to? Was I expected to inquire? It wasn't like he made any formal announcement about her, so I guessed that he didn't know that I knew about them. What he said... well, it didn't sound like the words of a concerned boyfriend. Time seemed like it slowed right down while I tried to think things through. I wanted it to get back to normal speed. Sitting here, doing nothing, certainly wasn't helping. I ran back down the stairs and ducked my head around Evan's office door. He pointed to his phone and I waited while he finished.

"I spoke to Gage," I told him.

Evan's eyes didn't darken like they normally did at Gage's name. "How's he coping?"

"He and Beau are going to try and reach out to some packs in England. I never knew we had any, you know. Anyway, he's talking about going there."

"Just because he is doesn't mean you can."

"I never said..."

"I mean it, Stella, I know you've been thinking about. If Gage can reach out to a pack, he's got back up."

"I have you," I countered. "And Étoile."

"And neither of us are going anywhere until we have more information."

131

"She could be dead by the time you get what you need." When I woke up, my temper had gone but now, I was seized by a sudden fury that bubbled inside me.

"I don't want to argue with you." Evan shook his head as he picked up his phone again. "England is not safe for you. Just wait this out and let the rest of us deal with it."

"The longer we wait," I pointed out, "the more likely it is the Brotherhood give up on me and kill her." Hearing any more platitudes wasn't what I wanted right now. I walked out, not bothering to close the door behind me, a plan forming in my mind. If Evan weren't prepared to save Annalise, I would have to be.

~

I felt guilty. I really did, but my loyalty to Annalise overweighed any hurt that I might cause Evan by sneaking out. I had the whole day, and night, after our cross exchange to think about what I would do. I didn't like to call it escape, because Evan wasn't someone I wanted to escape from, but, for want of a better word, that's essentially what it was.

The conflict in my heart weighed heavily on me. I knew Evan's intentions were good, that he wanted to save me from any possible harm. But so far, it didn't look like he or Étoile, or his demon assistant, could come up with any semblance of a plan, even with several hours gone. The lead from the shape-shifter apparently turned into a dead end, so far, and Evan still hadn't made contact with the shifter's employers, to my knowledge. Part of me was a little worried that I'd made a deadly enemy – even though the shifter's accident hadn't been one hundred percent my fault –

and someday it would come back to bite me. I pushed the thought away. I would deal with my own personal problems later. I had bigger worries for the moment.

Practically speaking, covering the thousands of miles between Texas and England was going to be difficult, especially as there was no way I could shimmer that far. Even if I were confident, the idea of materialising in the cold Atlantic was enough to make my stomach flip.

I couldn't use my magic in the house. I wasn't totally sure of my location, though I knew I was somewhere near Austin. I used the internet function on my phone to find a list of Texas' airports. Knowing the name of one was as close to directions as I was going to get. At least, I could reject all the non-international ones without physically going there to check each one out.

Once I got outside, I felt confident that my magic would reactivate. If I were unlucky, between getting outside and Evan finding me gone, I would probably only have minutes to shimmer. I felt a phenomenal sense of guilt at the idea of deceiving Evan and Étoile, but I swallowed it down. Once I had Annalise, I would apologise for as long as it took.

It wasn't until an hour later that I saw my opportunity.

Étoile was making a phone call in the living room and Evan was in his study, talking to Micah who had apparently returned. Slipping outside to the rear yard, I walked around, trying to sense my magic and ultimately realised that to shimmer, I needed to be off the property. It turned out to be pretty easy. I walked around the side of the house to the curved paved front driveway, then the double garage, and hit the open button on the electric gates. Slipping through, I paused on the sidewalk under the cool sun, looking to my left and right. We seemed to be in a pleasantly upscale neighbourhood with residential homes that stretched every which way. Behind me, the gates closed before my confidence dipped.

Concentrating on the airport I picked because of its international flights, I crossed my fingers for luck and shimmered.

The quiet of Evan's neighbourhood peeled away to the hustle of Dallas-Fort Worth airport. Thankfully, no one seemed to notice my arrival. I could hear families arguing and see sole travellers climbing out of taxis, hefting their luggage. So far, so normal. Forcing one foot in front of the other, my insides a bundle of nerves, I walked through the doors and entered the airport, looking cautiously around me.

The one and only time I'd been on a plane was a year ago when Étoile helped me escape from the Brotherhood. It seemed ironic now that everything had flipped on its head and I was escaping from my friends, heading towards my foe.

Tucking myself quietly away in a corner, I looked around. There were several desks, the queues growing longer with every minute that I watched. With dawning realisation, it occurred to me that I wasn't going to get anywhere without my passport and a ticket.

For once, I was grateful for Étoile's diligence in making me practice repetitively at using my telekinesis to move objects from different rooms, even through walls; but this was going to be a challenge. My wallet and phone were in my pockets and I identified the things I needed from my house: passport, clothing, a bag, and a jacket. I had no idea if I could shimmer objects this far. Yesterday, I sucked up the motivation to move myself, even if I didn't feel totally confident about it. Moving myself all the way there, even if I made it, would leave me exhausted and I'd still need to get to an airport. No, the best thing to do was bring what I needed to me. Out of necessity, I had to try.

I thought carefully about where my passport was, remembering that I kept it in the top drawer of my nightstand. Focusing on it, I held out my hand and summoned my magic, calling it to me. A smile of delight erupted on my face when I felt the low weight of my passport press down on my hand. *Okay, I can do this.*

Next I tried calling a small bag, and a few clothes, just enough to last me several days, and the jacket hanging on the rack near the door. The one I was wearing yesterday was still balled up in Evan's washing machine. Not wanting to get cocky, I ended it there and went to approach the BA desk.

I had to brush my hand against the saleswoman's hand as I showed her my passport, pushing the idea into her, the same way I'd seen Étoile and Seren do multiple times. I encouraged her to sell me a ticket for the next flight to London, and I actually did it! With my stomach continually flipping between panic and pride, I went through the motions of checking in, taking off my shoes and stepping through the scanners. An hour later, I sat in the departures lounge, fidgeting until my flight was called, expecting Evan or Étoile to turn up any minute.

It was only when I was on the plane and taking

off, the pressure on my ears suddenly heavy, that I relaxed. I was going home.

~

Standing in the cool drizzle outside Gatwick, I didn't feel the euphoric sense of homecoming that I anticipated. I thought I would feel something more, something more tangible. Relief, perhaps, or a rush of happiness. All around me, there were English accents; Southern, Northern, Midlands... accents I hadn't heard in months, but the ones I couldn't hear were what I craved the most.

Since I hadn't planned any further than hightailing it to England, rescuing Annalise, and getting the hell out of there, I knew I hadn't thought things through as strategically as I should have. That was no reason to stand in the rain, getting steadily wetter though. I pulled my wallet out of my bag, extracting the small piece of notepaper on which I'd written the address from the Brotherhood's original invitation. Hawkscroft, Yorkshire. Apparently, it didn't need a street address, and from the entry I found on the internet, I knew it was a very large, grand, country house. It shouldn't be hard to find. If I left now, I'd make it by early afternoon, which would give me plenty of time to scope out the area before dusk fell.

Nevertheless, I had at least a three-hour drive ahead of me; time enough to make a feasible plan, I hoped.

Walking back inside, I aimed for the nearest car hire service, showed them my licence, assured them I could drive on the left, and hired an inconspicuous Ford for the week. Slipping in on the right side seemed weird to me now, but I played with the gears for a moment, then cast a small confidence charm and drove out of the airport. Pointing the car north, I only crunched the gears once. *Fine, twice.*

After living most of my life in London, stuck in either school or an office, I never had much cause to drive north. Once I merged with the M23, I followed the signs for the M25, and, after an hour, switched to the M1, the motorway that would take me all the way to Leeds. Then I would have to take the smaller country roads to get to Hawkscroft.

As I sped past, I found I liked the rolling green fields, interspersed with the occasional pasture of cows and horses. Despite the motorway disappearing far into the horizon, dissecting the green, it was lovely scenery. It reminded me of the countryside around Wilding a little, though more open and barer, with animals that weren't about to get mauled by wolves. Everything, except the last thought that popped into my head, made my heart pang for my Wilding home.

Pushing all thoughts of Evan aside – especially the image of him discovering I was gone, causing him to probably start spitting feathers – I stepped on the accelerator and pushed on. A glance at the dashboard clock and a quick mental calculation told me I still had more than two hours. Not only did I need to explore the local terrain, but I had to find a bed for the night too.

Part of me wondered if the Brotherhood already knew I was here. It was wise to assume that they did, so, every few minutes, I glanced in the rear view mirror, but I didn't see any vehicle that appeared to be tailing me.

Originally, on the flight over, I thought about marching to their front door, demanding to see Annalise and shimmering us both out of there. But I knew that was ridiculous. They would certainly assume I would use my magic, and I wasn't sure if they would take some measures against that, most likely involving violence against me. I shivered and turned up the heat, filling the small car with warm air.

I thought about Evan a lot, the ring on my finger a constant reminder as I gripped the wheel, and how mad he probably was at me. I hoped he would understand. I wondered what would happen if it were me who were kidnapped and in danger, would he come for me quickly? I decided that he probably would and somehow, that made my decision easier to abide. I wondered if he would shimmer in his daemon way across the Atlantic, and if that were even possible. I wondered what Étoile was doing and if she were really all that surprised I was gone.

Most of all, what I tried to avoid thinking about was Annalise being hurt. Naturally, thinking about Annalise turned my thoughts to Gage. He and Beau would be worried as hell.

Pulling off at the next service station, I parked the car in one of the bays and reached for my phone, which I placed on the passenger seat, while my carry-on bag slumped in the foot well. It had half its charge left and I could see seven missed phone calls. Scrolling through, I saw five from Evan and two from Étoile and my voicemail showed there were messages. I winced. The voicemails I would deal with later. Or never. If I didn't listen, I wouldn't have to deal with how mad they must be. *Pathetic, I know.*

Holding the phone for a moment, I thought about what I'd say to Gage but really, I had nothing to tell him as Hawkscroft was still a couple hour's drive away. Right now, if he'd seen the notes on my laptop, he knew everything I knew. I tossed the phone back on the seat and switched the engine back on. All I could do now was drive and, in a couple of hours, I hoped I would know a little more.

With unexpected traffic delays through road works, then a crash, plus one service station sandwich and two black coffees later, it was dusk by the time the SatNav indicated the turning for the road to Hawkscroft. Reducing my speed, I made the turn, pressing on slightly slower than the speed limit, but not slow enough to look suspicious, taking my time to pass by Hawkscroft.

The house was set far back from the road, and in the cold dimness of twilight, it looked huge and imposing. A rolling mist settling in behind it gave it an ominously dark air.

Two large brick pillars announced the entrance to the grounds; a gravel driveway wound its way to a half-moon parking area, dissected in the middle by a brick fountain. Each pillar was framed by a wall, some five or six feet high that wound along the boundary lines, blocking my view as I passed by. Entering the woods, which bordered the road ahead, I drove slowly, finally parking my car in a small clearing a few minutes away before killing the lights.

Tucking my hair under a knit cap that I'd stuffed into my jacket pocket, I grabbed the flashlight from the glove box. I checked the battery level on my phone, making sure it was on silent mode and pulled on gloves. Walking cautiously across the road, I aimed in the direction of the house, staying in the shadows until I reached the wall. I was much too close to the road, and anyone who might happen down it, so, keeping the wall to my left, I started to edge around it, away from the road.

I couldn't hear anything but the wind whistling through the trees. So far, no dogs barking. A good sign, but I could sense the faint trace of magic on the other side of the wall. Something was protecting the house, a rudimentary sort of alarm; a bit more basic than the wards protecting my house and it continued the further I walked.

Passing what seemed to the tallest part of the wall, the woods flanking my side seemed to close in. The ground was soft, muddy, patched with grass, nettles and weeds. It didn't look like anyone ever walked here, but even so, I tried to stay on alert and not worry about walking into a lonely, dark wood while people minutes away wanted to kill me. All I had to do was keep quiet and just look. So long as I stayed unseen, I would be okay.

After five minutes of trampling through the undergrowth, the wall started to dip a bit until, if I stood on tiptoes, I could just see the house. There were lights on in the few windows here and there, their curtains already drawn. I could see bright light spilling across the terrace, onto the lawn at the back. I ducked when a floodlight suddenly lit the area just as a fox raced past it.

Keeping to a crouch, I moved on until the outbuildings loomed on the other side. Standing on tiptoes again, I tried to steal a look at the house, but I just wasn't tall enough, so I looked around for something to stand on. Spying a large rock, I scurried over and pushed it towards the wall. Rooting around in my pocket, I pulled out my phone, set the camera function, switching the auto flash off, and pressed myself against the wall, sliding upwards until I could peek over.

I was near what seemed to be on old stable yard. Two long rows of empty stalls were set at right angles around a concrete yard, a hundred yards or so from a rear entrance into the house. It looked deserted. I held up my camera and, moving it in a slow arc, started recording what I saw. After a minute, I stopped it and slid it back in my pocket to view later.

As soon as I drove past, I knew the front entrance was too obvious to try and enter unseen, but the rear entrance had all kinds of hidey-holes. I decided my best bet would probably be to scale the wall a little further on and try and get into the house that way, once I figured out what kind of magic was protecting the house.

First though, I needed to know where Annalise was. Evan and Étoile had been right, Annalise could be dead already. To me, however, she existed in a state of limbo, nothingness, until I knew one way or the other. Concentrating on her, I started to send out my magic to see if it would recognise her signature and tell me whether she was in the house or not. I felt the magic in the grounds give way. It was no match for mine. Whatever witch had spun the charm of protection was not a strong one, I decided.

I was so busy concentrating on detecting Annalise, that I didn't hear a thing until a twig snapped behind me. I started to turn my head to see what caused it, hoping it was probably the fox, or some other kind of small woodland creature.

A hand clamped over my mouth and another arm wrapped around my upper body, dragging me backwards. Then I was tumbling to the ground, my screaming muffled against the gag as I fought.

CHAPTER NINE

Instead of relying on my magic, I used my instincts and went for an old-fashioned elbow driven straight into my assailant's kidneys. When he yelped and staggered back, I wheeled away and kicked him hard on the knee, following that with a thump that connected with his cheek, knocking him backwards. I didn't waste any time waiting to see who it was or if I'd hurt him, instead launching into a sprint, not the least bit worried about the noise I was making as I crashed through the undergrowth.

I hadn't gotten far when something barrelled into the back of me, sending me sprawling, face first, into the wet leaves. A body pressed onto me, pinning my arms to the damp forest floor and I felt a knee in the small of my back. I wriggled and bucked, trying to throw my attacker off me.

"I'm not trying to hurt you," hissed a furious male voice, his breath cold against my cheek. "I'm trying to stop you getting yourself killed. Calm down, okay? I'll let you go, but don't make any noise. If they hear us, we're both dead."

The hands released my arms, slowly. Then the

pressure on my back was gone. I lifted my head and wiped off a leaf, probably leaving a streak of dirt in its place, and scrambled to my feet as quietly as I could, bracing myself to attack if I needed to as I turned around. "Who the hell are you?"

"Who are you?" The figure moved closer to me until I could see him in the moonlight, which pierced the shadows of the trees. He was dressed, head to toe, in black with a thick padded coat, and a cap pulled low over his forehead. His face was smeared black and brown; camouflage paint, I thought, but the whites of his eyes shone. He wasn't particularly broad, but he was tall enough that I had to look up at him.

"I asked first!" I tensed, waiting for any sudden moves.

The man looked at me for a long moment, his shoulders dropping, seeming to relax slightly. "You're a witch," he said, at last. I must have looked shocked because he continued, "I don't know you and I know all the witches here. I'm Anders. Anders Black and I'm not going to hurt you."

I focused on him and observed the register of difference around him that told me he was witch too, or a warlock, but nothing else, nothing that alarmed me. He definitely wasn't one of the Brotherhood, which gave me some relief. "What did you mean when you said you were stopping me from getting myself killed?"

"You can't go in that way. It's too obvious. I, uh, we've, been keeping this place under watch for months. Go in that way and you'll set off an alarm that triggers a trap."

"I know. It covers the whole grounds." I hadn't been planning on scaling the wall tonight, but if I had without realising what Anders was telling me... Well, he would have saved me. I appreciated him playing the hero card, even if he had no idea who I was. "Um, thanks, I guess."

"No problem." He looked at me expectantly.

"Stella," I said, seeing as he'd made an effort to save me, even though I hadn't actually needed it. "Stella Mayweather."

"Let's get out of here, Stella Mayweather, and you can tell me why you're so interested in that house."

"Presumably, you're going to tell me what your interest is too?"

"Maybe. Depends." But he didn't say on what. "We can't talk here. It's too risky. Come on."

He turned away from the wall, where I'd trampled in and moved off towards the woods, looking back to see if I were following him. He took us along a narrow path, barely noticeable through the undergrowth, to traverse the dark depths of the woods. Occasionally, he glanced behind him to check that I was still tagging along and hadn't been yanked by the Brotherhood's hands. Despite the twigs scratching at my clothes and nettles brushing my hands, he didn't stop to help and I pushed on, grumbling internally.

Some minutes later, we came out near a part of the road that was completely unseen from the house, the woods crowding the space between. Anders went over to some bushes and pulled at them until I saw he was unravelling a net hiding a dirt bike. "How'd you get here?" he asked, glancing at me as I hovered by the trees.

"Car. It's parked over there. I think." I pointed to where I thought my car was, probably only a few hundred feet from where we stood.

"I'll walk you to it. You can follow me into town."

"Why would I want to do that?"

"Because you want to know what I know about the Brotherhood," he said, though he held back from adding *obviously*. "And because a night in the pub is better than a night out here while nothing happens. For bonus points, we're less likely to die, too."

Well, he got me there.

He pushed his bike as we walked in silence to my car. I climbed in and turned the lights on because he said it would be more suspicious if I had them low, or off. Then I waited while he jumped astride the bike before sliding a helmet over his cap.

We parked alongside each other in the car park and I followed Anders inside, blinking until my eyes adjusted to the sudden light of the entry way. While Anders ducked into the men's room to wipe off his camouflage paint, I took the time to visit the women's bathroom to see the state I was in. It wasn't great. I washed the mud off my face, but there wasn't a lot I could do about the long smear that ran the front of my jacket. Losing, and/or ruining my outerwear was becoming an annoying habit.

Finally, we emerged into the light at the same time and I got a good look at him. Anders was a few inches taller than I, slimly built with sandy brown hair, cut so it waved around his head and eyes the colour of emeralds. He was easy on the eyes. His accent struck me as Northern, with flat vowels and a jocular, unpretentious way of talking.

The Rose and Crown was a typical English pub. Thick wooden tables and chairs, a garishly patterned carpet that had been trod on by thousands of feet over a decade or two, and the kind of regulars that prop up every bar throughout the country. A few of them sat at the bar, polished to a high gleam, while a few couples peppered the tables.

We settled into a booth in a corner, away from the regulars, and Anders paid for drinks and brought them over.

"What did you mean when you said you knew all the witches here?" I asked as he pushed a pint glass towards me, glad that he hadn't thought I was a wimp and ordered me a half.

"I'm coven master of this area. I know every witch in my district."

"I didn't think there were any witches left in England."

Anders raised his eyebrows and took a sip of his pint, looking over the brim at me curiously. "What made you think that?"

"Well... I was told that."

"By whom?"

I took my time taking a mouthful, mulling over what I should say as I swallowed. Anders was a witch, I was sure of that, but I didn't know him. Other than his not killing me when he had the chance, I had no reason to trust him. If I told him what I knew about witches, the Council, or the Brotherhood, he could use it against me, though I wasn't sure how. On the other hand, if I told him what I knew, he might share what he knew. I wasn't sure what to do.

"The Council," I said, at last, thinking it was best to keep it simple. If he knew who they were, I wasn't telling him anything fresh and, if he didn't, I'd told him nothing.

"US branch?" he asked. "I'm guessing, of course,

though you sound as English as I do. Londoner, are you?"

I nodded. "They said a few had gone underground, but all the witches of true magic left when the witch hunter killings started." Again, all stuff he would know.

"True magic, hmm?" Anders took a larger swallow this time and then set his glass on the table, his hands circling it. "I don't suppose it occurred to your Council that they don't know everything about the witches here."

I thought about that. It seemed at times that the Council didn't know what was going on in their own backyard.

"Witches would be hard to stamp out," Anders continued with an exasperated little sigh when I didn't say anything. "Witchcraft here dates way back, before Pendle even."

"Pendle?"

"Our version of Salem."

"Oh."

"The Council are insular, useless and badly organised. They need new leadership. Someone who can take them forward and put an end to the witch hunts," said Anders in a burst of anger.

"Is that why you were at the house? The Brotherhood's place? You said you'd been watching it."

"Not exactly. We know what they are, and we want to stop them. The Brotherhood a danger to us all, so we're gaining intel before we make a move against them. Aside from you being a witch, what's your problem with them?" he asked.

"They asked me to come to the house. When I

refused, they kidnapped my friend as retaliation, or bait. I'm trying to find her."

Anders chuckled and looked over me. I fought the urge to shrink into my seat. "And you thought you'd just break in and rescue her? All by yourself?"

Yeah. It didn't sound so great when he put it that way. I stared at the table and took a deep breath, exhaling slowly. "Pretty much," I admitted.

Anders laughed again. "You've got guts; I'll give you that. How do you know she's even in there?"

"I don't for certain. All I know is they brought her to England and this is where they wanted to meet me. She might be dead already, for all I know. I was trying to find out when you grabbed me."

"What does this friend of yours look like? Is she a witch?"

I shook my head. "She's a little taller than me, blonde with little pink streaks. She's a werewolf."

Anders whistled. "Haven't seen her. Don't get many werewolves around here, you know. The local pack is pretty small and spread across the whole county. If you can confirm your friend is there, they might help."

"Do you know how to contact them?"

"Of course."

"What about you? Will you help me?"

Anders looked uncomfortable. "I can't jeopardise my mission."

"What if your mission and my mission were one and the same? We both want to get rid of the witch hunters, and I want my friend back as an extra. We could help each other," I suggested, clinging to the rapid hope that our meeting might end up being fruitful. I hoped I wasn't being misguided.

"You're just one witch and I have a lot of backup," said Anders, sounding unconvinced.

"I have a lot of power. I've been training." I'd have liked to add that I had a daemon and a powerful witch behind me, too, but they were both probably pissed off in Texas right about now. I hoped I wasn't going to have a lot of explaining to do, but like so many other things, I'd deal with that later. "I can help you," I offered.

"You don't even know what we're planning to do."

It was my turn to hold back the *obviously*. "You want to take out the Brotherhood, and I'm going to help you do it."

"Interesting proposition." Anders looked thoughtful. He looked me over like he couldn't quite work me out. "I'll have to put it to the rest of the coven, of course."

"Of course."

"While we're talking about covens, where's yours? Why aren't they helping you?"

"I don't have one. I'm... a free agent."

"Is there any such thing in our community?"

I stifled a smile. "So far."

"And how's that working out for you?"

Let's see. I was abandoned as a young witch, through no fault of my parents who were killed when I was young. Then left to try and manage my own power alone, rescued at the last minute from the witch hunters, attacked by the Council's psychotic former leader, parted from my friends and Evan, which was partly my fault, and then targeted by a power-hungry necromancer witch who now had it in for me. And the Brotherhood kidnapped my best friend and wanted me dead. "Not too bad," I answered.

"Right," agreed Anders, his voice holding the slightest hint of scepticism. "Your name sounds familiar, you know. I'm sure I've heard it before."

"I can't see why. I've never been here before."

"Hmm, it will come back to me. Where are you staying?"

"Actually, I don't know. When I got here, I just went straight to the house to look it over."

"The pub has rooms, if you ask the landlady. Mrs. Peters is her name." He nodded towards the blonde woman cleaning the bar with the enthusiasm of someone who loved to polish. As if she heard her name being mentioned, she flashed a smile in our direction and Anders waved.

"Thanks for the tip. Do you live nearby?"

"Just outside the village."

"And the coven?"

"Here and there."

"I'm not a threat to them," I said, cautiously, wanting to set Anders at ease. "I'm here to get my friend, that's it. I've no interest in supernatural politics, and I'm not a spy trying to get access to your coven." Okay, maybe I sounded a little paranoid but Anders wasn't exactly forthcoming.

"Never said you were," he replied, but he did relax slightly.

I changed tack. "How did you know the Brotherhood were protecting their grounds with magic?"

"We've all felt it. There's various charms protecting the house, but they aren't particularly complex. I don't think they'll be hard to break."

"That's what I thought. I imagine they don't expect an attack."

"If they have your friend, they might be expecting an attack now." Anders drained the last of his beer and tapped the glass thoughtfully against the table. "I suppose the charms might be booby-trapped. We'll investigate further before we do anything."

"What were you planning on doing anyway?"

Anders shifted uncomfortably. "I'm not at liberty to say."

"I could just go to the house. They're expecting me." It sounded stupid even as it left my lips.

"You could, if you *were insane*. If you go into that house without help, you might not come out. You probably won't even be the first."

I slumped in my chair, folding my arms protectively across my body. He was right, of course. I could easily walk into the house, and find out what the Brotherhood wanted from me, but finding where Annalise was being held and getting us both out would be tremendously difficult, if not impossible. He was right. I had to think this through further, and spend some more time investigating before I did anything rash.

Anders went to the bar and came back with another round of drinks and some snacks. As he sat down, breaking open a packet of nuts, he asked, "What do they want with you anyway?"

"I don't know, but they were pretty insistent that I come. I think they want to talk to me about something."

Anders made a sceptical harrumphing noise. "Why would they want to talk to a witch?"

"Why would they protect the house with magic?"

I countered. "They hate magic, but they *use* it? They want to kill all witches, but are determined to talk to me. Unless they're hypocrites, there's something really weird going on, Anders."

"Agreed."

My phone buzzed. I checked the screen briefly and put it back in my pocket. I still wasn't in the dealing sort of mood.

"Aren't you going to answer that?"

"No." I eyed the snacks Anders brought over and he pushed a packet of crisps towards me. I really hoped he couldn't hear my stomach gurgle. It had been hours and hours since I'd last eaten. Between mouthfuls, I asked, "So, what's your plan for getting into the Brotherhood?"

"I have the plans for the house."

"And?"

"To be perfectly honest, Stella, I haven't made any effort to get inside. There are always a lot of men there and their fearless leader doesn't leave often, so he's not an easy target." He hesitated, like he wasn't sure what he should tell me. Probably in case I was a double-crossing spy. He seemed to think better of his reservations because he said, "There are floodlights on each side of the house. They patrol every hour in teams of two and they have dogs too, German Shepherds, I think. People come and go, men. I've never seen any women go in the house but that's not to say there aren't any. Occasionally, we've been lucky and gotten a decent picture. One of the coven has some police connections and they run pictures and names for us when they can do it without arousing suspicion."

"Why don't you just give the names to the police

in an anonymous tip-off or something? Surely they would be interested."

"You think we haven't tried that? The police don't do anything."

"But these murders have been the biggest series of killings in decades! There can't be a cop in Europe who doesn't want to be credited for breaking the case."

"Shh. Keep your voice down, Stella. I don't know why nothing happens with the intelligence we've passed on." Anders folded his arms and rested his head against the wooden wall of the booth. He looked as frustrated as I felt. "These aren't just any people we're dealing with. Our investigations have turned up all kinds of people working for the Brotherhood: murderers, bare-knuckle fighters, rapists. A lot of the henchmen have some kind of record; some have been flagged by Interpol. Any sighting should be followed up. The police force here would get a massive boon if they brought any one of these criminals in, never mind breaking the Brotherhood itself."

"What about the people further up the food chain? I was contacted by someone calling himself John Jones."

"Well that's more original than John Smith," Anders scoffed. "Don't suppose you got a picture?"

I shook my head. "Sorry." I hadn't thought to.

"Doesn't matter. The Brotherhood's officers, as we call them, tend to have clean records. They don't like to get their hands dirty. Or, if they do, no one finds out."

"My friends think someone is protecting them."

"That's the only theory that fits. The only one I've

come to," agreed Anders. "I wish I knew who had that kind of power."

I absorbed that then remembered there was something I hadn't asked him. "You haven't told me why you're so interested in them yet."

Anders was quiet for a moment. He reached into his jeans pocket and pulled out a slim black wallet. Opening it, he extracted a small, square piece of paper and passed it to me. There was Anders, looking younger, his hair a little longer and a girl with her arms wrapped around him, grinning at the camera. They looked very similar. When I looked up, question marked on my face, Anders said, "They killed my sister."

I didn't need to imagine how she had died. I knew. It would have been terrible. "I'm so sorry," I said simply.

We threw theories back and forth and my phone vibrated a couple more times, but I ignored it. Once, Anders excused himself to take a call, retreating to the foyer where I couldn't hear. Finally, he left with a promise to return the next day and bring with him his plans of the house and a map of the locale, along with another coven member, if they agreed.

I stayed in the pub, ate dinner alone at the table and asked about the rooms. The landlady, Mrs. Peters, was happy to rent me one and showed me upstairs, insisting on carrying my bag for me after I retrieved it from the car, even though I didn't need her to. The rooms covered the space above the pub and the one she allocated me was basic but clean, and not too expensive, which was good enough for me.

Standing alone, once she'd fetched towels and pointed out the door to the bathroom, I looked around. My room had a double bed with a thick duvet, an old-fashioned dresser with a mirror mounted on top and a small desk with a chair under the window. I dumped my bag on the chair, peeking outside. There was a single streetlight and I could just see fields stretching away as the road curved towards Hawksley village. I tugged the curtains shut and flicked on the lamp.

Since I packed hurriedly and at distance, I didn't have any pyjamas, meaning I would have to sleep in my tee, so I shucked my jeans, folding them over the chair and climbed into bed. I was too tired to brush my teeth and my eyes closed as soon as my head hit the pillow, even though my head was whirring with thoughts.

I wanted to make plans, I wanted to locate Annalise and get her away from that house. I didn't want to sleep but that's what I did.

Five minutes later, I woke up. At least, it seemed that way, but one look at my watch told me I'd been asleep for hours and hours. I rubbed my eyes, yawned without bothering to cover my mouth and stretched to ease life into my limbs, my mind already buzzing.

My thoughts alighted first on Evan and how angry he must be, not to mention worried. Annalise was either frightened or in a shallow grave. Gage was probably going crazy with anxiety. Étoile was... probably putting her make up on and rallying the troops. She might be pissed, but she always came through for me. I wondered if Kitty were safely at home.

I thought about Anders in his quasi-black ops gear and if he'd spoken to his coven about me. I wondered if the Brotherhood already knew I were here and if they were expecting me.

Reaching for my phone, I checked the call log. No new phone calls, but there were a couple of messages.

Gage sent: *"Made contact with local pack. Getting on plane tonight."* Given the time zones I wondered if that meant yesterday or today.

The other text was from Evan. It read: *"I can guess where you are. Stay safe until I can get there. X."* I breathed a sigh of relief. Perhaps the making up part wouldn't be so challenging after all. He had known exactly where I would go, and why, and he was on his way. That he was coming to help me made me feel a great deal more comforted than the idea that he was furious at me.

I smiled. A knock at my door made me sit up, tense. "Yes?" I called.

"Breakfast is downstairs if you want it, love," trilled Mrs. Peters, the landlady. "Cooked or cereal?"

At last, a question I could easily answer. "Cooked, please. I'll be down in ten minutes."

"I'll have it ready for you. Oh, and there's someone here to see you so I laid the table for two." I heard Mrs. Peters pad away before I could ask whom it was.

Dressing quickly, I pulled off yesterday's shirt, and tugged on a fresh one, then my jeans, still slightly mud-spattered, before quickly running through my bathroom routine. Finally I pulled on my boots and went downstairs; searching through the backrooms until I found the small dining room reserved for guests. I felt pleased that Anders must have come through for me already.

When I saw my guest, I stopped suddenly. "Étoile?" I gasped.

156

Étoile looked up from her cereal, her spoon hovering in the air, and smiled. "You could have told me what you were going to do," she admonished as I slid into the seat opposite. "It would have been nicer to get a flight together. Plus, now I owe Micah fifty bucks. I said you wouldn't go, he said you would."

I was starting to like Micah. Obviously, the distance helped. "What are you doing here?"

"Keeping you from getting killed… As usual," she said emphasising the last couple of words as she set down her spoon and rested her elbows on the table, clasping her hands together. "You're in trouble, by the way."

"I know that. I got Evan's message. Is he mad at me?"

"More at himself, I think. Though it's hard to tell when he keeps setting things on fire."

I winced, remembering his message saying he was coming. "Did he come with you?"

"No. He went back to Wilding to help Gage."

"Seriously? I thought he said it wasn't safe there." Also, I was more than a little impressed at his willingness to help Gage in his time of need, regardless of their personal opinions of one another.

"For you," Étoile pointed out. "Who's going to attack Evan? Forget I asked. He's rallying the troops."

"Rallying the troops?" I repeated, then sat back while Mrs. Peters put a heaped plate in front of me. With the mound of sausages, bacon, tomatoes, mushrooms and eggs, I was set for the day. Étoile looked at my plate, then back to her cereal and pulled a face.

"Mmm. Evan is going to help the wolf pack," confirmed Étoile. "He left a message saying they haven't found any trace of the Brotherhood in or around Wilding, so it's likely that they've left completely. Perhaps they all returned here."

"I found Hawkscroft, but I don't know for certain if Annalise is there."

"Given that she isn't anywhere else, it seems most likely that she is," Étoile stated in her assured fashion.

I looked around, but Mrs. Peters had gone back to the kitchen and there weren't any other patrons, so we were alone. "Étoile, there are other witches here."

Étoile looked up sharply. "How do you know?"

"I met one last night. He was watching Hawkscroft when I went there to scope the place out. Said his name was Anders Black. I thought all the witches were gone from here? Anders seemed pretty surprised when I said that," I said in a rush.

"You'd be surprised if someone told you that you didn't exist."

"I guess, but how come there are witches here, when the Council said they were all gone?"

"Have you noticed how economical the Council are with the truth?" Étoile considered that for a moment, her head tilted to one side then she waved her spoon at me. "Of course, there's always the possibility that they didn't know."

"I thought the Council were the omnipresent eye."

"They wish." Étoile snorted.

"Did you know?"

"What? That there were witches here? No, I didn't know. I saw enough of them die to think that you were the last, of any consequence."

"Of any consequence?"

"The ones with real power, not the dabblers and

hobbyists."

"I don't think Anders is a dabbler or a hobbyist. He seems to have power, real power." I'd ascertained that from his aura.

"Then, I think we can surmise that they didn't want the Council to know that they existed. Interesting."

I nodded, then, "Why not?"

"I've come to think it's because they are," Étoile stopped, correcting herself, "they were, egotistical and dismissive. Just so we're clear, yes, I'm talking about the Council."

"Anders said pretty much the same thing."

"Smart cookie."

I thought about that. The Council had been at the epicentre of so many problems. As a witch, I should have felt supportive of them, not just because they were supposed to regulate our kind, but because they were the defenders too. They should have been my ticket to meet other witches and earn a place in the community. Yet, all their secrets and lies had put me off. "Why did you work for them for so long?" I asked.

Étoile sighed. "We all do things we don't want to do. The things I did were supposed to be for a good cause. I'm strong, and they needed a strong witch to collect the others. Many of us were sent to different countries, you know, to rescue whom we could. My parents have always had an interest in you, so when the Council sent me to look for you, I honoured my parents' wishes as much as the Council's."

"Why didn't you tell me before?"

"Would it have made a difference?" Étoile picked up the cottage-shaped teapot and poured us both a cup, then added milk and sugar to hers. "Ah, I see. You would have trusted me more because our parents were friends. You're getting better at hiding your thoughts, you know."

"I've been practicing."

"Good for you. I've always been on your side, Stella. Always. I don't want you to forget that."

We sat in silence for a moment. I digested what she told me and it was like a small weight had lifted. I always had a problem trusting people, and it wasn't easy for me to accept someone being on my side, without complications. In the year since Étoile had found me, I'd gained so much and sometimes the thought of losing it, losing them, especially Evan, was crushing.

"There's always spells you can do to make sure that I'm telling the truth, or you can send your magic into me. That's a onetime offer, so if you want to be sure, do it now." Étoile held out her hand to me. "I've always been your friend, but I've also had a lot of other pressures. I want you to understand that. If you ever thought I left you willingly, you're wrong."

I set down my cutlery, placed my hand over hers and let my magic flow through me and into her. The power of it shone slightly between our hands. Étoile didn't put up any barriers and I had unfettered access into her very being. Her vulnerability in that instant made it a disturbingly powerful moment for me, and I willed our magic to offer me the truth, not just as I believed it to be, but as it was. Finally, I took my hand away from her and put it in my own lap and Étoile resumed drinking her tea, as if nothing happened.

Étoile hadn't shown me, but I wound my way unguided through her memories, like snapshots of the past and then reached into what I could only imagine as her soul. I saw her sisters, and felt the love she felt for them and the pain at her sister, Astra's mental struggles. I saw a handsome man, a man whom I thought she loved and missed. I saw how the Council really messed up her life, and I saw me through her eyes, that she wanted to help and protect me from the same problems that she faced.

I felt more than a little guilty that I'd taken her offer, but also glad, because I had no doubts now. "I'm your friend, too."

"I know." Étoile looked up briefly and smiled a lovely, uncomplicated smile, and then her face hardened. "Now let's talk business. How are we going to kill these bastards?"

CHAPTER TEN

Over the rest of our breakfast, I explained to Étoile what I had seen at Hawkscroft the night before (not that there was much to say), as well as what Anders told me about the patrols and security in place. It was still scant information, but she mulled it over while we ate.

"It's clearly going to be difficult to get inside, and I'm not sure that we should even try until Evan gets here," she said at last.

"That could be days," I pointed out. "Gage sent a message to say he was on his way. He made contact with the local pack."

"That's good. Does he know you're in the area?"

I shook my head. "I don't think so."

"Let him know, just in case. And, for the love of God, call Evan, too."

"I will."

"When you do speak to Gage, tell him not to tell the pack who we are. They will certainly know there are witches in the area because of Anders' coven, but

I'm uneasy about them approaching us without us knowing who they are. We are at a disadvantage here."

"You don't think they can be trusted?"

"We don't know them, that's all. Trust doesn't enter it."

"But they'll want to get Annalise out too, won't they? They won't want exposure either." At least, that's what I assumed and it ran along well with Evan's theory that no supernatural wanted to be revealed.

"So far, the Brotherhood have only targeted witches, so we might assume that wolves aren't high on their agenda. But remember, Annalise isn't one of their pack, so they don't have close ties to her, possibly not enough to risk their own members. Gage will be calling in huge favours if he asks them for help."

"I don't see what choice he has."

"I want to meet this Anders," Étoile said abruptly. "Is he coming back?"

"I hope so. Well, he said he would. I don't think he lives far, but he didn't say where. I guess we just have to wait for him to contact us."

"Good. We should check out Hawkscroft again too, maybe tonight. I'd like to get a feel for the place."

"I can take you there." I checked my watch. "It won't be dark for nearly nine hours. What do we do until then?"

"Keep planning until we find something that works."

After cleaning away the breakfast things, Mrs. Peters chased us out of the pub. She gave us directions to Hawksley, telling us to, "Make ourselves scarce now."

We walked along the winding country road that ascended to a moderately sized village after a few minutes. The houses were all nicely kept, with a cluster of identical, newly built homes in yellowed brick on the outskirts, giving way to terraced, row houses with thick wooden doors. They looked centuries old with their small sash windows. These older homes were chocolate box pretty. The local authority was clearly keen to keep the "Old World" style intact because the high street, instead of having garish hoardings, had neat signs that matched in complementing colours. It wasn't big enough for any chain shops or coffee bars. I counted the usual shops, a bakery and a butchers, a post office that doubled as a newsagents, and a hairdressers. Outside the bookshop, Étoile paused, grabbing my wrist.

"Do you see what I see?" she asked in a low voice.

"What?"

"I've counted three witches just from walking along this road."

"Are you sure?" I resisted the urge to look behind me.

"Absolutely. Each one of them recognised us too."

"Um, isn't that quite a lot, for one little town?"

"That's what I was thinking."

It was so like Wilding in that no one was what he or she appeared to be, that I laughed. Catching my eye, Étoile laughed too. "This never happened when I lived in the city," she said. "What is it with small towns and their freaky secrets?"

"Hawksley hardly qualifies as a town," I said, looking back along the quiet little street, burying the pang of homesickness that I felt.

It didn't take long to walk around Hawksley, just strolling casually, like we had nothing better to do with our time. After a while, we found a small library and went inside to get out of the cold.

As luck would have it, there was a small exhibition about the local area, just a couple of tables jazzed up with some beige cloth and a screen, covered in black cotton. We spent some time looking through the photographs of local industry, old journals and archives from the residents over the years. There were even some pictures of Hawkscroft in its heyday. It looked very grand despite the sepia. Pictures of horses and riders, the house looming behind them, and servants passing out drinks to the assembled crowd watching the hunting party ride out. Apparently, Hawkscroft had a history of hunters, in one form or another.

There were a few pictures of the grand families who once lived there, all predating the 1920s. Unsurprisingly, there was nothing about the current residents.

"Lovely house, isn't it?" said the librarian, coming to stand by me.

"Yes, it is."

"They've never opened it up to the public, like some of the grand houses hereabouts; but they used to hold a fête on the lawns for the village folk every summer."

"Do they still do it?" I asked.

The old lady shook her head. "Oh no, love. The current generation aren't so keen. Like to keep themselves to themselves, they do."

"Are they very rich then?" It was a crass question, but I wondered all the same.

"Mmm, yes, I should think so. The house is very well kept. You can go by it, if you like, just don't go onto the grounds, or you'll be chased off."

"Thanks for the warning," I said, as the woman shuffled off, taking up her position behind the oval counter, tidying up the already orderly surface.

"Did she know anything?" asked Étoile quietly.

I shook my head. "Nothing at all. Just that the owners of the house have got money and no one goes up there."

After we waved goodbye to the librarian and stepped back to allow a group of mothers to enter the building with their children, we left, turning back towards the high street.

Walking along the top end of the high street, we made our way across a small park, circled around a restricted area with children's swings and a slide, and walked on. Finding a bench, we sat. From this vantage point, which rose slightly higher than the village, I could point to Hawkscroft in the distance.

"So that's the seat of evil, huh?" said Étoile.

"The very same."

From here, we could scrutinise the lay of the land much better, though our only view was of the back of the house. Hawkscroft was surrounded on three sides by dense woods, a hill rising above them to the north. It looked very lonely sitting all by itself. The grounds were easy to see from our location and I could just make out the road that travelled across the front as it darted past the house, twisting into the woods where I met Anders.

From what I could see, the wall travelled all the way around the grounds. No parts of it had broken away, and it was all of a similar level, evidence of its upkeep. There was a walled garden close to the house, then lush green lawns that stretched across the grounds to the property lines. It struck me as strange that the property was walled off. The pictures in the library suggested the owners had once enjoyed hunting, so it seemed logical that they would own the woods too. Perhaps poor economics had forced them to sell excess land, or maybe it was just easier to guard a smaller property, even one as expansive as this. I said as much to Étoile.

"On the plus side, the woods will make it easier for us to get closer," she said. "Did you see anyone else in the woods last night?"

"Nobody. I got the impression from Anders that the Brotherhood didn't cross over." I recalled what Anders told me in the pub. "He said they might hear us, but not that they would find us."

"It's a big house. We can't possibly search it without being seen."

"Yeah. I figured we would need to locate Annalise before we tried to get inside."

As we watched, two dot figures moved around the side of the house, two more dots shooting off. Guard dogs, I assumed.

"Let's go back to the pub," said Étoile, standing and tightening her scarf. She looked at my muddy coat. "Maybe we can try cleaning that thing too."

Anders found us in the early afternoon, his night time spy gear replaced by jeans and boots. This time, he wasn't alone; two women flanked him. The first woman was around my age, a little shorter than I, and had neat, dark brown hair that swung around her chin. She was dressed for the cold weather in jeans, a thick, padded jacket and hiking boots. Her scarf was pulled almost over her chin and seemed to take an age to unravel.

"This is my girlfriend, Rachel Kelly," said Anders.

"Hello." Rachel smiled as she freed herself from the scarf.

Anders continued, "And this is..."

"Bree Thorne," said the second woman, her grip firm as she shook our hands before pulling out a chair. She took a seat at our table, sliding her jacket off and hanging it over the back of her chair. She was incredibly pretty with long blonde hair, almost white in hue, icy blue eyes, and very pale skin. Her hands were slightly rough, and her nails were chipped, like she was a manual labourer. She looked like a no nonsense type. "What brings you to this godforsaken place?" she asked without preamble.

"Didn't Anders tell you?" I asked as Étoile made her own introductions, shaking first Anders' hand, then Rachel's. I was under no illusions that she was just being polite; she was checking them out.

"Mmm, but I thought you probably wouldn't tell him everything after he pitched you into the mud." She grinned suddenly, her eyes lighting up. "He has terrible manners."

Anders scowled, but he didn't look particularly unhappy. "Not true." He reached into the rucksack he carried with him, pulling out some tubes of papers, which he laid on the table. "I've brought the plans you asked for. Bree knows the terrain around here better than anyone, so she wanted to come along." He didn't seem too happy about that.

"You're not a witch," I said, looking at her more closely.

"No, I'm not," she replied, "I'm a nymph."

The only nymph I could think of ended with "-omaniac," and I was fairly certain that wasn't why she looked so proud. "Oh?"

"A wood nymph. Traditionally, we live in forests, amongst the trees."

Étoile looked as interested as I did. Anders said, "We're very lucky to know Bree. Nymphs don't reveal themselves often."

"Why's that?"

"We don't like humans. The cut down trees and trample plants... They *litter*. The earth doesn't like that."

"We're not all bad," said Anders. "If we were, you wouldn't do our gardening. Bree is a landscape gardener," he added for our benefit. "She also knows all the paths and routes through the woods. She might help us find a better way through."

"But not into Hawkscroft. I don't like the magic there."

"Why's that?" asked Étoile.

"It's not that it's dark, it just seems confused. Like it knows it shouldn't be there, but it can't help itself."

"You talk about it like magic has feelings."

"Why shouldn't it?" said Bree, her silvery hair sliding over her shoulders.

I didn't know how to answer that, and apparently, neither did the other three witches sharing our table.

"Anders told us they've kidnapped a werewolf," said Rachel, her voice purposefully soft as she leaned in.

I glanced across to Étoile. "Our friend," I

corrected her.

"And you've come to get her back?"

"Yes."

"You've got balls, I'll give you that. No one goes onto Hawkscroft land." I waited for Rachel to say something like "and comes out alive" but she didn't. Instead, she asked, "How do you think you're going to get in? They never let anyone in, as far as I know."

"I don't know. We were hoping the plans would give us some clue."

"Best take a look then," said Rachel, reaching for the papers and unfolding them. "You'll be wanting to go in sooner rather than later, I imagine, 'specially with your friend in trouble."

After we studied the plans Anders brought, we didn't feel any wiser. The blueprints were old, showing the house as it would have been in the mid-nineteenth century. Despite the current zoning laws, since Hawkscroft was a listed historical building, we hoped that very little would have changed structurally.

Like many old country houses, Hawkscroft was a maze of work areas and living spaces. The kitchen led onto myriad smaller rooms; pantries or sculleries, I assumed, while the main living areas all sprang from one central hall. The plans marked a library, drawing room, and another reception room. Further along a corridor were a large dining room and several other rooms of indeterminate usage, Another corridor led to another set of smaller rooms. Upstairs was equally confusing with numerous rooms situated in each wing, every one branching from the central staircase.

Anders pointed out each exit. To the front, there were the main doors that I already discounted as being too overt. To the back, several sets of doors opened onto a terrace. The west side had a door, which led to a walled garden, while to the east, there was a tradesman's entrance that meandered into the disused stable yard.

"Every entrance is guarded twenty-four hours a day," explained Anders as he tapped his forefinger on each point of entry. "Even if one of us snuck in, it's teaming with people inside."

"There's been a lot of comings and goings over the past couple of weeks. Most of us locals don't like to go up that way, but we see the cars, of course," added Rachel. "Sometimes they come down to the village. Some of the locals, the ones who aren't in the know, think the owners just entertain a lot. Daft, if you ask me, why you'd want to entertain a bunch of scary fellas like that is beyond me."

Étoile looked up sharply. "Do they ever come into the pub?"

"Now and again," replied Anders. "But there isn't a bit of magic in a single one of them. Unless they know who you are, you should be safe. You might want to keep the accent to yourself though. Not a lot of outsiders come through Hawksley."

"Noted."

"Would they keep Annalise in one of the upstairs rooms?" I asked, keen to get us back on track.

"Unlikely. If it were me, I would keep her out of sight until they know what to do with her, somewhere easy to guard," suggested Bree.

"I've heard the house has a cellar," mused Anders, shuffling through the papers looking hopeful that he might have plans for them too. "That would be a good place to keep someone. No windows, probably only one exit, dark. It would take minimal manpower to keep someone under guard there."

"We need to confirm it."

"We've tried everything to find out what's in there, but we've never gotten anything. None of our charms seem to work, and the spells aren't much good either. We haven't wanted to dabble too far, in case someone realises we're on to them."

"I'm happy to give it a try, if you don't mind?" suggested Étoile.

"We'd have to go up there."

"It's too light right now. You would need to wait for nightfall again," said Rachel.

Étoile and I got a message on our phones at the same time from Gage saying he had landed and would be in Hawksley as soon as possible. There was nothing yet from Evan and, as it turned out, my phone was fine for receiving, but couldn't send anything. It was as good as useless.

As it would be long past dark by the time Gage arrived, we made the decision to go and check out Hawkscroft before he got here. At least, then we might have some confirmation of where Annalise was being held, information that would help us plan her rescue.

"A friend of ours is on his way. I'd rather have something to tell him, than nothing," I told them. My next question was for Anders, "Will you take us up there?"

"Yes, but I don't want to stay long. One of their lot nearly caught one of ours a few nights ago. I'm not sure how often they patrol outside the walls so we'd have to keep very quiet. Bree? You in?"

He didn't need to spell out that getting caught would be a catastrophe.

"Yes," she agreed simply, "but perhaps we should approach a different way from where you normally keep watch?"

"Which way do you suggest?" asked Rachel.

"From the west. We'll get a better view of the back, including the outbuildings and some of the front."

"Wish you'd mentioned that a few weeks ago," said Anders. He started folding the plans away and stacking them.

Bree looked at him in surprise. "You didn't ask. Besides it's a longer walk. We should take one vehicle and leave it over here," she pointed to a spot on a beer mat, her finger travelling around the logo in the centre as she added, "We'll cross the woods this way, and arrive over here. It won't take us more than an hour; and, if there's anyone else in the woods, we can leave this way, by crossing the stream. The wood exits out onto fields here."

"What time do we leave?" Rachel asked. "I've got work for the rest of the afternoon, but I can finish by five."

"Let's meet back here at sundown," decided Anders and we each nodded our agreement.

Rachel got to her feet, winding her long scarf around her neck, pulling it up slightly to cover the back of her head. "See you later. Bye, sweetie." She dipped her head to Anders, kissing him quickly, but long enough for me to feel the pang of missing Evan, even though it had been little more than twenty-four hours.

~

The five of us returned to Hawkscroft an hour after sundown. Anders left his car, a large, rumbling Land

Rover Defender, in the pub car park and climbed into my rental, which was smaller and quieter. He took the passenger seat, directing, while Étoile, Rachel and Bree squashed into the back.

Parking in the same spot as I did the night before, we got out, shutting the doors lightly behind us, keeping our mouths shut even though it was unlikely anyone would hear us. Crossing the road, we walked the short distance to the woods, then followed Bree in single file as she pushed on, keeping to the country tracks that she knew so well, with only the single beam of her flashlight lighting the way. The further we travelled in, the more I realised there was no way I'd be able to find my way back on my own, so I kept in close file behind Bree, with Étoile right behind me, Anders and Rachel bringing up the rear.

After a while, Anders called to us to stop and we huddled in a circle. "We're just going to look, okay?" he told us again. "Don't do anything to attract attention and don't put even a finger over that wall."

"Then we'll move around to the back of the house," added Bree.

We nodded solemnly. A howl echoed in the darkness, somewhere in the distance, and Étoile and I looked at each other with grim expressions. I didn't get the feeling we were alone in the woods anymore.

"Let's go," said Bree, turning off her flashlight.

"Wait!" Anders looked around, like he was searching for something. "I forgot. The watch earlier said there had been a lot of movement by the stable walls today. Let's go around back instead. Like Bree said, we'll be able to see more over there anyway."

"Okay," agreed Bree. Then to us, her silver hair almost glowing in the dark, "Stay close. The woods are more overgrown that way, but there's some good vantage points. I'll show you the patrol points too."

As we walked, I counted twenty-seven things I'd rather be doing than this; Evan was items one, five, nine, thirteen and twenty. Not only was it cold, but also eerily quiet. The only noises I heard were the occasional squawk of a bird or snuffling in the undergrowth. At least, I knew there weren't any dangerous, indigenous creatures out here, and the chances of stepping on a poisonous snake were so remote, most British people never saw one in their lifetime, never mind fell afoul of one. All the same, I kept on alert, aware that the howl we'd heard earlier might be a signal from the local wolves. Perhaps Gage had managed to get their support, I hoped, though I wasn't sure I wanted to run into them tonight. It occurred to me, however, that at least, they would be familiar with Anders.

The going was tougher here, the trees knitting together, a tangle of bushes and thorns catching at my coat. Bree seemed to make her way through easily enough, as if the woods recognised her as one of their own and allowed passage for her. The rest of us should be so lucky.

"We're heading west now," said Bree, the murmur passing back through the line. "We're also going to pass close to the wall before we can turn, so try not to make too much noise."

We followed her, the path leading us so close to the wall that I caught sight of the house briefly before we swung right, and the path got wider. I heard the howl again, a mournful whine that seemed to carry through the woods and was returned by another.

I caught Étoile's sleeve and tugged. "There are at

least two wolves in the woods with us tonight," I whispered and she nodded, putting a finger to her lips.

I quickly closed the gap I'd left between Bree and us. Her flashlight was off completely now, and it was getting difficult to see where to place my feet, or see overhanging, spindly branches until I was right on top of them. I checked my watch, the little hands glowing. We'd been walking for a good thirty minutes.

"Just a little further," called Bree, loud enough that we could all hear. After another ten minutes of trampling in the dark, she stopped. "This is it. We can climb those trees there to take a look. They aren't hard to climb."

She scrambled up the nearest tree, her hands and feet sure as she used the branches for a ladder, hopping neatly up until she was around five feet from the ground. Securing herself, she called down, "The lights are on but I can't see any patrols. They might be changing shifts."

"Take that one," said Rachel, nudging me and pointing towards a tree a few feet away. "It has lots of branches and you'll be able to nestle against the trunk where those two branches fork."

"If you look straight ahead you'll have a great view of the rear of the house," said Bree. "Hurry up."

The tree was easier to climb than it looked and, with the exception of pulling off some bark (I didn't dare look to see if Bree winced), I made it up quickly, sitting in the junction of the tree as I held onto one branch. A side door was open and I could just make out a couple of men who stood there. One had a cigarette in his mouth, the embers glowing red as he flicked it onto the grass. They seemed to be talking. I looked beyond them. Several windows were lit, the drapes undrawn and I could see people moving about and a number of screens. I couldn't make out what was on the screens, but I assumed it was closed circuit television and this was some sort of operations room. After a few minutes, a man stood at the window, looking out, then he grabbed the drapes, shutting the room from view. Further to the left, what I assumed to be the walled garden blocked my view. I couldn't be sure, as some of the people kept moving around, but I thought I counted ten men.

"I think I hear something," said Anders, his voice somewhere off to my left. I squinted, looking for him and found him in a tree, Rachel close by his side. "I'm going to take a look."

"Stay in the tree," hissed Rachel. "No one comes out here. We're mad to."

"Just wait here. I'll be back in a few minutes." Anders clambered down nimbly and disappeared into the dark. I sat, immobilized, watching Hawkscroft. I didn't see any patrols, which struck me as odd, but maybe they had cameras covering the grounds as backup.

After a few minutes, Anders came back. "There's someone out there," he said, beckoning us down. "Let's go. I don't want to run into whoever it is."

"Could it be one of your coven?" asked Étoile.

"Unlikely. I told them all to stay away tonight. We weren't finding anything out anyway." He held his arms up to Rachel, catching her as she jumped from the last branch to the floor. "Did you see anything useful?"

"Only that we can hardly stroll across the grounds into the back," said Étoile.

"There's a control room in the corner on the right wing," I added. "I think they were watching camera feeds."

"Interesting. Let's get out of here. Which way, Bree? We can't go back the way we came."

"This way then. We'll have to cross a river, but it's shallow."

"Lead on," said Étoile. Bree took off at a jog and we hurried along after her, falling quickly into single file again. We reached the bank quickly, standing shoulder to shoulder as we looked down. The river had shrunk back from its banks, leaving just a shallow strip of water.

"As soon as we get across, head straight and you'll... shit!" Bree ducked as something whistled past our heads, thudding into a nearby tree. "Was that a...?" She stopped and shrieked. A shout echoed behind us, then I turned and saw figures rising, as though from the earth, taking lurching steps towards us.

"Go! Go! *Go!*" yelled Anders, no longer caring about being overheard as he pushed us, sending us scrambling down the banks. At the bottom, I tripped and fell, twisting my ankle as I struggled back to my feet. I was halfway up the bank when something grabbed my injured ankle causing me to cry out. Fingers dug into my flesh and yanked me backwards.

The last thing I saw, before falling into the darkness, was Étoile's horrified face as she reached for me. Then hands were grabbing me, rolling me over, shouting. I remembered staring into a pair of narrowed brown eyes right before something very hard connected with my head, and the world went black.

CHAPTER ELEVEN

When I came to, I was lying on a stone floor, my cheek pressed uncomfortably against the tiles. Cranking open one eye felt like running a marathon: enormously challenging and utterly exhausting. My hair stuck in patches to my face and the cold had made its way through my layers to my bones, chilling me to the core.

I raised one hand, groaning as my body protested against the sudden movement, and brushed the hair out of my eyes, momentarily surprised that my hands were free. I tested my feet next, wriggling my ankles and found they weren't tied either. As I lay there, blinking, I wondered who decided it was a good idea to leave me unbound. They must have been confident that I wasn't going to escape.

The air smelled damp, musty, like it didn't have much cause to move, or anywhere to travel if it did, and it was very dark. I could barely make out the outline of anything in the room, not even where the darkness ended and the walls began, but that might have had a lot to do with the buzzing in my head.

To make matters worse, something was licking my face in long rasps. I drew my knees up, rolling into a foetal-style ball and pushed at whatever it was. Instead of a hideous monster, I got a wet nose. My hands ran over it to find a muzzle, then fisted in coarse hair. The licking stopped, and was replaced by a short, low, whine with an impatient push of the nose into my cheek. I squinted in the darkness and could just make out the soft pink-tinged, pale fur of my best friend.

"Annalise?" I asked, keeping my voice low, the hope evident in my voice. I had no idea where I was or who else could hear me or if we were even alone. My head hurt, my mouth was dry, and my body ached. I desperately wanted something to dull the pain.

The wolf yapped, just once, but it was enough.

"Why are you in wolf form?" I whispered.

Annalise padded in a tight circle for a moment then rattled her head to and fro until I saw the thick collar around her neck. A chain clanked and rattled as the links fell back onto the floor. I could just make out a curved panel bolted to the floor, the heavy links secured to a circle that ran through and under it, ensuring Annalise couldn't move very far at all. I hated to think how long she had been kept like this.

I reached for her and she shuffled forwards, nuzzling into me. Normally, I'd keep my hands off the werewolves when in wolf form unless they offered permission because it seemed impolite. Simply stated, I wouldn't run my hands through their hair when they were human, so why do it when they were wolf? But this was an exception. Running my hands over the cold hard collar, I sighed. The basic signature of the magic was clear enough, sufficient to recognise that while the collar was in place, Annalise couldn't change back to her human form, even if she wanted to.

"Magic," I said, like she hadn't already guessed. Annalise yipped and sat back on her haunches, her front paws tapping from one to the other.

"This sucks," I muttered and she yipped again.

Wrapping my arm around her neck, I held on to her while I shuffled into a seated position, Annalise half pulling me upwards, as dizziness overcame me. "How long have I been down here?" I asked, reaching up to touch the back of my head. The steady hum that sounded in my skull was bad enough; but as I ran my hand around to the front, I could also feel something sticky that had dried in a trail from my forehead to my cheek and stuck my hair together in clumps. Someone had hit me hard enough to knock me out and cause damage. Peeling the hair off my face wouldn't be too bad, but tackling the wound was going to hurt like a bitch. I unstuck a few strands, wincing, and tucked them behind my ear, almost glad for a moment that it was so dark. Seeing as I didn't have any bandages or anything to clean the wound, I left it alone.

Annalise twisted her head and looked at me, her eyes sad, and nudged me a couple of times with her nose, then licked my cheek. She sidled closer, pressing her body against mine and flattened her front legs to the floor, crossing them and laying her muzzle on top.

"Right, can't speak. Gotcha." I puzzled it over for a moment. We needed a way to communicate, something basic at the very least. "One yap for yes, two for no?" I suggested.

Yap.

"Have I been here a long time?

Yap.

"Days?" Wow, I hoped not.

Yap yap.

No, less than that. "Hours?" I tried.

Yap

That I could deal with a bit better. It was just past dusk when we'd trampled around the perimeter of the estate and we were there for a little more than an hour when it all went wrong. It could be evening, or the early hours of the morning now. Without any clue from the moon or sun, I couldn't be sure. "Do you know what is going on?" I asked her.

A whine.

"That a maybe?"

Yap. Then she edged forwards and nuzzled at my wrist, pushing the cuff back to show the slim silver bracelet that had been Gage's Christmas present to me, a match to the star-shaped pendant Annalise bought. It was quite plain with four little discs hanging from the catch, each one representing a stage of the moon. I thought it was enchanting.

"Gage is here?"

Yap.

"Can you communicate with him?"

Yap yap.

No. That sounded slightly less promising. Gage once explained that they were able to communicate telepathically as wolves, but it could be the magic, or the distance interfering. All the same, she knew he was here, and that was reassuring. I hoped Evan was close behind. Letting out an exasperated breath, I asked, "Are we completely and totally screwed?"

Whine.

That sounded like a definite maybe.

"Talking like this is going to take freaking hours. Is it safe for me to look around?" I hadn't moved since I sat up and I was starting to feel aches running up my legs and into my back. My left calf was starting to seize like I had a cramp.

Annalise just nodded this time. After stretching my leg, I massaged it until the pain was gone, then scrambled to my feet. I made a vague, pointless attempt at dusting my clothes with dirty hands and walked the few paces of our small cell, feeling my way around the edges, trying not to jump when something ran across my foot.

I expected to find something in the room, something to sleep on, a mattress roll or maybe some blankets, or some kind of bench or chair but the room was absolutely stripped bare. Or had never been furnished in the first place. I could just about reach the ceiling if I stretched my hand and stood on tiptoes and, from running my hands over the walls, I could tell that they were bare brick, some of the mortar crumbling under my probing fingertips. There weren't any water pipes or cables for electricity, nothing that could be broken, or torn apart, or used as weapon.

There weren't any outside windows that weren't concealed by shutters, and the only apparent opening was a thick wooden door set into the wall. It had a slim viewing hole that let in a sliver of light, just enough that we weren't in absolute darkness. By pressing my head against the opening and rolling to either side, I could just see another room and a slim passageway extending from that. Both appeared empty. From the cold, and the musty smell, I figured we had to be somewhere under the house, perhaps in the vaults or a wine cellar of some sort – they hadn't been on the plans but Anders mentioned them – and it figured this would be where they would hold us. With only one entrance/exit, it was easy to keep us prisoner and away from prying eyes.

Holding out my hand, I willed light to flow from it. I couldn't summon anything. I tried again, this time trying to create a little fire. Still nothing. Something was blocking my magic. I didn't know whether to hope it was something to do with the head injury I'd sustained. If that were the case, I didn't know if it were irreversible or if my magic would even return. No, that wasn't right; I could feel it inside me. It just wasn't coming out.

I tried the door by pulling on the bars embedded in the viewing hole – there wasn't a handle on the inside – but it was obviously locked. I ran my hand over the keyhole, in case I could somehow trip the lock, but my magic stayed firmly within, dormant for now.

The irony struck me again. For people who professed to hate magic, they sure used a lot of it. I had no doubt that whatever was suppressing my magic now was a direct result of something they had done.

"How come they're using magic?" I asked Annalise as I turned back to her. She sat up, then lay down again, her tail thumping against the floor. "Sorry, forgot. Can't talk, gotcha." As I moved back to her, I stooped to one knee and ran my hand over her collar again. It didn't seem right that the Brotherhood would employ magic, especially not in their home. I couldn't understand it. Magic was everything they hated, everything they stood against, everything that united them in their crusade; at least, that's what I thought until now. Why they would use magic for their own purposes was altogether puzzling. Over the past year, I assumed that because they hunted witches, they didn't have any of their own. They shouldn't even be able to perform magic, certainly not want to. I was going to have to revaluate everything I'd ever thought, or assumed, about the Brotherhood.

"Weird, huh?" I said to Annalise. I crouched next to her and put my arms around her, feeling dejected. I couldn't see any way out of this mess. She nuzzled my face. I guess she felt the same way. "I'm, we're, going to get you out of this," I promised her. I hated the idea of her being held prisoner down here since she'd been kidnapped a few days ago. Her fur didn't have that light, fluffy feel that I'd felt before when she was out running, not that I made a habit of petting her. Instead, it had taken on a dry, coarse feel and was matted in places. I rubbed the matted part and raised my fingers to my nose, inhaling it. Blood. They'd beaten her.

Putting my hand over her collar, I felt around for a catch. After a moment, I found it and let out the breath I hadn't realised I had been holding. I was afraid there would be a padlock holding the collar closed but instead, there was a simple catch closure held together with some kind of pin. I worked the pin backwards and forwards until it loosened, falling to the floor with a little clink.

I pulled the collar apart and carefully placed both pieces on the floor next to the wall, just in case anyone was listening. Days of wearing the collar had forced Annalise's fur apart and her skin felt bare and sore from the rubbing, so I smoothed the fur gently back into place. It occurred to me that this was possibly the longest time she'd ever maintained this form and I wondered how tiring that was on her.

There was nothing else to do but sit down and rest my back against the wall. Annalise snuggled up to me so I put my arm round her and hugged her and there we waited, cold and frightened, trying to keep each other warm, wondering who was going to come for us... and even worse, if they ever would.

Since she couldn't talk, I told her about what happened since she'd been kidnapped; about Evan's swift removal of Étoile and me to his home and my mixed feelings on that. Still, I thought he probably made the right choice, given the circumstances. I told her how I had come to England alone – I mentioned we were in Hawkscroft, just in case she didn't know – and how Étoile had just shown up, like a good guardian fairy. Annalise snuffled at that. I told her that we made plans to find her and rescue her, plans that had obviously come undone. "I can't believe I tripped on a damned root," I said, disappointed in myself. After that, we were quiet.

It's easy to lose track of time when you've lost all relativity to it in the first place. My phone had been confiscated and I wasn't wearing a watch. Plus, with the artificial light beyond the door, it was impossible to know whether it was minutes or hours that slipped by in our dark little cell. It felt like we'd been waiting an awfully long time when there was a scraping noise and the door suddenly opened a little bit, just enough to slide in a tray. I didn't even see who it was, just a hand as I blinked against the sudden light. The door slammed shut again.

We both sat there and watched the tray like it was something ominous. We looked at each other. "Fine, seeing as I'm the one with hands, I'll get it."

Annalise made a little huffing noise that sounded like a laugh.

I crawled over and reached for the tray. When my fingers connected with the plastic, I dragged it towards us. A couple of plastic bottles of water lay on their sides and there was a triangular shaped package. Sandwiches. There was a tin of something, too, with a ring pull top. I held it up to my face, squinting. Oh. Dog food. Yuck. That answered my question of how long she'd been kept wolf.

"You want to go human and share a sandwich?" I suggested, snapping the cap off a bottle of water. Annalise shook her head, her tongue lolling out one side of her mouth. I tipped the water close to her mouth and she lapped it up. When she finished, I capped it again and set it at her feet. Then I unwrapped the plastic packaging of the sandwich, offering her half. After I finished swallowing the sandwich, which felt like cardboard in my mouth, I took a sip of water from the other bottle in a vague attempt at washing it down before shoving the tray away.

We dozed a while longer, huddled in the furthest corner of the room, propped against each other for warmth. I was deeply uncomfortable sitting on the cold floor and couldn't imagine how Annalise had endured it alone. Aside from the sounds of our breathing, quiet filled the small room, punctuated every so often with the squeak of a small mammal.

Once I thought I saw a mouse run over the tray.

I was too tired to stay awake, and too frightened to go to sleep, so I tried to relax into a half-state of being neither one nor the other, anything for some rest. There was no telling what would happen later so it was sensible to conserve our energy. I said as much to Annalise.

The first I knew that someone was in the passageway was when I heard the key in the lock and the heavy bar slide free. My eyes shot open as the door opened a crack and Annalise and I huddled further together, away from the sudden burst of light that penetrated the anteroom beyond and was now flowing into our light-starved eyes. For the first time, I saw Annalise's sorry state; she was dirty and bloody. Then the door was fully open; a man filled the doorframe, blocking the light. Extending a hand, he indicated to me with one finger. "Get up," he said, his voice gruff. I smelled the heavy odour of cigarette smoke on him; he was clearly a heavy smoker.

I felt Annalise tense, then rock back on her haunches. With a snarl, she leapt at him, knocking him backwards to the ground, snapping at his neck. A swat from her claws had him bleeding from a wound to his cheek and she kept up a relentless snapping, biting him. I kept low and made ready to run the moment the man gave up.

"Get it off me!" he shrieked, his hands flailing at Annalise's brute strength.

Another man appeared in the doorway, his eyes darting over the scene of his fallen comrade. There was a brief flash of blue light and, with a howl, Annalise fell back, falling into a shaking heap on the ground. Her eyes were open but glazed over and I realised she'd been hit with a taser, the shocks still ricocheting through her body.

Just as I was about to scramble towards her, the second man rushed into the room, stepping over Annalise's shaking body before grabbing me by my shoulder.

"Step back or I'll tase you too," he said, his voice emotionless, "and the master won't like that." He wrapped his arms around my waist and carried me kicking and screaming out of the room. The bleeding man had already scrambled into the anteroom, a wad of paper towel pressed against a cut on his face. As we cleared the door, the bleeding man stepped past us to slam the door shut and turned the key, turning slowly to face me.

"She'll be fine. Now stop kicking or I'll have to knock you out," the man holding me murmured into my ear. He was dressed much nicer than the first, in black trousers and a polo shirt, and he smelled like mints and bread dough, fresh and warm. It was a strange contrast to the first man, who was looking at me with undisguised disgust.

"Pretty thing, ain't she?" The first man looked me over slowly. "Bit scruffy, but definitely a pretty lass. Wonder if she's got some magic in the bedroom, eh, Pete?" He stepped closer, a toothy grin on his face and stroked a calloused hand over my cheek.

I landed a kick firmly in his groin and watched him drop to his knees, howling, before the man holding me, Pete, hauled me back.

"The master said she wasn't to be hurt," Pete warned him. "And getting nasty with women isn't my bag, my friend, so I reckon you deserved that."

I continued struggling, but his arms were firmly

hooked under my shoulders, forcing them upwards and pushing my shoulders to painfully over extend. I managed to stamp on his instep and he let go, smoothly grabbing my wrists behind my back with one hand, and pushing my arms upwards. "Despite what the master said," Pete hissed in my ear, "I will knock you out if you do that again."

I stopped struggling, falling limp. There was no point; I couldn't get free from his tight grip and getting knocked out twice in one day seemed a little excessive, even for me. He waited until I calmed down before gripping each wrist and moving my arms down so that my wrists rested on the small of my back, his one, mitt-like hand wrapped around them both.

The nasty man in front of me straightened up, glowering, but he didn't approach me again. Instead, he put his face to the door and looked through, nodding to himself. Stepping to the right, he hung the key on a hook above the door. Now that I wasn't flailing, I could see a corridor that stretched far into the distance, but it was too dark for me to make anything out.

Pete gave me a little push towards the open archway. "That way," he instructed, adding, "Mind your step!" as I tripped on a flagstone. I winced as the ankle I'd twisted previously sent a jarring shock through me. He caught me, helping me upright, without relaxing his grip once. I heard a small click and a light flicked on; long florescent tubes flashing on one by one. It was basic and austere and everything looked sinister in the unnatural glow. We faced a long corridor that seemed to pass through a number of interconnecting rooms via a series of archways.

"Where are you taking me?" I asked, a small shove in my back making me move forwards, my captor propelling me along. From the looks of it, we were definitely in the cellar of Hawkscroft and it was a long winding path from our cell to wherever our destination lay.

"Upstairs," Pete surprised me by answering, his footsteps echoing with mine.

Behind me, I heard Annalise whimpering, then Pete pushed me on, hurriedly. The second man limped behind him, cursing, as we walked on into the unknown.

CHAPTER TWELVE

On our way up from the cellar, we passed through a series of other rooms, each with barely enough clearance for me to be able to walk through without ducking my head. I took some perverse pleasure in how annoying it must have been for my two attackers to have to keep bending down. With the speed of the walking, and the constant pressure on my back from the man named Pete, I didn't see much as we passed through each room. Finally, we stepped into a room larger than all the others. It seemed to be some kind of storage area. Shelves ran across the walls, each one packed with boxes, lids taped down, like it was some kind of archive.

If I hoped that was it, I was wrong. From there, we changed direction, passing through another series of other rooms, each getting increasingly larger, the air slightly clearer. They were cluttered with large pieces of furniture; chairs, tables, consoles from all different eras, and dozens of boxes, thickly taped again. Passing through another corridor, we arrived at a set of steps.

Pete, the prison guard, gave me a rough shove forward, simultaneously releasing my wrists. Momentarily unbalanced, I slipped, throwing my hands forward, and scraping the heels of my palms on the steps. I bit the inside of my cheek to stop me from wincing because there was no way I was going to give them the satisfaction of seeing me in pain before I scrambled back up. I grazed some of the skin. Blood was already beading on the surface and it stung like a bitch as I started to ascend.

At the top of the staircase, Pete took my arm again, half pushing, half pulling me into a small room. Just inside, I bent over, resting my hands on my knees to catch my breath as if I were recovering from the fast walk.

"I'm going to let go of you. If you try to run, you'll regret it," said Pete. "All I have to do is yell and there will be twenty men in here."

I looked up at him, then over to the second, still nameless, man who lumbered up behind us. He grinned again; his lips peeled back to show his missing teeth. Nameless took one last look at me, winked, and slid out of the room.

"He'll be first in the door," Pete warned in a low voice.

Yuck. "You win," I sniffed, straightening up. I took a moment to take in some air and regulate my breathing after the power walk. It wasn't that I was out of breath; I just wanted it to look that way. Months of running almost every day had paid off; I was fit and healthy, but feigning a stitch meant I could take my time in looking around the room. It was windowless and seemed to serve as some sort of large catchall closet for household things like brooms, mops and other cleaning equipment. I guessed this was where they stored stuff ready for transport below ground and brought things back up again. *Like prisoners*, I thought ominously. Unfortunately, it looked like this room was the only way out of the cellar and, as we stepped out into what looked like the foyer, I realised that was a problem. It would be almost impossible to return unnoticed, or to leave.

Pete didn't give me much time to look around, but I saw that the ceiling must have been twenty feet high, a huge glass chandelier twinkling under it. The walls were painted a rich, dark red and there were dozens of portraits of men and women in period dress in huge frames. The furniture looked old and heavy and the wood gleamed from decades of polish.

"Let's go." Pete nudged me forwards, but not before I scanned the room quickly, making a count. Four men flanked the tall double doors, the front doors I assumed; two more, sat at a table pressed up against the far wall, playing cards. Another man walked past, entering the foyer from one corridor and exiting by another. He didn't even glance in my direction, though some of the others did. That made eight including Pete and this was a big house; Pete had already intimated twenty men were in earshot. It was best to assume he wasn't lying.

The chances of me being able to get past all these guards and into the cellar, breaking out Annalise, then leaving the cellar by the same route and exiting the house, without getting caught, was looking decidedly sketchy. My heart plummeted and stopped somewhere around my toes.

"Through here," Pete snapped, reaching for me

again.

"Get off," I hissed. For a moment, he stood there, staring down at me, like he was having some kind of internal struggle about whether he should take hold of me again or not. He must have concluded there were enough guards about that I wasn't going to cause trouble because he just shrugged, pointing towards a set of double doors across the foyer, saying, "That way." Where else could I go? If I attacked him, I'd have eight men pummelling me in an instant. If I ran, I'd get five feet before the same thing happened.

"Who's there?" I asked, after a moment of staring up at the man. With his bland, emotionless face, I couldn't fathom why, or how, he had gotten involved in this. Was he just a brutal killer or had he been sucked in by the lure of a cause intent on "defeating evil"? Was he a bad man doing bad things because he enjoyed it? Or a good man doing bad things for what he felt were good reasons? It was impossible to tell. Perhaps the lines had been drawn too closely together.

"You'll find out, won't you?" Pete was expressionless. For the first time, I got a good look at him. He was bald with a pale white face, probably somewhere in his early forties. He was well built, broad and muscular without an inch of fat. I wondered if he had been one of the witch hunters that chased me through the streets back when I was alone and afraid. I might have been alone and afraid now, staring up at him almost defiantly, but it was a different sort of fear. I had friends now, not to mention, hope. All I had to do was stay alive, which sounds so simple until you have to do it.

Call me crazy, but I was pretty certain that behind

the doors now facing me, there wasn't going to be anyone I liked or wanted to see. I thought about shimmering, but although I could feel my magic within me, I knew it wouldn't do what I wanted while something else was suppressing it. Without my magic, I didn't have a choice. If I were going to get Annalise and me out of here, I'd have to go forwards.

By the time I realised that, and made my decision, we had crossed the floor, coming to a stop outside the closed doors. Pete knocked and dipped his head towards the door, listening momentarily for something I didn't hear. Then, he twisted the knob and opened the door, signalling for me to enter. When I passed through, Pete stepped back. The door closed behind me lightly and, for a moment, I was too surprised to do anything but stand still and wait.

At first, I thought I was alone. I was in a library, a very beautiful library. The ceiling was as high as the foyer, which was split in the middle by a narrow mezzanine floor, just room enough for one person. A matching pair of slim, spiral staircases stood at each end so that you could walk the entire circuit and exit without having to retrace your steps. Three walls of the library were covered in dark wood shelves, each one stuffed with books from floor to ceiling. The only exception was the door interrupting the shelving behind me. The fourth wall, facing me, had a large fireplace, probably just tall enough for me to stand in upright. Right now, it was blazing, the wood crackling in the grate and kicking heat out across the room.

Two leather wingchairs sat a little way back from the fireplace and between them was a low table, scattered with an open book, reading glasses and a notepad. All fairly innocuous things until I wondered whom they belonged to. To my right, there was a couch, set at a diagonal so people could move around it easily and access the books. A small table was parked in front of it and it also had a shallow stack of books, all very old volumes in excellent condition. Someone really took care of their books.

"Pleasant isn't it?" said a voice. "I haven't quite read every book, but I plan on doing so during my lifetime."

I looked around, trying to locate the voice when I saw an arm reach out from the recesses of one wingchair and point to the other. "Sit down, Miss Mayweather. I insist."

I skirted around the table and chair, keeping my distance from the arm that rested on the side of the chair, as well as the body attached to it. The man didn't move at all until I was facing him, the empty wingchair between the two of us, giving me several feet of distance in which to appraise him.

He was sitting ramrod straight, legs crossed, a book open and face down over one leg. He was a solid looking man, not fat or particularly broad, just well kept with a neat beard. I guessed he was somewhere in his late fifties or early sixties. He wore a dark grey three-piece suit with a tie in muted stripes, giving him the air of a university professor or a businessman. I was sure I'd seen him before, but I couldn't place him.

"Sit down," he said again.

I walked slowly around the chair, keeping my eyes on him while he turned his attention to the fire as if I were of no consequence to him whatsoever. I sat uneasily waiting for him to speak, but he stared at the flames for a while. Just when I was starting to fidget, he looked at me and smiled. It was a cold sort of smile, the sort that didn't reach his eyes, or make me feel that he was in any way happy.

"Wouldn't our meeting have been so much more pleasant if you had simply accepted my invitation? Oh, that's a rhetorical question." He slipped a leather marker into the book he was holding, closed it and leaned forward to drop it lightly on the table between us. "I've looked forward to meeting you, Stella. May I call you Stella?"

"No."

He ignored me. "I've known about you your whole life, of course, but you've been hidden such a long time. When you finally surfaced, I sent my men to find you as soon as I realised you had come into your powers. Such a shame. Magic is an abomination. Blights so many lives, you know."

A year ago, my life was changed in the course of just a few hours. I had a dull job, a dull life, but it had been all mine. Like every other woman, I was well aware of the witch hunter murderers. One night, I was chased by a group of men who were intent on killing me. I narrowly escaped them twice; the second time with Étoile's help.

It came to me then. That was why the man looked so familiar.

I'd seen him once before on television. It had been that same night that Étoile rescued me. A broadcast went out across all stations simultaneously, announcing that the Brotherhood claimed responsibility for the killings of witches throughout Europe.

The common feeling amongst the media, since that broadcast, was that this Brotherhood was comprised of mad, deluded serial killers, though it did add extra drama to their reports. Only a small faction knew the truth about what they were and that they really were assassinating witches. The killings had spread briefly from Europe to the United States, and further afield. Then they stopped, just as abruptly. Things had been quiet for a while, not that any witch dared to take a relieved breath and think it was all over.

No, everyone I knew had been waiting tentatively for the Brotherhood's next move.

Strangely enough, I hadn't seen them on television since then, but their one and only broadcast had been enough to fuel the hysterical websites that I spent so much time picking through on my quest for information. It also added some weight to Anders' suggestion that this man was somewhat untouchable. He was able to broadcast his responsibility for murder, and yet, here he sat, in the comfort of his home. Someone was protecting him. The Brotherhood went further than this.

"You're the Brotherhood's leader," I said, concealing my thoughts. "Your men didn't come to find me. They firebombed my flat."

"Some of them are quite enthusiastic." The man shrugged, like it wasn't anything of consequence. "They were reprimanded, of course."

Like that made me feel any better. If anything, I felt more nervous than ever. Suppose those men were here tonight? After having been punished, who knew what kind of grudge they held against me now? I had the uncomfortable thought that, aside from the cellar prison, this room was probably the safest room in the whole house for me right now. Thinking of the cellar reminded me of Annalise, alone in the dark, and I concentrated on my breathing, instead of flying into a screaming rage, which was tempting.

"Why are you doing this?" I asked, because simple questions are sometimes the best ones.

"To rid the world of something that should have never been in it. No one should have such power, no person should be able to teleport, or use telekinesis, or all the evil things you do." If he'd been thirty years younger, I would have expected him to add *well, duh!*

"We're not evil. We don't kill people!" I fought to keep my composure. I didn't have much choice. Arguing might have been a foolish move, but it went against my nature to meekly take what this man was dishing out.

"We're a necessary evil, like executioners, politicians and taxes. We do the dirty jobs no one wants to think about." The man leaned forward, his eyes boring into me. "We keep the world safe without them *ever* having to lift a finger."

My voice was cool and calm, icy even, when I said, "You're ruthless murderers."

He smiled unexpectedly, but it was such a cold expression. "Such a pejorative term, don't you think?" he asked.

"Who are you anyway?"

"I didn't introduce myself? Do forgive my manners. My name is Auberon Morgan. You can call me Uncle, if you prefer."

"Why would I do that?" I frowned.

"It's a polite way to address one's relative," he answered succinctly, before dropping the bombshell. "Your mother was my sister."

"You have got to be kidding me."

"Do I look like someone who... *kids*?" He looked at me like I just said something completely absurd. I suppose I had.

Auberon Morgan rose and walked around the wingchair to a table nestled in one of the large windows. When he returned, he had a large silver picture frame in his hands, which he passed to me. I had no choice but to take it and study the photograph it contained. There was a couple, aged around forty or so, with two children, a boy in his teens and a slightly younger girl, probably around nine years old in a pale blue dress, her hair in bunches. All four of them were sitting with their backs against an ancient oak tree, parents behind, children in front. A check blanket was spread out in front of them with the remains of a picnic and an open wicker basket. There was something content and lovely about the faded scene.

"Isadore was eleven then. She was four years younger than me. This was taken when I was home from boarding school for the summer." Auberon returned to the window and was looking out as he raised one hand, waving it off to the left. "You can just see the tree from this window if you crane your head a bit."

"So, you're a witch too? A warlock?"

"Oh no, only your mother was unlucky enough to inherit that curse, but she loved it, loved the things she could do. She wasn't the type who taunted, or did anything cruel, but it was unnatural the way she could be there one moment, disappearing the next." Auberon turned back to me but his eyes were far away, somewhere in the past. "I always felt sorry for her, tried to help her stop but she couldn't, she insisted it was part of her. Then she married your idiot father and he was just as bad, whispering spells. She brought you here once, when you were a baby, and I begged her to stop with the magic, for you, but they wouldn't listen."

"They're dead."

"I know, and I don't mean to speak ill of the dead, but perhaps it's for the best." Auberon slid back into his chair, resting his head against the back, closing his eyes for a moment like he was so weary of the world that he couldn't keep looking at it.

I was still struggling to take in what he told me. I couldn't fathom how this awful man could possibly by my mother's brother, and my uncle. My only living relation was the man who masterminded dozens of murders? Who for the past year had made me live in fear? Anger bubbled inside me, and I felt my magic agitate.

"You tried to kill me once, why not just do it now?" I hoped I wasn't having a too-stupid-to-live moment, but the question just begged to be asked. He hated witches; he wanted us all dead, so why keep me alive?

"I don't have much family, I'd hate to destroy what's left," said Auberon, ruining the warm, fuzzy, family-bonding moment when he added, "so I'm giving you a choice."

"What kind of choice?"

"Work with me."

I raised my eyebrows. "Seriously?"

Auberon seemed to have expected that because he was ready with his answer. "You can't be enjoying the life you have, Stella. Parents dead, attacked by witches – yes, I've done my homework – the strange little town you live in, under a constant threat. And what's the common theme here? Oh, yes! Magic!" Auberon shook his head like he couldn't quite believe the predicament I'd gotten myself into. One hand reached up to smooth his beard. "Help me get rid of the witches and I'll help you bind your magic. You'll be able to live a nice normal life without fear and I can give you everything in return: a family, safety, money. You'll never have to worry again."

I couldn't lie to myself. There was a part of me that thought if he'd found me in my teens, and asked me then if I wanted my magic bound, in exchange for a family, I might have said yes. But I had a family now, my very own, and powers that I controlled. I couldn't ask for a normal life in return for betraying everyone I now held dear. What he was asking was untenable.

"What's the alternative?" I asked.

Auberon turned sad eyes on me. "Death, Stella. That's the only alternative."

We stopped talking then because the door was opening, letting in a little rush of cool air. Auberon leaned back in his chair again, not bothered by trivialities, while I craned my head around to see. Two men entered. One carried a tray with a teapot and cups with saucers. The other stood with his back against the door, like I was even going to bother trying to escape.

"On the table, here, man," Auberon instructed, clearing the few things off the table between us, setting them on the floor under his chair. The man holding the tray crossed the room and set it down between us, not even glancing at me. Picking up the teapot, he poured each of us a cup, adding sugar and milk to Auberon's, none to mine. When he was finished, he backed away silently; then they were both gone.

Something else occurred to me then, something to keep me from having to choose between life and death. "Why do you use magic here if you hate it so much?"

"You noticed? When one is trying to defeat evil, one must also be protected from it."

"So, who's doing it?" They must have a witch, someone who'd turned against the supernatural world, or someone who was being forced into performing magic for them. My questions came thick and fast. "Is that how you found me? And the other witches? By magic?"

"You don't really expect me to answer your questions, do you? Don't let your tea get cold." Auberon leaned forward, stretching his hands towards the fire, warming them, while I picked up the delicately striped china cup. Just as I was bringing it to my lips, I noticed it swirl strangely, far more than it should. I paused and stared at it as two very distinct letters formed.

NO.

No? I frowned at it. Someone, or something, was interfering with the liquid, and whoever it was, apparently, didn't want me to drink the tea. Puzzled, I put the rim of the cup to my lips, pretending to drink as Auberon turned to look at me, silently watching.

While I pretended to sip, I took a moment to think. Of course, I didn't expect Auberon to answer my questions, but if he were planning on killing me, it would be useful to have a little extra knowledge. If nothing else, I might be able to transmit it to Étoile before I bit it. Besides, the bad guys in movies always gave terrific soliloquies and admitted everything right before the heroine was saved, and they got their comeuppance, so I really, really hoped we were going to have one of those moments.

I should be so lucky.

Auberon might not be willing to tell me much, but at least, I did know now that there was someone supernatural working with them and that person was willing to risk sending a message to me. Maybe that meant there was another prisoner in the house, or, at the very least, someone who wasn't so enamoured with the Brotherhood that they wished to sit idly while I drank... well, it clearly wasn't just tea. Poison, perhaps, or a sedative would be easy to conceal. Maybe they knew other things that would help. If I could just get to them, maybe they would help me. There were an awful lot of maybes to consider there.

"Drink, dear Stella. You must be cold."

I pretended to sip again, careful to make sure that not a single drop of the tea landed on my lips.

"I imagine you're tired after your flight, and, well, everything else. I'll have one of my men escort you to your room so you can rest. You must have a great deal to think about. We can talk over your decision at dinner tonight."

"You're not sending me back to the cellar?"

"Of course not." Auberon sounded surprised. "We're not uncivilised here."

What about Annalise? I wanted to ask. Was she okay? Hurt? I hoped Nameless wasn't mistreating her. I hoped his cuts from her claws got infected.

"Take a moment or two to clean up when you're in your room. Someone will collect you for dinner." Auberon turned away, and just like that, I was dismissed.

I was going to protest, but a man hauled me up by my arm. I hadn't even seen him enter the room. Before I could ask any more questions, I was marched towards the door, now standing ajar, and Auberon sat back in the wingchair, out of sight.

Just as we reached the door, it opened further and a young man stepped through, causing me to immediately step back. The guard barrelled into me and I started to fall. The newcomer, a young man, grabbed me and set me to rights, holding me up for a moment longer than was necessary; our hands touching. As our eyes connected, I caught the faintest scent of magic from him. He wasn't much younger than I, maybe only a couple of years and he had sad eyes.

I knew I should have ignored him, shrunk away, pretended I didn't feel a thing, but there was no denying what he was. As I recognised him, he knew it too. He shivered for a moment, his eyes burning into me, but didn't say a thing. Then he stepped past and I was propelled outside, the door clicking shut behind us. Our brief encounter couldn't have lasted more than a few seconds.

The house was less of a rabbit warren than the cellar and I tried to draw up a mental blueprint from Anders' old plans. We crossed the foyer but, instead of turning into the room that led to the cellar, I was pushed towards the stairs, almost tripping as we ascended quickly. Halfway up, I paused when I saw a picture of a lovely woman, her dress formal but in a much newer style than any of the other portraits. She was breathtakingly pretty. My mother. The guard pushed me on and I tried counting the turns we made before he paused at a door. I was hungry and disorientated and wasn't concentrating as well as I should be so, instead of being able to pinpoint my location, I simply felt lost.

Opening the door, the guard pushed me inside with a firm shove between my shoulder blades. As I skidded to a halt on the carpet, righting myself, the door shut quickly, a key turning. I hammered my fists against it even though I knew it was fruitless. After a while, I just stood there, resting my forehead against the wood, breathing hard.

Turning around, I leant my back against the door and looked at the room. Dominating the large room was a four-poster bed, piled with cushions and a thick quilt, and velvet drapes that were tied at each corner. There was a wardrobe, and an armchair, and a tall chest plus a nightstand. The walls were covered in floor to ceiling tapestries hung in long panels. I couldn't make out the pattern so, curious, I stepped forward and found them embroidered with flowers and birds. It was very pretty, accentuated even more by being in this place, which deserved nothing beautiful. Though the room was distinctly nicer than the cell below the stairs, I was still a prisoner all the same. If Auberon thought that being in a comfortable room would make me forget that, or even find his offer more appealing, he was wrong.

There were two other doors, so I tried them quickly. One led to the attached bathroom, definitely a modern addition. The other was locked and I couldn't see anything when I peered through the keyhole. It looked like something was pressed up against the door; furniture, perhaps. The window looked over an enclosed courtyard, featuring flowerbeds, but when I tried to open it, the sash was stuck. I flopped onto the window set and rested my head against the pane, suddenly smiling when I realised I knew where I was. Despite losing my location in the house, I now knew I was on the west side of the house, the furthest side from the woods where I was captured. It might seem like inconsequential information, but I knew in the woods, there were eyes I couldn't see.

My whole day might have been a bust so far, but at least, I knew one thing, the young man with the sad eyes had felt my magic as surely as I felt his. For the brief moment that our hands touched, he drew my magic forth, not through him as Étoile had, but to intertwine with his because his ran free. He tacitly let me gauge his power without a single word.

I had an ally.

CHAPTER THIRTEEN

I paced around the room for what seemed like forever. I couldn't rest even though my limbs felt heavy and sluggish; it felt wrong somehow – Annalise lying on the cold stone floor while I occupied this plush bed. When I first heard a soft creak, I almost dismissed it, until I heard it again, this time with a scraping sort of sound. Initially, I was paralysed by indecision, not sure whether I should retreat into some corner, or investigate. If there were a chance to exit, I wanted to know about it and that's what won me over. I kept my footsteps light as I navigated the room. The scraping noise wasn't coming from the door I'd entered, or the bathroom, or the locked door. I turned around, puzzled, trying to trace where the noise was coming from. I even looked upwards to the ceiling, even though I knew that was a little foolish.

When a figure emerged from behind one of the long tapestries, I jumped backwards with a start; but something about him told me that I shouldn't be afraid. He stepped forward, holding his hands up, then putting one finger to his lips. It was the young man from the library.

"Hi," he said softly.

"Hi."

"Did you drink the tea?"

I shook my head, no. "That was you? Sending the message?"

The young man nodded. Now I had a chance to look at him a while longer. He was probably a little younger than I originally thought. Maybe in his late teens, or just tipped over to his twenties. He was gangly and tall and walked in a way that made me think he'd shot up suddenly and didn't quite know what to do with his long limbs. His chestnut hair was tucked behind his ears and he smiled uncertainly.

"The tea was spiked with a sleeping drug," he explained. "They expect you to be unconscious for the next couple of hours, so you'll have to pretend to be sleeping if you hear anyone near the room. When you woke, your power would have been neutralised, to make you less of a threat. I don't know how long it lasts."

That sounded ominous, and I was grateful that he warned me. It was also interesting that, despite the Brotherhood using some kind of magic to suppress mine, they still weren't confident that I wouldn't be able to do something. I felt a little more positive at that. "Thanks."

"I'm Daniel." He didn't try and shake my hand, instead, just slumped against the wall. I thought he was trying to appear as unthreatening as possible, staying his distance but close enough that we could talk in hushed tones. On one level, it was working. I wanted an ally. I wanted to know I wasn't alone; but I wasn't prepared to put all my faith in a stranger, certainly not one connected to the Brotherhood.

"Stella," I replied, but he probably already knew that. "Are you a prisoner here, too? How did you get here?"

"I'm not a prisoner, well, not as such. I came through the passageway." Daniel beckoned me over to the tapestry, which he pulled back to reveal a doorway where the panelling slid backwards. A long tunnel stretched into the dark and there was a large flashlight sitting on the floor. Daniel continued, "There's lots of these passageways, all over the house. Some were for the servants to get about without being seen in the old days when the below stairs people were not allowed to be seen or heard. Some were for the original owners to come and go as they pleased, invisibly. Not many people know about them and I'm the only one who uses them now."

"Are there any that can take us outside?"

"I think so, but it's too dangerous, so I haven't tried. A couple of the tunnels that lead from the house caved in years ago. There's two more that I know of, but, like I said, I haven't tried. They might be blocked too."

I sat on the bed with a sigh and watched Daniel. "So, if you're not a prisoner, what are you?"

Daniel hesitated a moment, looking deeply uncomfortable, before answering, "Auberon is my dad. I, uh, that makes us..."

"Cousins," I finished solemnly. "You know, I went my whole life without family? Then, in a few hours, I find out I've got a serial killer uncle, and a cousin who... What are you doing here, anyway?"

"I want to help you."

"How?"

"Well," Daniel thought for a moment. "I didn't let you drink the tea, and I let you look over me, so you knew what I was."

"A witch."

"I prefer warlock," he confirmed.

"Whatever." I knew I was being a touch dismissive, and I appreciated Daniel coming to me, if he were being genuine; but I was having a hard time wrapping my head around the whole family reunion thing. Another realisation dawned and it wasn't a nice one. "You're the one who's been practising magic for Auberon."

Daniel nodded, his head bowed. After a moment, he came and sat on the bed beside me but I didn't move away. He was quiet and I got the impression he wasn't just uncomfortable with his role in the Brotherhood, he was deeply ashamed.

"You helped him find me?" I asked.

"Yeah."

"And the other witches? You know he kills us when he finds us?"

Daniel didn't move for a while, and then nodded, just once, his eyes closing for a moment. I remembered how Auberon had offered me a position with the Brotherhood: finding other witches in return for my life. Maybe Daniel had been given a similar option. Maybe he'd always had to do what his father told him, no matter how awful. I wonder how long it had taken him before he realised what he was doing for them.

"Why hasn't he killed you, too?"

"I expect he will, when I've served my purpose, or

bind my magic. I'm not a particularly strong warlock. No training, see? So, I can't do a lot of the things my dad needs me to do, or I muddle them. He needs a stronger witch, like you." Daniel said all this without any particular emotion. It stood to reason that he'd had a long time to think this over. What a horrible thought that was. I couldn't imagine the hell of growing up knowing all that.

"What did he want you to do?"

Daniel looked up then, cocking his head to one side. "Someone's coming. Pretend to be sleeping, and I'll come back soon. I'll tell you everything then." He started to slip behind the tapestry, pausing to grab his torch from the floor.

"Wait! Can you get Annalise and me out of here?" I whispered frantically, but the panelling was already creaking back into place and Daniel was gone.

I had enough time to leap across the room and skid into the bed, slumping into a ball as the door opened. I could feel someone's eyes on me, as I lay there, rigid, but no one came any closer to check and, after a few seconds, they went away. I hoped they would forget to lock the door but I heard the unmistakable sound of a key turning, locking me in again. Except this time, I knew there was a way out.

Rolling onto my back, I lay on the bed, waiting, wondering what I should do. There wasn't much in the room, certainly nothing to occupy my time.

Daniel hadn't shown me how to open the passageway from inside the room, so I got up and walked over to the tapestry, pushing it to one side and running my fingers over the panelling. While I could feel the shallow grooves of the opening, barely perceptible unless you were looking, I couldn't find any sort of handle. It made sense that there would be a mechanism to open the door somewhere in the room, so I pushed, prodded and pulled at all kinds of things, hoping to find it. I tried everywhere from the floor, pushing with my foot in case there was a hidden lever, to running my fingers over the tapestry, hoping for some kind of pull cord. Wherever it was, it was so well concealed, I couldn't find it.

By now, I also hoped Gage had reached Étoile and that they were making some kind of headway with the local wolf pack. Perhaps Evan was here too, or on his way. I couldn't imagine him staying out of the fray too long. Combined with Anders' coven, they would make a formidable force, if they could find a way onto the grounds, and the house, without attracting attention. Perhaps that was something that Daniel could help with. I didn't like the idea of relying on someone so entrenched in the organisation, but Daniel didn't seem like he wanted to hurt me, unlike the others. Perhaps he was trying to make reparations in some way. I admired him for that. Another thought occurred to me; perhaps he saw me as his way out, too. I couldn't be cross with him about that. It must be frightening for him, living in a house full of people who hated his kind, being forced to use his magic against us. If I could help him, it was the right thing to do, I decided.

Making my way over to the window, I sat on the broad seat that spanned its length and stared out over the gardens, almost barren after the winter hibernation. The sky was cloudy and overcast but the sun seemed to be at full strength, even if it were only weakly making its way through. I guessed it must have been mid-afternoon, so I had been here for around twenty hours. That meant Annalise had been here for close to five days.

Somewhere below me was a door that opened onto the garden, but I had no way of reaching it. I could just about pick out the door set into the wall that led beyond to a wide expanse of lawn. It was almost completely open for several hundred yards before trees started dotting the grounds and there were several people walking around. They seemed to be assembling something with wood. Whatever it was, I couldn't make it out because it was in the very early stages of construction. Even without the people currently working there, trying to escape that way would guarantee my getting caught. But that was a moot point, seeing as I didn't know how I would get there anyway.

Twisting the ring on my finger, I thought about Evan again. I wondered when he would come for me, and what would happen if he did. Then I remembered that sometimes you didn't wait for rescue, you had to do it yourself.

I didn't dare sleep, so I dozed again, my back pressed against the wall. My mind was racing with possibilities and I was so sleepy I must have dropped off because I woke with a start when the door opened. Pete, the prison guard, stood in the doorway.

"The master says you're to dress for dinner." He hung a dress over the wardrobe handle and placed some shoes below. It was velvet, cut quite high on the waist, with a long skirt that flared a little. It was in a red so dark, it was practically black. The shoes were black, plain and flat like ballet slippers. "I'll return for you in twenty minutes. Please be ready."

I nodded and that seemed to be enough because

he left, turning the lock again. I didn't hear his footsteps so I assumed he was standing just outside the door, waiting.

The idea of changing didn't appeal to me, but my clothes were filthy and the mud had dried on both my jeans and sweat top where I'd fallen. My jeans were still a little damp and they clung to me, but somehow I hadn't really noticed it until now. Blood and sweat mingled to give me a generally yucky air. I wouldn't want to have dinner with someone dressed like me either.

I washed up the best I could in the bathroom, giving my face a scrub. I couldn't wash my hair so I settled for running my fingers through it and tying it back in a knot with a band I found in my pocket. Looking in the mirror, I wasn't very pleased with the results, but I wasn't here to impress; and frankly, the less appealing I could look, the better in my opinion. I changed out of my dirty clothes and ran a flannel doused in warm water and soap over my body, drying quickly on the hand towel.

The dress fit well, skimming over my hips to end just at my ankles, but the shoes were a little tight. So long as it was only for one night, I would put up with it. After all, my only mission was to stay alive until I could get Annalise and me out of here.

Pete knocked the second time before he entered. He didn't say anything about my dress, which was good, and didn't hold onto me either, which was even better. Instead, I walked alongside him as we made our way downstairs. I followed him through the foyer and the guards, past the library and along a corridor before he stopped and opened a door, indicating that I was to go through.

The dining room was decorated in sombre greens and a long table ran almost the length of the extensive room. Only one end was set for dinner and that's where Auberon sat, at the head. Daniel sat to his left, his back to the windows. The curtains were still open and even though the light had dimmed significantly, I could just make out the lawn beyond.

"Good evening, Stella. Your mother's dress fits, I see." Auberon didn't stand as he appraised me, and Daniel gave me a quick smile before dropping his eyes to examine the tablecloth.

I tried not to focus on the idea of wearing my mother's dress, even if the thought warmed me for a moment, like Isadore was with me, protecting me. Then I felt cold as the thought flitted through my mind that dressing me in my mother's things was all part of some grander plan. No matter how much I wished my parents were still alive and that I had a family, Auberon was a poor substitute. I couldn't, wouldn't, let him cloud my judgment by offering me things, token connections to what I'd lost, as if he were the only one who could do that; as if I needed him.

Pete pulled out the chair opposite Daniel and waited for me to sit, pushing it back in politely. He left without uttering a single word.

"My son, Daniel," Auberon nodded to Daniel. "Your cousin. Isn't it nice to have two young people in the house?"

We exchanged flat "hellos" as if we hadn't met, and didn't really want to while ignoring Auberon's question.

"Daniel suffers from your affliction, but he bears his shame well," Auberon told me. "He is a great asset to our cause. We do not have many young folks here, so it is a pleasure to have you both."

Daniel didn't look like he felt he was an asset to anything. He coloured slightly and Auberon smiled fondly, seeming to take that as chagrin, or pride. I wondered what skewed reality Auberon lived in to find anything pleasant about this situation, but I wisely kept my mouth shut.

A suited man served the first course, tomato soup with warm bread rolls. I looked at it for a moment then dared to flick a look at Daniel. After a quick glance, at Auberon who was already lifting his spoon to mouth, Daniel just nodded. Seeing as no warning appeared in my soup, I could only hope it was safe to eat. My stomach certainly wished it were. If I were lucky, Auberon already believed my magic was neutralised by the poisoned tea.

"Very nice indeed." Auberon patted his mouth with a napkin, then continued to eat, talking between mouthfuls. "Isadore and I used to attend dinners in this very room. Our parents were very fond of parties and Isadore loved dressing up for them. We had all kinds of people, so it was always very interesting, especially to a young boy." He smiled into the distance. "We do not use this room nearly enough now, do we, Daniel?"

"No, Father."

The same man returned to clear our bowls, leaving swiftly again. It occurred to me that I'd yet to see a woman in the house. Perhaps it was hard to sign women up to such a cruel cause? Maybe they just had better things to do.

Auberon kept up a steady patter of conversation throughout the main course and into dessert. He didn't seem in any hurry, but I stayed tense while I waited for him to say something again about joining the Brotherhood, or at least to threaten me. Daniel studiously avoided meeting my eyes. Some of the time, I stared out of the windows while Auberon kept up his patter, reminiscing about the old days and my mother. I spent a lot of time staring out the window. We were at the front of the house and all I could see was a long swathe of grass, stretching far away to the gates. I was hoping I would see some sign, some clue that my people weren't far away, but there was nothing. I tried not to let my heart sink. I told myself to be realistic, that no one would linger near the house while there was still some light.

"Let's talk business," Auberon said once coffee was set before us. I knew Daniel tensed the same moment I did.

"Business?" I asked.

"You've had some time to think over my offer." It wasn't a question.

Daniel caught my eye, and gave a single shake of his head, sipping his coffee. "I've been asleep," I told Auberon. "I guess I must have been tired."

"Of course." Auberon seemed to accept that. "I must ask that you continue to think of your options, Stella. My men are uneasy with a witch in the house, and they are hard to placate. We must come to an agreement soon."

"About whether I live or die?"

"It's not a hard decision, really, is it, Stella? Think of everything you have lost through witchcraft: your parents, your life, your job, your country. You live under constant threat, you have no family. You have nothing!"

Like all good lies, his were partly true, but I thought of all the things I had gained. Friends, a home, a job I enjoyed rather than tolerated, magic at my fingertips, a man who loved me. All that went a good way towards outweighing anything negative, but somehow, I didn't think Auberon would understand that. He didn't want to.

"And when you grow older, Stella, what happens then?" Auberon continued. "Will you subject your children to the pain you have suffered? Will you risk them growing up with magic, a danger to humans? Or would you rather your children live a normal life, doing normal things, and grow old safely?"

I held my coffee cup and stared at it, stunned momentarily. It wasn't what he said, it was the reminder that children could be in my future, a very near future given the exciting night of birthday sex Evan gave me... as well as the next night. The realisation I had, days ago now, in Wilding, had gone clean out of my mind with everything that happened since then. It wasn't something I could address now. I worked hard to keep my face emotionless.

"Your home is here at Hawkscroft, with your family, if only you'll join us, if only you would help us rid this world of witches. Keeping this world safe is our calling, it is what we were born to do."

Some calling.

"Where is my friend?" I asked abruptly.

"Ah, your friend. She's still with us. She won't be a problem much longer. Do put her out of your head."

Daniel was watching us with interest.

"She's hurt. She needs to see a doctor."

"She needs to see something far more than a

doctor, Stella. She's an unnatural beast, little more than a filthy animal."

"She's my friend. Please don't hurt her." I looked up at Auberon, but there was nothing in the cold eyes he turned on me.

"I can assure you that abomination is of no interest to us. She was merely the means of getting to you, and I had stern words with my men about bringing her. I can't say immigration would be too happy."

It struck me as so absurdly odd that Auberon would be concerned about border controls that I almost burst out laughing. Then something he said made me ask, "What do you mean she won't be a problem much longer?"

Auberon placed his hand over mine and it was everything I could do not to fling it back. "She'll be put down, dear Stella. It's a kindness, I assure you."

I struggled to maintain my composure, magic fizzling though my veins in a desperate rush to flatten Auberon. I breathed in and out through my nose, my calm demeanour threatening to flee any moment. While I clutched the edges of my chair, Auberon stood and crossed to the long windows, sipping his coffee as he looked out into the dark.

"When?" I asked, after I was sure my voice would be even, devoid of emotion.

"Tomorrow," replied Auberon. His reflection showed a small smile. "My men are most eager. Many of us have not seen a werewolf before. It will be a quick, clean kill."

"You're going to burn her?"

"Of course not. That's just for witches. The fire negates their magic as they leave this world. We've never captured a werewolf before; but all the old texts suggest silver bullets are the most efficient." Auberon turned back to us. "I am sure you will see things in a clearer light when you are no longer affected by ties to our other... guest."

I glanced at Daniel who was studiously staring at his cup, trying his best to look like he wasn't even there. So far, he'd said very little. I wondered if that was always the way between them, or if Daniel were being cautious not to give away that he had secretly made contact with me. Later, I decided, I would ask what he knew about Annalise's planned execution. It seemed imperative to me, now, that we escape. Annalise could die tomorrow if we didn't and I couldn't let that happen. If we were to have a chance, it would have to be some time through the night. Darkness might give us some cover of escaping unnoticed, but I would need my magic returned to give us a fighting chance. I wasn't weak, aside from the head injury and the twinges of pain in my ankle. I'd never been fitter, but I was no match for twenty or more men, especially when each one of them believed emphatically I should die.

"Please don't kill her," I said in a weak voice, thinking quickly for something that would save Annalise. "Maybe she'll be useful. Maybe she'll..."

"Enough!" Auberon dropped his cup on the table, where it rattled in the saucer, whirling for a moment until, tipped in mid-air, it stopped, held its position then settled flatly. Really, it should have fallen on its side; the liquid spilling across the table. I tried to catch Daniel's eye but his were fixed on the table. Auberon sucked in a breath, his cheeks pinched, but when he spoke next, his voice was soft again. "Let us talk some more of you joining our little family. Your homecoming would be so welcome. We should celebrate it."

I imagined being served cake while dozens of eyes stared at me in hate. A celebratory tea party with the Brotherhood was not on the cards.

"You will live with us in the house, of course; it is the family home. You can move around the house as you please, once we are certain of your loyalty. I'm sure you will find it to your liking. Daniel will enjoy your company and he will learn with you. Two strong witches will propel our cause significantly."

"Is that what Daniel wants?" That got Daniel's attention and he frowned at me.

"Of course it is," answered Auberon. "Isn't it, Daniel?"

"Yes, Father," muttered Daniel, lurching forward when Auberon clapped him on the back.

"Life has been hard for you, Stella. It needn't be. Look around you; look at what you could have. Money, power, significance, a cause to direct you, a family who will guide you to the light, away from the terrible darkness that surrounds you."

Death, fear, destruction... Yeah, Auberon really had it going on.

He seemed to be getting into his stride, his eyes taking on a faraway look. "We have saved so many who have fallen away from the light. We embrace them, give them purpose. We take them away from their sad, aimless lives and help them towards improving the world. We are the soldiers of humanity!" Auberon nodded sagely to himself.

I wanted to punch him. Instead, I tried appealing to Auberon's sense of family. "Why not just let me go? Isadore wouldn't have wanted you to hurt me."

"Isadore was a simple soul, given to flights of fancy. It is fitting that you should be returned to your family so that you can be cared for, so we can relieve you of this deviance. Our cure is the only answer for you, niece."

The door opened then, preventing either of us from continuing what was becoming a cyclical conversation. A man, not Pete, but dressed in similar clothing – black jeans, t-shirt straining across muscles – entered and crossed to whisper in Auberon's ear. "There's a phone call, sir. A miss..."

"Not now." Auberon waved the man away impatiently. "I'll return the call later."

Another man burst into the room, just as the messenger was exiting. "There's been a security breach, sir," he told Auberon, ignoring Daniel and me. Pete stepped into the room and waited by the door.

"Where?" asked Auberon calmly.

"Front entrance. We're sending patrols out across the perimeter. Shall I initiate..."

"No, no." Auberon's jaw set in a stern line as he looked around, seeming to notice Pete and beckoning him forwards. "Take our guest to her quarters."

I looked over at Pete approaching, but he stopped halfway and signalled to me with his fingers. I knew it would be useless to argue, so, with a quick glance to Daniel, I got up and walked towards him.

"Stella?" Auberon followed me across the room and when I turned to him, he placed cold hands on each of my arms, looking down at me for a moment. "I shall expect your decision tomorrow."

"If I say yes, will you let Annalise go?" I knew the

answer already, but it was worth asking all the same.

"My men are expecting an execution. I cannot disappoint them. You know as well as I that we cannot let such a thing return to the population. It's too dangerous. Remember, you are with family now. Do not let the lure of the evil in your life influence your decision. We will protect you."

The only thing I needed protection from was Auberon but he had already turned his back on me, ushering quiet instructions to his man. Pete extended a hand towards the door and I followed him out along the corridor.

The foyer was a hive of activity. Several groups of five or six men stood waiting. They were dressed in uniforms of black; combat trousers with pockets on the legs, or jeans, thick fleece tops and knit hats. They seemed to be of different ages, different builds; some of them weren't speaking in English, but each one of them was armed with a pistol or rifle. I spotted hunting knives, little canisters and other weapons slung on belts around their waists. They were armed and ready for action. As we crossed the foyer, each man turned to me, their voices dying away until the air was heavy with silence. I listened for other sounds instead: voices and footsteps from elsewhere in the house.

Witch, witch, witch. The words followed me up the stairs. I tried not to show my fear. I could run, take the stairs two at a time, but that might encourage them and I didn't want someone taking a pot-shot at me when I couldn't defend myself. Despite Pete's instructions to safely deliver me to my room, I sincerely doubted he would step in if one of these men decided taking me out were a good idea.

Auberon would be briefly pissed, but even that might not be enough to defend me against the hoard of witch hunters below. I increased my pace slightly, forcing myself not to look back. When we passed a window that looked out over the driveway and front lawns, I counted a bunch of cars parked in an orderly fashion and two minibuses. I wondered if more men had been bussed in during the night, ready for tomorrow's spectacle.

As I watched, two patrols fanned out across the drive, moving towards the open lawns, weapons drawn, but Pete nudged me on before I could see what they were looking for. I hoped it was Anders, luring the men from the house to count them and determine what the opposition was, how many there were, how well-armed they were, how fast they responded, which was what we should have done. Even with the little I'd seen, it seemed apparent that patrols were ready to move quickly.

When I heard a burst of gunfire, I froze for a moment. Pete took me by the arm, driving me forwards so I had to jog to keep up with him as he took the turns to my room. Earlier this evening, I'd counted the turns on the way out, so I could just anticipate how many paces, and which way we'd go. It gave me some small satisfaction that I might be able to exit this way without getting lost.

"Inside," Pete grunted and pushed me into the room, apparently all done with niceties. Crossing to the window, I strained to see if I could see anything at all but, aside from patrols crossing the lawns and sweeps of flashlights, nothing was happening this side and it was too dark to see. The lights, however, gave me an idea.

Crossing to the door I'd entered by, I scrabbled in the dark for the light switch. When I found it, I flicked it on and off, counting to twenty. Sure, if any of the patrols looked back at the house, they'd see it, but I had to hope that any flickering could be blamed on faulty wiring; after all, Hawkscroft was an old house. More importantly, if anyone were watching from the woods beyond, they might take it as a signal of my location, that I was alive. I just wished I learned Morse code. What I really needed to do was send a message, and for that, I needed Daniel.

I left the light on when I finished flicking. Someone had come into the room while I'd been at dinner and left towels and wash things on the bed, but no clean clothes. After a quick look in the bathroom, I saw that my dirty clothes had disappeared; leaving me with only the velvet dress and flat shoes to wear.

I stayed at the window watching until the patrols were just dots moving about. I couldn't see anything aside from them but I had to hope someone was there in the woods and that my signal had been enough.

When the door opened softly, I didn't turn round at first. I guess I assumed it was Pete, or maybe Daniel.

"Hello, love," said a different voice, a far worse voice and, with a sinking feeling, I turned around.

Nameless pressed the door shut and leant against it, grinning at me. His eyes took me in, then flicked across me to the bed and back again.

"What do you want?" I asked, gulping.

"How about a little cuddle, love?" Nameless curled back his lips revealing his charming array of missing teeth that left a dark void in his yellow smile. I suspected he had a bigger void where his brain was supposed to be.

"Get out," I hissed.

"Oh, don't be like that. Not when that nasty little bitch downstairs already bit me." Nameless took a step towards me. Like a dance, I stepped backwards, then moving away from the window, I kept my back to the wall as I tried to maintain distance between us. There was precious little I could use to defend myself and Nameless knew it as he moved closer.

"The boys and me, we share rooms in the attic." He jutted his chin upwards, then looked around. "Now, this is cushy. Four-poster, eh? I quite like the idea of roll in a big bed like that."

"I don't." I sidestepped as Nameless lunged at me. He fell against the chest of drawers. Pushing on them, he righted himself and turned, looking for me. I had no choice but to move closer to the bed. Looking around myself, I saw I had few options. Get to the bathroom and hope to God there was a lock, or at least a bolt. I hadn't thought to check earlier. Or, I could try and get the key off Nameless, unlock the door and get out before he could grab me.

Or scream the place down and hope that someone gave enough of a shit about Auberon's orders to rescue me. Except... What if I got someone who wanted to join in with Nameless' sick little plan?

"Play nice, you naughty little witch, or I might have to get nasty with you just like I did to your little wolfie friend."

"What have you done to Annalise?" The constant simmering of my magic, unable to find an outlet, was giving me a headache that hovered behind my eyes.

"Gave her something to think about." He wrinkled his nose. "Don't be disgusting. I'm not into animals. I like my women two-legged."

"If you've hurt her, I'll..."

"You'll what?" Nameless sneered, moving slowly closer to me. "You ain't got no magic here, 'ave you? You ain't got nothin'."

I tried sidestepping past him to the door, but he was faster, manoeuvring so he stood in my path. He grabbed at me, his sweaty palm wrapping around my wrist, one foot swiping my ankles as I raised my knee, aiming for his nuts. Down we went in a messy, smelly tangle of limbs. He planted himself over me, forcing me to the floor. I screamed when his hand slid up my leg, pushing my skirt up around my thighs.

"Like the floor, do ya?" He laughed, teeth nipping at the top of my dress. I wriggled a hand free from his grasping paws and punched the side of his head repeatedly until he slapped me, my head bouncing against the carpet. "Was looking forward to a nice, comfy mattress, but I'll take what I can get." He planted his mouth on mine, his tongue wriggling against my lips as I clamped them shut. In a swift, sharp move I drew my head back and head-butted him. Bloody hell, if that didn't hurt like a...

Nameless screeched and raised an open hand. The sound of the slap rang in my ears and, for a moment, I actually saw stars. I kicked and thrashed and grabbed his ear, wrenching the lobe until he screamed; his hand rained down on me, slapping and hitting. Stunned, I barely noticed as he pulled at my dress. A seam tore, the ripping sound nothing compared to his rank, heaving breath.

It felt like a fog surrounded my head. Everything

seemed dim and distant. I could hear shouting and footsteps but they could have been a hundred feet away, or merely two, then Nameless lurched backwards, flailing, screaming curses.

Someone was kneeling beside me, a hand stroking my hair almost gently. I blinked, and must have lost consciousness for a moment because when I opened my eyes I was in a man's arms and being deposited on the bed.

"Evan?" I whispered. My throat felt scratchy, raw, and I whispered his name again, waiting for the answer I wanted to hear.

CHAPTER FOURTEEN

"What's that?" said a man's voice as I struggled to sit up. A pair of hands went under my armpits, boosting me upwards, and a pillow was moved behind my head. The voice continued, "Sorry about that." Pete's voice, I thought, with a flash of annoyance. Pete, not Evan. "That dick, Barker, sees a woman and thinks he has a chance."

"What's it to you, prick?" shouted Nameless, his sudden screech making me shiver. The name, Barker, seemed strangely appropriate for him. "That whore needs to be taught a lesson."

I blinked a few more times before I could focus properly. Moving my neck hurt but if I rolled it gently to the side I could see Nameless. Blood ran down his nose and smeared his mouth like he'd just eaten raw meat. As I watched, he spat on the carpet and something small and white shot out. One of the men holding him let go, stooping down to pick it up, rising slowly. He grabbed Nameless' hand, forced it to uncurl until his palm was facing up, then dropped the little object in it. *Oh, a tooth.* Served him right, I thought with a flash of anger.

"Not by you," admonished Pete, returning his gaze to rest on me. He didn't look compassionate, or concerned. He didn't look anything. I'd never seen anyone so devoid of emotion. "Are you hurt?"

I thought about it, wriggling my fingers then my toes, raising my shoulders and testing each limb. The whole process took only a minute or two. My head hurt and my arms and back from the fall and being pinned down, but nothing else. "No," I said, "I'll be okay."

"Someone get a first aid kit," Pete barked and footsteps shot off. He nodded at Nameless. "Get rid of him."

I watched as Nameless struggled, no match for the burly pair holding on to him. "You'll regret this, you bitch!"

"Wait!" I sat up straight, my head pounding, the sudden dizziness making me nauseous. The men stopped, watching me, traces of fear flitting across their faces. For all their armaments, they were still afraid of me. They were probably waiting for my head to spin, or a curse to fall from my lips, but instead, I said clearly, so they would all hear, "If you got bitten, you'll probably turn into a werewolf." I'd no idea if it was true, of course, but Nameless paled. "Enjoy the next full moon!" I called brightly, laughing as he was dragged, cursing, from the room. I knew I sounded slightly hysterical; right now, that was part of my charm.

"That true?" asked Pete, after a long pause during which we listened to the sounds of the three men retreating, the stomp of their feet against the carpet,

Nameless shouting.

I shrugged. "We'll have to wait and see." Maybe they would shoot him instead of Annalise, just in case? One could live in hope.

After a moment, one of the men came back and, keeping his distance, tossed a white box on the bed. Pete opened it, extracting a few things. After putting on thin plastic gloves, the kind a doctor wears, he sat on the edge of the bed and ripped open a small packet. He smoothed an antiseptic square over the few small cuts I'd sustained. I tried not to wince as it stung.

"My shoulder hurts," I said as he screwed the wipe into a ball, dropping it on the nightstand.

He manipulated it while I winced. "Not broken, or dislocated. Probably just bruised."

"Yay."

"Did he..."

"No," I replied quickly.

"I would have shot him if he had."

"Don't hold back on my account." I think Pete smiled then, but it was so fleeting, I couldn't be sure.

He packed up the medical kit silently and stood, peeling off the gloves. "We're not the bad guys, you know."

"Neither am I," I shot back.

We looked at each for a long moment. One of us was lying.

"Keep still for a while. I'll post a sentry on the door so you don't get disturbed again."

There wasn't a whole lot I could do after Pete left, so I lay on the bed, staring up at the ceiling. Every so often, I could hear voices outside the door, so, good to his word, Pete had posted at least two men on the door. They may have been fine for blocking anyone's entrance, but they were also blocking my exit.

After a while, when my head stopping hurting so bad, I got up and walked over to the window. Pete, or someone else, had drawn the curtains so I peeled them back. It was dark outside, the moon full and heavy in the sky. Nameless was going to have a bad couple of nights, wondering if he would turn. I couldn't see any patrols crossing the grounds, but that didn't mean they weren't there. I wondered if they found anything, but I supposed I would have heard some kind of excitement if they had.

I didn't hear Daniel enter the room this time. One moment I was alone, then I turned, starting suddenly when I saw him standing in front of the tapestry.

"You came back!" I think the surprise in my voice was evident.

"What happened to you? I heard there was some kind of commotion."

"One of those creeps thought he'd try attacking me."

Daniel looked appalled. "Are you okay?"

"Bruised and a few cuts, but nothing worse. Do you know if Annalise is okay? He said he hurt her."

"The wolf-girl in the cellar? I don't know. I haven't heard anything. Maybe he was bluffing?" Daniel didn't sound too hopeful.

"Maybe. Do you know what they're going to do with her tomorrow? What Auberon has planned?"

"I heard one of the guards say the execution would be before dusk tomorrow. They invited a lot of people. No one knows there's a werewolf, they just think it's some kind of special event."

"Some event!" I sat on the edge of the bed,

feeling glum. "We've got to get out of here, Daniel. They're going to kill Annalise tomorrow, and probably me too, after I tell Auberon no."

"Couldn't you lie and say yes?" Daniel looked at me hopefully.

I'd thought about that. "Auberon will want me to prove my loyalty and it will be something cruel and vile that I can't... Annalise will still be dead. I can't risk someone else to save my ass."

"I guess not." Daniel held up the cardboard tube he was holding and started pulling off the top. He knelt on the floor, pulling out the papers inside and unrolling them, revealing plans that looked similar to the ones Anders showed us, except these were older and the plans looked hand-drawn. "I've been looking at the floor plans and there's a passageway that we could use to get out of the house. I tried it earlier and it's clear. It leads to the stables. That's the place closest to the perimeter." He pointed to the place on the map, then swept his finger along where the wall stood.

"The stable yard is booby-trapped. The whole of the grounds are protected by magic," I pointed out, even though I figured he probably knew that already. He'd probably done it. "Is there any other way out?"

"Front entrance, but it's completely open from there to the drive. Anyone leaving that way would be picked off easily. The rear door leads to the courtyard, then the stables. The east wing has doors that go to the walled garden and out onto the grounds. There really isn't anywhere to hide, and I doubt we could sprint for it."

"What about the other tunnels? You said there were more."

"Three. One of our ancestors was a smuggler, so he added extra ones. They run here and here." Daniel pointed to two other spots on the map. "But, like I said, I think this one has caved in, and I haven't tried this one. This one might be okay, but it leads to a cottage on the grounds. No one lives there now, and it's kind of a wreck because there was a fire a few years ago. The tunnel might be fine, but I don't know if we can get out when we reach the end. I haven't tried it."

"Where is the cottage?"

Daniel searched the map, placing his thumb on the map somewhere beyond the stable yard. It wasn't far from the perimeter either and a river wound its way past, a couple of hundred yards north.

"I can take us through the secret passages; but our biggest problem is being seen once we leave them. As well as the security, there's cameras, too. Lots of them."

"I saw the control room the night I was captured." I stared at the map, my options limited. "So the tunnel to the stable yard is our best bet?"

"I think so. I can disable the traps when we need to go outside for the last part, but I don't know if the tunnel is still accessible. I've never tried it and, as far as I know, it's been disused for decades. Plus, the moment anyone notices we're gone, the alarm will go off and even if we get over the wall, without some way to flee, we'll be caught." Daniel's voice rose in panic and I crossed over to lay a hand on him. It was small comfort, but I needed him to be strong.

"What if we had outside help?" I asked.

Daniel thought about that for a moment. "There's a coven that's been keeping an eye on the place. I sense them sometimes."

I nodded. "I've met them, and one of my friends who came with me met them too. They know who your dad is, what he does." It occurred to me then that Daniel had never reported them, even though he knew they were there, and that gave me a little more hope.

"I thought as much. Even if we get away, my dad will know I've helped you and he'll still be able to come after us. Maybe we can turn him over to the police? If they know he's responsible for all those deaths, they'll arrest him, right?"

"You got any evidence?"

"No." Daniel leant against the wall, his arms crossed. "I'm just as guilty as he anyway. I didn't know what he was doing at first, I swear. Then I saw the news one day, and I knew. I knew he was killing all those people. I didn't want to help him."

"Daniel, he forced you. It wasn't your fault."

"I should have stopped him earlier."

"You couldn't have. He's got an army of goons killing for him. My friends say they've tried reporting him to the police but they don't do anything. Someone's protecting him," I explained. "Look, can we talk about this later? Let's just get out of here first." I thought for a moment. There had to be some benefit to my being here. If I could find out the Brotherhood's next moves, I'd have something to take back to the Council, something that might help other witches. Maybe it would help contribute towards a time when we wouldn't have to worry about being hunted. "Do you know what he wants me to do, aside from hunting witches for him? You said he needed a stronger witch to do stuff you can't do."

"I'm not sure, but I think it involves money. I've tried various schemes for him, messing with computers and stuff to create money, but I can't do it. I'm good with growing plants and herbs, but not technical stuff like that."

"I don't understand. I thought he was all about getting rid of witches?"

"Yeah, it started like that, but he knows what they can do. He can be rich and powerful in his own right if he has a powerful witch serving him. He can annihilate anyone who stands in his path. He could even rule the world. Who would ever stand up to him?"

"And that's what he wants me for, so he can be rich and powerful?" I waved my hand around the room. The house wasn't exactly in disrepair. If anything, it was warm and comfortable. Plenty of people seemed to live here and that had to cost a lot. "Isn't he rich enough?"

"Is anyone?" Daniel countered.

I thought about that, about what Auberon would be able to achieve if he had unlimited power and money. It wasn't a comforting thought. "We are definitely getting out of here."

"I'm coming with you. You can't leave me here, Stella. For years, I've been wondering if this will be the day when he kills me, when he realises I'm useless."

I watched Daniel, the morose, slumped way he sat, the hopelessly sad eyes and thought about everything he'd had to deal with, how even though he was afraid, he still hid the knowledge of Anders' coven from his father. Not to mention, how he'd helped me so far. He was right, I couldn't leave him behind. "Okay, you help us get out of here, Annalise too, and we'll take you with us. Deal?"

He didn't hesitate. "Deal."

"And if we die, no hard feelings, okay?"

Daniel pulled a face, for the first time, showing a spark. "There might be some hard feelings."

"Fair enough. Here's what I want you to do. First, we need to get a message to my friends and for that, I need the barriers to be down long enough that I can send one without anyone noticing. Can you do that?"

"I think so, yes."

"You also need to explore that other tunnel, find out if we can definitely get out that way, too. Can you try it?"

"Maybe. No one's expecting me for a while. What about the wolf-girl?"

"Annalise," I reminded him, because it seemed important that he saw her for what she was: a person with a name, not just an animal. "Are there any secret tunnels to the cellar?"

Daniel searched the map, then shook his head. "None that go directly to where she, sorry, Annalise, is kept." He pointed, tapping the map. "There's another stairwell that goes from the kitchen here to the storage cellar. It's not used often because we don't store much there anymore and it's not really as direct as the other staircase."

"How do we get past all the guards?"

"I don't think I could take them all with magic. They're built like brick shithouses."

"I get the picture. How many of them are there?"

"At least twenty at any one time, though there will probably be just over thirty, maybe forty, when all the patrols come back in. Easily double that tomorrow."

"Too many to be certain that we can knock them all out together," I mused.

"Yeah, plus they are all on alert. They know you have friends, so I guess they're expecting an attack. That's what was going on earlier. Something tripped the perimeter alarm. It might have been an animal though. We have foxes and deer pass through occasionally, especially now, when it's cold and they're looking for food," Daniel explained.

"There were only two guards covering Annalise and me when we were in the cell and I didn't see anyone else in the cellar on my way out."

"They've been taking turns. Shift changes every two hours. I listen in from the secret passageways sometimes."

"If we can get into the cellar unnoticed, we could deal with those two guards. No one will notice for two hours, right?"

Daniel nodded. "So long as no one goes down there between shifts, no one will notice. I could knock them both out, I think, if I gave them sedatives."

Getting us out of here wasn't going to be as easy as it looked. If we could even get to the cellar to get Annalise, there was no guarantee that we'd be able to get out again. If we left without her, we might not be able to get back before she was killed. Even if we all got out together, the chances of us being picked up close to the house were high. With a maximum of three of us, two wounded, though I was already feeling better, against thirty-plus heavily armed men, our odds of escape were depressingly low.

Another idea popped into my head, and it seemed

almost ludicrous. "What if we had more witches in the house?" I asked.

Daniel looked confused. "There's only us."

"But what if we can get the local coven in? That would give us a fighting chance, right?"

"I guess, and they won't expect an attack from the inside."

"Exactly. They're prepared for someone to storm the house, an explosion, not an implosion. If something lured them outside, it would reduce the numbers in the house."

"If I can disable the traps around the stable yard for a few minutes, that might be long enough to get them in that way and bring them here." Daniel looked excited. "If we could get Annalise up here, we could all leave the same way."

"What are the chances of getting noticed?"

"Still high. What's going to happen to my dad?"

"I don't know. He's dangerous, Daniel, really dangerous and... Have I mentioned this? He wants to kill us, all of us, and I don't know if any witch is going to let him go scot free."

"Yeah, figured you'd say that."

"Are you okay?"

"You know, I am. Dad, he wasn't always like this, but I can't accept what he does. I've had a long time to think about this."

"But you're worried about killing him?"

Daniel stared at the carpet, picking at bits of it. "Yeah. I've done a lot of bad stuff, but I'm not a killer, and I don't think I get the right to pick and choose. I don't want to kill because that will make me like him, and I'm not. I'm nothing like him."

"Let's just get out of here first, Daniel, okay? We'll

work the rest out later."

"I have to go. I'll come back later, okay? I have to show my face a few times just so that they don't notice something is up. If I don't come back in time, send a message to your friends at midnight. I'll make sure the barriers are down for a couple of minutes. Do you think that will be long enough?"

"Yes." It would be enough to send a message anyway. "Can you meet them, let them in through the tunnel?"

Daniel grimaced. "If the magic drops for too long, an alarm triggers and someone will come looking for me. I can stop the alarm briefly; but I won't be able to hold it for long. If they can make a diversion, that would help." Daniel got to his feet, turning to slip behind the tapestry.

"I'll try. Uh, Daniel?"

"Yeah?"

"Can you bring me some clothes next time you come? Something practical?"

He gave me a tight smile and nodded. "See you later." And I was alone again.

I literally watched time pass by on the small electric clock on the nightstand, willing the numbers to click over faster and faster, formulating a plan on how I'd get a message to Étoile. I hoped she was with Evan and Gage, and some of the Hawksley coven members. My telepathy was weak and unpractised, and I'd only ever tried it once, so that wasn't going to fly. Finally, I remembered the spell I'd seen in the borrowed spell book that I had for a short while. It was the last spell I'd read before the book disappeared. It was a simple one, perfect for sending messages. I scrabbled through the drawers of the nightstand, then the chest, and came up with some pieces of notepaper and a short, stubby pencil.

I tried to keep my note brief and to the point: *I'm alive. Annalise is being held in the cellar. She's been hurt, but alive too. Thirty-plus guards and leader here. Go to stable yard wall, secret tunnel to inside. Daniel Morgan coming to help you. Diversion needed for front.*

I cursed when my pencil snapped, leaving a dull end too blunt to even scratch out a few more words. Around me, I could feel the magic protecting the house. Daniel hadn't let down the barriers yet so I folded the paper into small squares and concentrated on the power, waiting for it to fade.

A minute to midnight, it suddenly ebbed and gave out, and my magic surged. Holding the paper in one hand, I focused on it, closed my eyes, whispering the spell as I imagined it in Étoile's hand, wherever she was. I didn't feel it disappear, but opening my eyes, my hand was empty. I waited, rooted to the spot for any sign that she had received it and I wasn't disappointed. The air in front of me thickened into a white smoke, arranging itself into words:

We're coming.

As suddenly as the barriers went down, they were back up again and my magic was shoved deep back inside me. I had a scant minute to send and receive. If it had been more, I could have shimmered to the dungeon and grabbed Annalise, whipping us out of there to deal with the fallout from Auberon later. But every fibre of my being told me that attacking from the inside, with help, was the best course of action.

Yawning, I pressed a hand to my mouth and curled up in the big window seat, the curtains parted. I could see two-man patrols walking the grounds, closer to the house now, occasionally lit by flashes of torchlight, and dogs; big, ferocious, mean-looking dogs, straining on their leashes beneath the moonlight.

Sleep was pushing on my tired eyelids. I'd been unconscious in the cellar so that didn't count, and I'd dozed slightly earlier, but not enough to really refresh me. Now, so close to escape, knowing my friends were coming, the best thing I could do would be to grab some shuteye, so I'd have enough energy to run when I needed it.

Somehow, I dozed on the window seat, tucked in amongst the pillows. When I heard footsteps in the room, I thought I was dreaming at first, then almost tumbled from the seat in my haste to throw myself at Evan.

"Thank God you're okay," he mumbled into my hair, embracing me fiercely. He looked tired and drawn, with days-old stubble. A quick glance at the clock told me it was one-fifty in the morning.

"What are you doing here?" I asked, looking past him. Daniel was standing awkwardly by the secret entrance and Étoile and Gage were stepping past him, then Anders and Bree.

"Saving you," Evan said, and I thought I might have heard him mutter *again*.

Gage hugged me, just a brief squeeze about the shoulders and stepped away quickly, but not before whispering against my ear, "Glad you're okay. I was worried about you."

I put my finger to my lips, signalling to them to be quiet, then to come as far away from the door as possible. Just in case anyone was looking up, I pulled the curtains together.

"There are two guards at the door," I told them in a soft voice as they huddled around.

"We got your message. Obviously," said Étoile. She seemed to be dressed in some sort of "fatigue chic" – black turtleneck, tight black pants and boots. "How'd you do that? The shields haven't dropped once all the time we've been watching."

"Daniel lowered the house's protection so I could send it."

"Can he be trusted?" Étoile asked bluntly, looking at him. He shifted uncomfortably.

I shrugged my shoulders. I wanted to say yes, but truthfully, I didn't know. "He's helped me this far," I said, which was fair. I hoped he wasn't double-crossing us, that this wasn't some elaborate scheme of Morgan's to show me how little hope I should have of ever leaving. Something nagged at me when I thought that, but just as the idea was about to form, it went again. "Were both tunnels clear?" I asked him.

"The one to the stable yard was clear, but it's not all that stable anymore, excuse the pun. I didn't have a chance to try the second one. Sorry."

"You find out what the Brotherhood wanted with you?" Evan kept his arm around me, but I could see him assessing Daniel, probably wondering if he should take him out.

I nodded. "A more powerful witch. Daniel is untrained and can't do everything the Brotherhood wants him to do." I thought it might be easier for Daniel if I kept his parentage out of it for now. I wasn't even sure how I was going to break my heritage to my friends. There was more, of course, but all that could wait until later. "They gave me the choice to stay and work for them or die."

"And they actually thought turning traitor was an option?" Étoile scoffed. "They clearly don't know you at all."

"Thanks."

"Plus, the health benefits would have been crap," Étoile went on. "Bet the salary sucks too, right, Daniel?"

"Where's my sister?" Gage cut in, saving us from Étoile's amused ponderings. I noticed how strained he looked as he said to me, "Your note said she was hurt."

I tried to keep it brief, to spare him the extra worry of how poorly Annalise had been treated. "When I woke up, I was in a room in the cellar with her. She'd been kept in wolf form and collared. I took the collar off but she stayed that way anyway. When they came for me, she went for one of the guards and he tased her. By the time they released me, she was out cold and I haven't seen her since."

"She's alive," added Daniel. "I haven't seen her, but I've heard the guards talking. She'll be kept alive until her execution, uh, obviously. Most of the Brotherhood have never seen one, uh, a werewolf that is, before. Auberon's planning on making a big spectacle out of her. Like team bonding or something..." He trailed off, as Gage glared at him.

"This Auberon is the Brotherhood leader?" Evan asked.

"He's the man from the TV; that night you saved me from them," I told him, looking to Étoile. She and Anders nodded thoughtfully. The transmission was sent across every channel that night. Alone, that should have been enough to secure a conviction.

"They won't stop with witches once they have

werewolves on the agenda," mused Gage, flexing his hands like he was getting ready for a fight. His eyes had taken on a dark hue, and he looked distinctly wilder tonight. "She'll be their first kill."

"The execution is planned for tomorrow," I interjected, wishing I could give him some more assurance than that.

"Good thing we have a full moon tonight. Some werewolf rumours are true, you know. We'll be at our strongest tonight," Gage promised.

"Speaking of tonight," Evan continued before I had a chance to ask about the possibility of turning from a wolf bite, like I'd threatened Nameless, "We need to get Annalise and go. Stella, it's too risky to leave you here in this room. Daniel, how long do you think it will be before someone comes to check on Stella?"

I looked at Daniel. "No one's been in for a few hours," I told him.

"Probably not 'til dawn, I guess," Daniel said hesitantly. "It'll be trickier getting Annalise out, I think. She's been guarded constantly since she was here."

"Will they let you down there?" Anders sat on one of the velvet chairs, crossed his legs and waited while Daniel shrugged.

"I haven't been down there the past couple of weeks, so I don't know."

"So what do we do, storm the place?" asked Evan. We were still talking in low voices but that didn't stop the threat from sounding in his voice. "That's going to wake up some pissed-off killers."

"What about that concoction Auberon tried to make me drink?" I asked Daniel. "You said you could spike their coffee or tea, or something? If they were knocked out, we could get Annalise easily and no one would know a thing until the next guard came."

"That might work. I do make them drinks sometimes. I could add a charm to make sure they drink it."

"How long will it last?"

"Depends how strong I make it. A couple of hours, at least."

"More than enough time to get Annalise back to the tunnel and get the hell out of here?" Evan asked.

Daniel nodded, pulling his wrist up to squint at his watch. "The shift changes in ten minutes. It'll take us five minutes to walk there." He thought about it a moment longer. "Getting to the cellar will be difficult though. Like I told Stella, there aren't any tunnels directly into the cellar, so we can only go so far until we'll need to cross the kitchen. People are in and out of there all the time and that's where we might be seen. At night, there aren't as many guards usually, but closer to dawn, there will be more people awake."

"Étoile, did you arrange a diversion for the front of the house?"

"Anders?" she said.

"Got that covered," he grinned. "The first phase distracted them long enough for us to get in. Phase two is being put in place as we speak.

"If we're going to go, we need to go now," said Daniel. He handed me a small flashlight and that's when I noticed everyone else was carrying one too. "When we go through the tunnels, stay close together and don't make any noise. We're going to pass a lot of rooms and go downstairs. I'll tell you when we get to the exit. I'll slip out and make the tea, then come back for you. From there, we'll have to cross the kitchen, but it's best if we don't all go. There's too many of us to go back and forth. When we've got the were... Annalise, we'll take the tunnel I brought you in through."

"I'm going," said Gage. "She's my sister."

"Me too," I added quickly.

"Then I'm going as well," Evan threw in, just for good measure.

We had minutes to huddle together, working through our plan. It was flimsy at best; hopeful at worst, but it was all we had. After a few minutes, when we seemed to all be in agreement, Daniel handed me the bundle of clothes he brought, and my boots. Someone had laundered them and my boots had been cleaned, not polished, but the mud had all been knocked off and it looked like someone had even thought to rinse them.

I stood in the bathroom, the light off, Evan filling the doorway. Beyond, our small group were talking quietly so I peeled off my mother's old dress, tossing it over the side of the bath. I wished I had time to take a shower, but that would have to wait until later. Evan stepped forward, and I relaxed against him when he put his hands on my head, examining the wound. "It doesn't look deep," he said.

"I got knocked out... and earlier, well, I hurt my head again."

"You might have a concussion. Headaches?" He looked into my eyes, searching. "Blurred vision? Any sickness?"

"Just a headache and I'm tired; but it's been a bad few days so that's hardly surprising." I stepped into my jeans, then pulled my t-shirt over my head, careful to avoid the parts of my head that ached.

"As soon as we get out of here, I'll heal you. I promise."

"Thanks." I smiled up at him, already feeling reassured by his presence. "That would help."

"How did your dress get ripped?" asked Evan, quietly, so no one else could hear.

I paused. I hadn't realised he'd noticed. "One of them tried to attack me."

"Did he hurt you?"

"No," I said, bluntly. "He tried, but he didn't."

"If you see him tonight, point him out," Evan replied in a thick tone that held the promise of nothing pleasant. "That asshole is going to pay for that."

I squeezed his hand, because there were no words to reply to that. Despite his pledge, and the comfort I got just from his presence, there was nothing that could stop the heavy beating of my heart when I thought about how dangerous the next few hours would be to us all.

CHAPTER FIFTEEN

The passageway was narrow, dark and draughty, much as I imagined it would be. We filed in, one-by-one, Daniel taking the lead, then Evan, then I, still holding his hand, then Gage and finally, Étoile, Anders and Bree. We had to press ourselves against the wall for Daniel to slide back and fiddle with a pull cord that closed the door behind us. Then, he pressed again before moving back to the head of the line. Evan's thumb stroked the thin section of skin between my thumb and forefinger, and I rested my head against his arm for a moment while Daniel readied himself. At last, a beam lit the way ahead and we were off.

Daniel had travelled the secret tunnels for years so he was surefooted and quick, while the rest of us just concentrated on making as little sound as possible as we passed between rooms, only a few bricks separating us from our enemies. Upstairs, the house was quiet, the rooms either empty or the inhabitants sleeping. When we descended a steep flight of stairs, with barely enough space to put a whole foot on a tread, I started hearing noises from the adjoining rooms, snatches of conversation, a scrape of a chair. Obviously, some of the household were still awake. Bad news for us.

As we reached a bend in the passage, Daniel stopped and we shuffled to a halt. I could just make out his face as he turned to us. "The kitchen is that way," he whispered, pointing into the dark. "Wait here and I'll make the guards their drink. I've already got the sleeping draught." He patted his pocket. "I'll be five to ten minutes, tops."

"Be careful," I whispered as his flashlight bobbed away from us. We switched ours off rather than waste the batteries. Crouching on our heels in the dark, we waited for what seemed like forever, until there was a scuffling in the corridor. Evan swung his flashlight up, the beam lighting on Daniel's face. He recoiled, shielding his eyes and squinting.

"How did it go?" asked Evan as he lowered the light.

"Well, they were kinda surprised to see me, but I was right, they just started their shift. I added a charm so they would drink it and I tipped in the whole vial so they should be out cold in five minutes."

Gage leant forward. "Did you see Annalise?"

"No, but she's definitely in there. One of the guards was looking through the little hole in the door. I think he was taunting her."

"What about the keys?" I asked, trying to ignore the last part because getting angry would only cloud my head more.

Daniel looked alarmed. "I don't know. I didn't think."

"They were hung on a hook near the door when I was taken out. Did you see them there?"

Daniel thought about that for a moment, his mouth twisting in frustration. "Yeah," he said finally. "I think I saw them. There was a big ring of keys up there."

"What now?" asked Étoile.

"I'll go and get Annalise," said Daniel.

"You can't go alone," I pointed out, exposing the first flaw in our plan. "What if someone chances on you? Or Annalise gets scared and attacks you?"

"We can't all go. There's too many of us," Daniel whispered back.

"I'm coming with you," interjected Gage, and no one could possibly refuse him.

"Me too," I added.

Evan sighed. "Then I guess it's going to be the four of us. Étoile, Anders and Bree can wait here."

"Fine by me," said Anders. His head was bowed as he fiddled with his watch and I saw two short luminous lines spring up. "Sooner we get out of here, the better. We have a diversion going off in twenty minutes, enough to draw everyone out front while we head out back. Be quick."

"Okay," Daniel nodded. "This tunnel takes us to the kitchen." He paused for a long moment when some voices, somewhere on the other side of the wall came closer, then receded, reminding us how close we were to the enemy. "We cross the kitchen, into the pantry where there is another set of stairs to the cellar. Once we get there, we come out into a little room and we need to cross two more to get where

Annalise is being held. The kitchen is the place we're most likely to be seen. People come and go at all times."

"Then let's get our asses in gear," grinned Gage. His teeth looked awfully sharp in the gloom, but then, it was the full moon, the time when the wolf pack was at their most primal, and therefore, most dangerous. If we were at home, he'd be out in the woods surrounding our homes, leading the pack on the hunt. Tomorrow, he'd sleep in all morning. No such luxuries here.

"Be safe," said Étoile, dropping a kiss unexpectedly on my cheek.

The three of us followed Daniel and, as we got to the door, he raised a hand, signalling us to stop and keep quiet. Someone was in the kitchen. I could hear whoever it was whistle as they walked around. A few minutes later, they were gone and Daniel was pulling a lever. The door opened slowly and Daniel had to push it the last little bit. When I stepped out, and moved around, I saw the secret door wasn't part of the panelling, like in my room, but built so that it was part of a cabinet.

With a quick heave from his shoulder, Daniel shut the cabinet on the passage and we followed him, running across the broad kitchen, our feet flying over the flagstones. He waited until we were inside the pantry and shoved the door closed, just as Gage slipped inside. He pushed a sack of something in front of it, blocking the entrance. "Just in case someone comes back," he whispered, "If you need to get back into the tunnel, and if, for any reason, I'm not with you, go to the fireplace. The second brick down on the left is the lever, push it and it'll open;

then pull the lever once you get inside to shut it again. I gave your friend Étoile a rough map showing you how to get out." We nodded and I wondered if I were the only one thinking how hard that must be for Daniel, still helping us escape, even if he weren't sure he would make it.

Daniel searched the shelves for a moment and grabbed a packet of chocolate biscuits. We followed him down the winding staircase, pressing our bodies close to the wall where the brick treads were at their widest. The temperature dropped a few degrees in the cellar and I shivered, despite my jacket.

"You okay?" asked Evan. I nodded quickly and Gage squeezed my shoulder, then pressed a pair of gloves into my hands. I pulled them on gratefully.

Daniel walked ahead, biscuits in hand, as we followed him through the small rooms he'd mentioned. With a flap of his hand, he signalled us to one side and we fell back, letting him go on alone.

"Oh hey, man," I heard him say jovially. "Thought you might want these with your tea. I meant to bring them down before, but forgot."

"Thanks, kid. Hey, no dozing on the job." There was a sound like a kick, then a heavier sound. I saw an arm land across the doorway on the floor, and the top of a head. "What the hell happened to..." The man never got to finish his sentence, because Gage stepped forward just as the man stepped into the archway. Pulling back his fist, Gage planted it firmly in the guard's face. He stumbled backwards and hit his head against the wall, sliding into a slump on the floor, unconscious.

"They're out," confirmed Daniel, gingerly checking them over. Evan and I moved forwards and

I reached for the keys on the hook, bypassing each key until I found what looked like the right one. Holding my breath, I slipped it into the lock and turned. It unlocked and I swung the door open.

Annalise lay in a heap on the floor. The collar was around her neck again and when she staggered to her feet, I realised she had been hobbled too. Thick iron cuffs were wrapped around each leg, connected by chains that clanked horribly.

"Oh no," I sighed as she limped forwards, her eyes lighting up in recognition.

"Let's get her out of this," said Gage moving forward to kneel down and wrap his arms around her in a brief hug. While Evan and Daniel stood watch on the door, Gage and I worked the restraints. The collar was easy but the leg cuffs were a little stiff, rusty with age, and I had to find a very small key on the keychain to unlock them completely. Annalise lay on her side, panting, then springing up when her last leg was freed. She nuzzled her head into me and I crouched down so my mouth was level with her ears.

"We're getting out of here right now," I told her. "Evan is here, Étoile too. The guy at the door is Daniel and he's helping us. Can you walk okay?"

Annalise raised a front paw and put it in my hands. Through the light filtering in from the guardroom I could see it was sore and blood-soaked.

"It's going to hurt, I'm so sorry, but we'll be out of here soon." In the gloom I locked eyes with Gage. He never looked angrier.

"Let's go," said Evan, glancing into the room. Annalise stuck close to Gage's legs as we walked out. I could tell she was being very stoic as she limped after us as quickly as she could, every whine of her pain swallowed down. Evan and Gage moved the unconscious guards into the cell and locked it behind them. In a moment of pique, I took the key chain with me. *See how you guys get out of there now.*

The pantry was exactly as we left it, the sack still blocking the door and, if anyone had tried to open it while we were in the cellar, well, I couldn't tell. I turned behind me, checking as Evan climbed the last step. Gage appeared a moment later, Annalise slung over his shoulder. He lowered her to the floor and she lay there. When she moved, I saw bloody paw prints staining the floor. "Ready?" Daniel asked, waiting for us to nod. He pushed the heavy sack out of the way and swung open the door, saying, "All clear."

We followed him into the kitchen and made it only a few steps when two men walked into the room, talking quietly to each other. One of them was Nameless and he stopped suddenly, his arm flying out to knock into the other man's stomach. He looked at Nameless in surprise, then followed his eyes to us.

"Daniel?" said the second man in surprise, a frown spreading across his face as we fanned out behind. "Who are they?" He spied Annalise, lowering into a crouch, a growl ripping from her throat. "Oh fuck." Turning on his heel, he went for the door. Gage leapt after him, his body changing as he flew through the air. When he landed on the second man, taking him down, he was wolf; his ferocious teeth snapped at the man lying prone under him, fists thrashing and shouting obscenities.

"Well, well," said Nameless, dropping into a fighter's stance as he edged away. He pulled his fists up in front of his face and circled, bypassing the table and edging close to us. All I could think was, *just how stupid is this man*? "Looks like we've got a little escape party here," he snickered. Someone had bandaged his nose, a thick strip of medical tape securing it across his cheeks.

Evan looked at him, then down at me. "He's the one who tried to attack me," I confirmed, noticing Gage's ears flick forwards then back as he snapped at the man he'd taken down.

Evan turned back to the man, his expression blank. "That so?" he said.

"C'mon," said Nameless, motioning to Evan. "Send the witch slut over here and we'll go easy on the rest of you."

"Did you just call my girlfriend a slut?" asked Evan slowly. I could see a glow lighting his hands, not fire but something else, something almost imperceptible. Clearly, Daniel hadn't thought to protect the house from a daemon; he probably didn't even know they existed.

"Slut. Slut. Slut," repeated Nameless, cackling, proving just how stupid he really was. Behind him, on the floor, his comrade whimpered and I saw him thrashing still, but less so now. He'd stopped shouting too. I don't think Nameless even realised he was levitating until he slowly rose above us and began floating backwards. When he did, I saw the frustration on his face as he tried to move, his limbs unyielding. "What are you doing to me?" he shrieked, his face contorting in terror under the medical tape.

"Guys, uh guys?" Daniel's voice rose above the two guards, panic edging in. "We are making way too much noise."

"Help!" shrieked both men at once. Nameless

shot backwards, landing hard against the wall, his feet helplessly dangling.

"Can you shut him up?" I asked, frightened that any moment, the noise would bring countless more guards upon us.

Evan's eyes didn't leave Nameless for a second. "Sure," he said. A cloth lifted from the counter and flew across the room, jamming into Nameless' mouth so his voice was just a hum. Evan stepped closer. With a flick of his hand, the man under Gage seemed to sigh and lose consciousness.

Gage crawled backwards, the front of his fur now mottled with blood. Circling around, he searched the kitchen for Annalise, licking her head affectionately after he found her, then trotting over to press against my leg, while growling at Nameless. I stooped down and buried a hand in Gage's fur and he turned big, angry eyes on me. He buffeted my shoulder with his head and, when he looked at me again, I knew he wasn't angry with me, but the situation. "Go back to Annalise," I told him. "She needs you."

"You tried to hurt a defenceless woman," murmured Evan, stepping closer to Nameless. The cold of his voice seeped through the room. Nameless did nothing but stare, his nostrils flaring as Evan stepped closer. There was a large table running along the middle of the room and, with the barely damp surface and stacks of clean crockery, it looked like someone had recently cleaned up after the evening's meal. A block of knives sat at the end closest to us. Evan slipped each one out of its slot, lining them up on the table. Nameless watched with wide eyes as he completed the task, and then picked up the biggest, scariest-looking butcher's knife. He held it in his hand, weighing it. Then, with a flick of his wrist, it flew across the room. I held a hand over my mouth, trying not to squeak as the knife lodged in the wall. Evan repeated the action a few more times, the knives landing with absolute precision, bare inches away from his arms, legs, head. The final knife landed about two inches lower than Nameless' crotch and I'm fairly certain he wet himself, judging by the growing stain. I couldn't bring myself to feel one bit of sympathy.

"We have to go," said Daniel, tugging at my arm and looking up to where Nameless was pressed against the wall. His voice dropped to a whisper, "But I can't open the tunnel without him seeing and telling everyone."

"Evan, this has been fun, but can you knock him out so we can go?" I asked, my voice shaky.

Evan glanced over at me and, for a moment, there didn't seem to be anything human about him at all. His eyes were hard, his face completely blank, then he seemed to shake out of whatever had gotten hold of him. "Sorry, what?" he said, like he hadn't heard me.

"Time to go, Evan."

Evan looked at Nameless for a long moment, raising his hands. Light seemed to pour from them, brilliant and strong. Nameless struggled and screamed against the gag, then went limp, his chin slumping forward to rest against his chest.

"Is he...?"

"Unfortunately, no," said Evan. "Dead, that is, but he'll be out for a while. Let's go."

Daniel jogged over to the fireplace, pushed the panel and the concealed door opened. We piled through, leaving the unconscious guards in the kitchen. As I was last, I found the lever and closed the door after us. Evan waited, then reached forward to give the door a tug, when it stuck. Finally, ensconced in darkness again, he grabbed my hand, pulling me after him.

Étoile, Anders and Bree were where we left them, except now we were two witches, a daemon and two wolves. None of them said anything, though Bree did give a little squeak when she saw the wolves' eyes. She was probably worried they were going to pee on one of her precious trees. To be fair, they probably would.

"We'll just have to hope no one finds them for a while, though we should have put them in the pantry, I guess. Never mind," finished Daniel. "Let's go. This way." We jogged after him as he twisted and turned through the passage. Every so often, I caught the flash of conversation again, my heart leaping as I realised how close we were to the Brotherhood, how easy it would be for them to discover us. I wished there was something we could do to disable them as we left, but in my heart, I knew it was more important to escape than to stay and fight.

A distant rumble had us stop, bumping into each other.

"What was that?" I asked, almost forgetting to whisper.

"Our distraction," replied Anders. "We called in a few reinforcements and they're setting off alarms all over the front of the property."

Bree added, "The local wolf pack are going to run interference. The terrain will feel particularly hostile tonight."

"Let's keep going," Daniel urged as feet ran past us on the other side of the wall, and orders rang out.

"Everyone will be awake in a few minutes."

We sprinted the rest of the way along the passage, descended some more stairs, until I felt we must be parallel with the cellar, as the temperature dropped again. The passage widened a little here and I knew we were going outside the house, somewhere under the grounds; but it felt very disorientating. Daniel and Evan took the lead, the wolves next, then Bree and I, and finally Étoile and Anders.

Bree grabbed my hand, lurching to a halt. "The earth says something is wrong." Her hands trailed against the walls where they were crumbling, soil and roots sinking through the cracks. "We're..."

Just as I was about to shout a warning ahead, something barrelled out of the darkness and knocked Daniel and Evan flying. "Go back!" shouted Daniel. "It's a trap." I could see Evan grappling with someone, fists flying in the darkness as Evan sprang back to his feet, giving Daniel the chance to scramble to his. Evan and the stranger were pounding each other and I heard a grunt as Evan shot his knee up, connecting with his assailant. A blast of light shot from Evan and his foe was down, at least, but there were more swarming out of the darkness. I could see the whites of their eyes.

"This way." Étoile grabbed Bree and me, her fingers tightly closing over our forearms, forcing us to sprint backwards the way we had come, the wolves on our heels. As we reached the junction, I realised she was aiming for the house.

"No this way! Daniel said there's another passage but he didn't get a chance to check it," I argued as I signalled the turn that would take us towards the untested exit. Daniel thought it would be safe. I thought it was a hell of a lot safer than heading back to the house, especially when we could be discovered missing any moment.

Bree pushed her hand into the soft floor, springing up quickly. "It's clear enough, but it's weak. Let's go." She pushed us on. "The others are right behind us. Do not wait," she hissed at me, seeing my hesitation. A moment later, Anders and Daniel came into view.

"Take down the shields," yelled Étoile. "I need my magic!" I half expected her to stomp her foot if she took a moment to slow down.

"I can't. Not down here. I won't be sure the shields are gone until we're above ground." Daniel sprinted past us and we followed him, pushing on hard. At first, the passage looked okay, just as stable as the other one. Then I noticed the cracks in one of the supporting struts as I fled past and saw, in the glow of the torchlight, how the roof struts bowed under the strain of the earth overhead. Annalise and Gage were much faster on their four legs and they sped ahead. I held on to Étoile, each of us pulling the other along. Anders and Bree seemed pretty fit. I couldn't resist looking backwards for Evan, tripping on a thick root and almost falling, pushing off the walls to right myself.

"I'm here," said Evan. "But they're following. I'm going to collapse the tunnel. Go. Go!"

I sprinted on, the sounds of shattering wood behind me. When the first section of the tunnel began to collapse, dust and rubble exploding every which way, it felt like the world was folding in on itself.

"Evan!" Hands pulled me after them as another section collapsed, sending splinters and soil spraying into the tunnel behind us. Ahead, I saw a faint shaft of light and I was pulled towards it, forcing my legs to run, tears streaming down my face as I yelled for Evan.

Daniel and Anders had already scrambled up through the opening, and were pulling us through. The wolves sat back on their haunches, firing themselves upwards and we grabbed their bodies, hefting them the last little bit. It was the longest few seconds of my life as I waited for Evan to appear in the hatch. Then he was sliding through, swinging his legs over the top and I threw myself at him, relieved to feel his arms wrap around me.

When I let him go, I could see we were inside a derelict cottage. Its roof had long since caved in, and the windows were either cracked and grimy or missing completely. There was evidence of fire damage everywhere. Daniel hovered by the trapdoor for the ensuing few minutes, listening to see if anyone managed to follow us through. "I think we're good," he said, lowering the trapdoor. We helped him move some things on top of it, bits of broken furniture and other debris that would weigh it down. Although I doubted anyone had gotten through the tunnel when it collapsed, it seemed wise to take precautions.

"Take down the barriers, Daniel," I said, giving his hand a quick squeeze. He looked terrified.

"They'll know. The alarm will go off."

"And the whole house and grounds will be unprotected. Our people are fighting for us out there," I jabbed a hand towards the house. "They need their magic and so do we."

"Plus," said Evan, his chest barely heaving from the run, "they already knew we were coming. That, back there, was an ambush, my friend."

"Wasn't me!" Daniel squeaked in terror. I reached over and gave his hand a little squeeze, not wanting him to think that we were about to gang up on him. He closed his eyes for a moment and, when he did, he seemed to relax a little, his face taking on more colour.

"Didn't say you did," said Evan, "but someone let them know. How far to the wall?"

"Not far."

Étoile had picked her way across the debris and wiped a spy hole in the filthy glass. "Every light is on in the house," she said. "I can see a lot of movement."

"Any of it coming our way?" Evan asked.

"No."

"Let's go. Which way out, Daniel?"

"There's a door over here, it leads towards the rear of the property." Daniel led us into a smaller, and just as damaged room. Between Anders and him, they levered the door open. The wolves went first, sniffing the air. Despite Annalise's injuries, they sprinted for the wall, the six of us following behind as fast as we could.

Behind me, fire erupted from one of Hawkscroft's large windows and I turned away as the glass blew out. I could hear shouting over the sound of the alarm ringing, and the frantic barking of the dogs.

"Keep going," Evan hissed. "Don't stop for anything."

Ahead of me, Daniel stumbled and clambered to his feet again. "I..."

"Don't even say it, Daniel. Keep moving." I gave him a shove forwards and he started running again, aiming for the wall Anders and Bree had just vaulted over. "There's nothing you can do to help."

"Except shut up," said Étoile. She skidded to a stop in front of the wall and Evan cupped his hands together, taking her foot and launching her so she could slide over the top. Annalise and Gage sailed over the top and I heard the wet rustle of leaves as they landed. Daniel climbed over next, then I put my foot in Evan's hands and he hoisted me up so that I was sitting on the wall. I leaned forward, swung my leg over and slid down the other side, waiting as Evan appeared over the top a moment later.

"The protections are gone," said Daniel. "We have two minutes until the main alarm goes off and Auberon knows what I've done."

"We can make a run for it through the woods," said Anders, bending forward, panting, his hands on his knees.

Daniel nodded, adding, "The village is two miles north of here."

Étoile shook her head. "We're going a lot faster than that. Stella, we're going to shimmer all of them."

"I don't know if I'm strong enough," I protested.

"It's a short trip, and you can draw some of my power." Evan linked his hand in mine and I could feel the familiar flow of magic start to trickle from him to me as my energy levels rose. We didn't exchange power often, but I'd had enough lessons that I knew how much I could reasonably take without weakening him or overloading myself. It was like an energy boost on the last leg of a marathon.

"What about you?" Anders asked him.

"I'll follow. Witches don't like the way I travel."

"You're not a witch?" asked Daniel, bracing

himself as Étoile tutted and I shot her a glare.

"No, I'm not. Werewolves and witches aren't the only thing on this earth, Warlock." Evan looked down at the wolves. "You two are going to have to run for it."

"I'll go with them," said Bree. "The woods like me and will let us pass easily."

Gage wrinkled his nose. "I think he wants to know if you can keep up," I told her.

Bree smiled down at the wolves. "Of course."

"Where are we going anyway?"

"Where's safest?"

"My house," said Anders.

"Never been there. Anywhere we can visualise?" I asked, knowing we were wasting precious seconds discussing this.

"The pub car park?" he suggested.

"That'll do." I could create that in my mind. "Gage, do you know where to go?" The big wolf lowered his head in a nod and turned, thrusting himself forward through the undergrowth, Annalise on his heels. Bree sprinted past them, her silvery hair streaming behind her. Her speed was impressive. She must have been holding back in the tunnel.

"Let's link hands," Étoile said as she drew us into a circle. Daniel stood between us on one side, Anders and Bree on the other. "Close your eyes, it'll only take a moment." Magic flowed through us, the circuit travelling between the five of us and I felt it complete just as a huge roar echoed behind us and I stumbled forward, hands catching me. We'd been found.

"Go NOW!" shouted Evan I forced myself to stand up straight, even though there was a flash of pain that ripped through me. With a nod from Étoile,

I rejoined hands with Anders and Daniel either side of me just as something punched me hard in the stomach and we flashed out of the woods.

The Rose and Crown car park was empty and still. A few cars were dotted around and the lights were off. I could hear music playing from somewhere, one of the bedrooms, and the sound of someone laughing. I felt cold, dreadfully cold and started to shiver. It was fright, I told myself, and exertion. My breath was coming quicker and my teeth chattering.

So far, only the four of us had made it to the rendezvous. Gage, Annalise and Bree wouldn't arrive for another few minutes, at least. Just as my heart started to constrict, with the fear of what happened to Evan, he appeared next to me, perfect as always.

"You're okay!" I felt an enormous rush of relief.

Evan nodded and grinned. Then his smile faded as his eyes travelled down.

"What's wrong?" I looked downwards, remembering the unfortunate incident with the shape-shifter, which felt like weeks ago now. I hoped I hadn't brought something with me. I twisted, wincing, to look over my shoulder. Nope, I looked extra limb-free.

"Are you okay?" he asked slowly.

"Sure, I'm..." I followed Evan's eyes down. He wasn't looking at the ground. He was looking at the dark patch spreading across my jacket, through the ragged edges of the torn material.

I wasn't okay. I really wasn't okay. Touching a finger to the centre of the dark mark, I drew it to my face. Blood. I was bleeding. That's when the world started to get dizzy and wobble from side to side like I was on a carnival ride. I felt sick.

Evan caught me as I fell, lowering me steadily to the asphalt. I looked up at Étoile crouching beside me, Daniel hovering, looking sick. I looked up at the beautiful black sky, the pinpricks of golden stars and the moon that watched over us. Some distance away, I heard an explosion. I expected to hear sirens, shouting, but a blanket of calm seemed to descend over the deserted car park.

"I've been shot," I whispered, my hands pressing over the wound in my side.

CHAPTER SIXTEEN

"We've got to get her inside." Evan's voice sounded like it was coming from under water, very faint in contrast to the sound of the blood rushing in my head.

"My house," came Anders voice, soft and far away. Then Evan lifted me, his arms wrapped under my shoulders and knees and we were running so fast, the world became a blur around me. That was probably when I lost consciousness.

When I awoke, I was lying on a sofa in a warm room, where a white plastered ceiling replaced the dark sky. I felt wet and scared and my hands were sticky with my blood. My side throbbed horribly and I couldn't resist letting my fingers stray to where it hurt most, yelping when I touched the soft, damaged part of my body through my layers.

Étoile crouched next to me, peeling back my sweater to see the wound and I had to mash my lips together to stop from screaming.

"Is she going to be okay?" Daniel's voice was laced with worry. I could just see him hovering somewhere above my head, but I had to blink twice before his face swam into focus. I searched the room for Evan, found him; then my eyes drifted in search of Annalise and Gage, but I couldn't find them. I hoped they would get here soon. I hoped they were safe.

"I think so." Étoile said. Then I screamed as she pressed my ragged flesh, her cold hand travelling around to my back, which didn't feel quite as bad. "I think the bullet is still inside. There isn't an exit wound. She must have been shot just as we shimmered. Otherwise, it would have been a through and through."

"Can you get it out?" I whimpered, tightening my hand around Evan's. I hated to whine but I could barely think properly and everything was flickering, except it wasn't a faulty light, it was me. Evan's face, close to mine and full of concern, wavered in and out of focus.

"Yes," she said. Through my half-closed eyes, I saw her grimace. She didn't need to add that it was going to hurt.

"Can you do that thing you do, where you make me feel sleepy? I don't want to feel it."

"Sure."

"Sorry for being a wimp." I breathed in and waited for Étoile's suggestion to seep through me once she placed her hand on my forehead. Before, when I was weak and not in control of my magic, she used her influence to knock me out. I told her and Seren to promise never to use their sway on me again and, to their credit, they hadn't. It helped that I could block them nowadays. I let my defences down to allow Étoile's magic to work through me, lulling the pain until I felt sleepy and distant, like I was floating away from my body.

I was only vaguely conscious of Étoile's hands over my wound, then the bullet sliding out of my body, pushing past my flesh. Étoile's hand disappeared for a moment; then she placed both hands on me and began to heal my internal wounds as well as the entry hole the bullet made. I couldn't watch what she was doing, even though I was horribly numb, so I focused on Evan's stricken face, swallowing up every last lovely look of him. Then I was out again.

When I woke up, I felt like I'd slept for days. My vision was back to normal and I took my time looking around before I even tried moving. There was a large teapot on the table and a rack of toast. Annalise and Gage were there, both in human form. They both looked like hell. Annalise had red eyes like she had been crying a lot. When she saw I was conscious, she flung herself across the room, kneeling by my side and taking my hand. She started to speak too fast and faltered each time. Finally, she just said, "Thank you."

"For nearly getting you killed?" I croaked. "No problem."

"For saving me, silly. Gage told me that you came here all by yourself and that you even got yourself captured because of me. I know that part obviously." She took a deep breath, reliving the horror of the cold cellar. I glanced over at Gage, watching us and he met my eyes momentarily, before Annalise's voice distracted me. "And getting us out of there, too," she added, with another squeeze of her hand.

"That wasn't me," I protested weakly. "Daniel knew the tunnels. Evan destroyed them."

"But if it weren't for your note, no one could have gotten in," Annalise persisted before rubbing her eyes when a tear slipped out. "And we wouldn't be here now."

Speaking of here... "Where are we?" I groaned, reaching down to where my wound had been. I was still slightly damp, and the blood had crusted my sweater and tee, soaking into the waistband of my jeans. I gingerly peeled back the stiff fabrics, straining to take a look. Étoile walked quickly around the sofa and, between Annalise and her, they helped me sit up, nestling me against the back and arm of the sofa. My wound was gone, just pink flesh and a faded white scar left, marring my otherwise flawless right side. Annalise winced at it and walked stiffly back to the chair she was occupying before I woke.

"My house." Anders pressed a mug of hot black tea into my hand. I wriggled my toes and stretched my legs, encouraging my circulation to start moving again.

"Everyone else okay?" I looked from Gage to Annalise, then to Daniel, hunched over in an armchair in the corner, who nodded glumly. Étoile walked across to my cousin and perched on the chair's arm, patting him softly; keeping him calm, I thought.

"It's nice to have two arms and two legs again," said Annalise with a little smile that tried to cover how hoarse she sounded. Someone found her a pair of baggy jeans and a shirt to wear and she looked fresh and clean, like she'd just taken a shower. Her face, hands and neck, however, were covered in angry red wounds. "Spending that much time as a wolf was a challenge. How're you feeling?"

I tried shifting my muscles a little and tentatively raised my arms. There was no pain, just a dull ache in my right side. "Sore."

"I'll make you a poultice," said Anders, "to draw the stiffness out."

"Thanks." I looked around, realising there was something wrong with the picture. "Where's Evan?"

Anders gulped and looked at Étoile, who shrugged. "Hunting," she said.

"Hunting what?"

"Whoever shot you," she said succinctly. "He waited to make sure you were okay, then shot out the door."

I looked at her, my eyebrows raised.

Étoile pulled a face right back. "Sorry. Too soon to make bad puns?" she apologised.

Anders passed me a blanket when I shivered and tucked it around my shoulders. Placing a bet, Anders claimed the odds that whoever shot me would live were pretty bad. Cautiously, I drew up the hem of my top and poked at the pink flesh. It was healing fast. The small scar I'd have to live with, but I was alive and that was a lot to be thankful for. Someone cleaned my wound, but my top and jeans were still encrusted with my blood. I probably stank too. "Has he been gone long?" I asked.

Anders checked his watch. "You've been out for two hours, so a little less than that. We're just coming up to dawn."

"The Brotherhood didn't track us here?" I asked, frowning.

Anders shook his head. "Too busy dousing the fire at Hawkscroft. They haven't come here, at any rate. We'd have noticed."

"What about your coven?"

He smirked. "Stoking the fire."

"Oh." I sipped the hot tea. It tasted perfect, the way things do when you've had a shock and suddenly everything seems bright and wonderful. When my stomach rumbled loudly, a hot, buttered slice of toast was pressed into my hand and I ate it in just a few bites. Although it stopped the rumbling, it didn't stop the sick feeling I had when I remembered what Evan told us in the derelict cottage.

"Étoile, can you help me up so I can get clean?" I asked. I probably could have made it without help, but I wanted to talk to Étoile alone. I figured that what I had to say probably wouldn't go down too well with Anders. I was grateful for his hospitality and for coming to help us escape Hawkscroft, but something was niggling at me, something that told me someone we trusted had betrayed us.

"I put more towels in the bathroom," Anders said. "Étoile knows the way."

"Thanks." I started to get to my feet and Gage half stood, ready to help, but sat again when Étoile slid a hand under my arm and another around my waist. She pulled away when I winced. I was sore and tender but alive, so there was much to be grateful for. First things first, I had to get clean. While I knelt by the side of the bathtub, Étoile washed my hair. She had to shampoo it three times before it felt clean, and the rinse water no longer ran with blood. Then I patted it until it wasn't dripping wet. Finally, Étoile took over and coaxed it into a braid. With all the gentle tugging at my scalp, I realised someone had ministered the cut on my head while I was unconscious and my headache finally, was gone. The rest of me could wait, I decided; there were more important things to attend to.

"Étoile, we were ambushed in that tunnel," I said softly, not knowing who was in the house and if anyone would take it upon themselves to eavesdrop. "Someone knew we were going to escape that way and they were waiting for us."

She considered that, asking, "You think Daniel double-crossed us?"

It was an obvious suggestion, so I wasn't surprised. It had crossed my mind too, but I quickly discounted it. "No, I don't think he would do that. He's frightened of the Brotherhood."

"Frightened enough to set us up to save himself?"

"No." I thought that too, but Daniel seemed so genuine, so afraid of his father and he'd been thinking about escape for so long, it was unlikely that he would try to save his own hide. "He could have stayed behind if that were the case. No, I think this was someone in Anders' coven."

"What reason would they have to set us up?"

"Bribery? Blackmail? Fear?" I shot off the most obvious motives.

"Anders wouldn't have betrayed us. Not after what they did to his sister, surely?" pondered Étoile. Ahh, so she knew about that. She sat on the edge of the bathtub while I washed my face in the sink and brushed my teeth using a squirt of toothpaste on my finger.

"I don't think so. Who else knew we would use the tunnels to exit the house?"

"Gage, but we can rule him out obviously. Bree. She was with us, but I can't see why she would try and hurt us either."

"Maybe she doesn't want them in her woods?"

"I don't see how ambushing us would stop them going in her woods."

"Was anyone with you when I sent the message? Or maybe came to the tunnels with you?"

"Only Rachel. She was there for both. Her team were supposed to guard that section of the grounds until we came out."

"Then where the hell were they?" I asked. The woods seemed completely empty until the point when we were encircled and made to shimmer.

"Anders has been trying to find out. He's worried something happened to Rachel. Evan said he would look for them while he's out."

"I don't like this. If there's a traitor and we're all here together, we're..."

"Sitting ducks," finished Étoile. "I don't like it either."

I heard a door bang downstairs and we both looked over to the bathroom door. Étoile, being a little faster than I right now, and closer to the door, poked her head outside. "Evan's back," she said, returning her eyes to me.

My heart thumped with relief.

"What should we do about the, uh, problem?"

"A spell would bring the traitor, if any to us," she suggested. "But it would be polite to ask Anders first, seeing as this is his territory."

Étoile made to leave but I grabbed her forearm, stopping her. Pushing the door closed, she sat back on the tub again. "What is it?" she asked, her eyes searching my face as I gulped. There was only one small thing I hadn't told her yet.

"There's something else I need to tell you. About the Brotherhood... and Daniel."

"Go on."

"Daniel and I are related. Cousins, actually." Étoile raised an eyebrow, waving a hand for me to continue. "Auberon Morgan is my mother's brother, my uncle."

"No shit?" she breathed.

"When all the killings were happening a year ago, when you came for me... Auberon told me that they weren't going to kill me that night. Instead, they were supposed to bring me here, recruit me, even though I wasn't much of a witch."

"Funny way of 'rescuing' you." Étoile waggled her fingers for air quotes, her voice dripping with sarcasm. "The fire and the axe in the door made me think they wanted to hurt you."

"Yeah, that's what I said."

"Good job I got to you first, huh?"

I nodded, thinking about what Daniel had to put up with. The fear, the coercion, the co-habiting with people who simultaneously hated and needed him, knowing that the things he was forced to do put us all in danger. "You saved me from a hell of a lot worse than death."

Étoile shrugged. "So, you think Daniel is okay? Trustworthy?"

"I really do. He's practically been a prisoner there. His dad made him locate the witches so that they could attack them. Daniel didn't know at first, but when he realised, they forced him anyway."

"So he says. Let's keep our cautious heads on

here, okay, Stella? We can't just blithely trust because we want to."

"I know that. That's why I told you who he was, how we're related."

"Stella?" Evan's voice floated up the stairs.

I cupped my hands to my mouth. "Be right there," I called back, softening my voice to speak to Étoile again. "But can we at least give Daniel the benefit of the doubt? The Council might be interested in what he has to say. What he knows could help all of us."

"I'll contact them." Étoile brightened. "We have very little intelligence on the Brotherhood. Daniel's knowledge will be welcome, I'm sure. Perhaps give them something to actually talk about, rather than squabbling until the summit. Now, there's a man down there who needs to know you're okay. Go. I'll clean up here."

"Thanks." I hugged her quickly and ran down the stairs as fast as my aching body would let me.

It didn't take me long to find Evan standing in the kitchen, talking to Anders. I caught the tail end of the conversation: that Rachel was nowhere to be found, but some of her team hadn't fared too well and that Hawkscroft had sustained a lot of damage. When he heard me at the door, he pulled me over and hugged me, quickly releasing me to check me out, seemingly pleased with what he saw. He ran his hands over my hair and I felt it dry immediately in the braid, which was a good thing. I didn't want to trouble Anders for a blow dryer. Evan's hands paused to cup my face as he looked at me with absolute relief. "Nearly lost you there," he murmured.

"Never gonna happen," I whispered back.

"Not on my watch. Been awake long?"

"Not long, just enough to start getting cleaned up. Can you do anything about my clothes?" I asked, knowing his skills would come in very handy right now and wishing I'd had the foresight to have him teach me. That would be the first thing on my agenda when I got home. "I'm pretty grubby."

"Sure." My clothes melted away, immediately replaced with black jeans and a fleece top – warm, clean and practical. It's amazing how being fresh can make you feel more capable, more ready to face the day and I had an inkling that the coming dawn was going to be the start of a very long one.

"Do you take requests?" asked Anders, looking down at his own mud-spattered clothes. He looked tired, dark circles smudging his eyes.

Evan eyed him sceptically. "This is not 'Daemon Eye for the Magic Guy'."

"Fair enough." Anders seemed jovial enough. He picked up the teapot he'd been filling with hot water from the kettle and left the narrow room, leaving the two of us alone.

"Are you okay?" I asked, taking Evan's hand, winding my fingers through his. He didn't look out of breath, or exerted, or angry. He looked calm.

"I found the man who shot you."

"Okay."

Evan said it in such a calm, disinterested way that I wasn't sure how to take his news. I felt certain nothing good resulted from their encounter, but I was hard pressed to feel bad for whoever was on the receiving end of it. They shot me, after all, trying to kill me. Perhaps I was wrong to be glad I was the one standing. Perhaps I was losing my morality, but I knew one thing: if it were a choice between the Brotherhood and me, I'd pick me every time.

Evan watched me while I came to my own conclusions. Slowly, he asked, "Do you want to know what happened to him?"

"Yes... and no," I replied as honestly as I could. After seeing what Evan was capable of, and his explanation of what his lineage could do, I could imagine, which was a lot different from knowing. I didn't know which would be worse. Part of me didn't want my high regard for Evan coloured in any way. Another part of me told me that was stupid, and that to love someone, you have to know them completely. For a moment, we stood in an uncomfortable silence while I tried to make my mind up if ignorance were bliss, or just foolhardy.

"I have some things to report on. Let's find the others," said Evan, making the decision for me. I had no illusions that this was the end of the conversation, just a reprieve. When he turned to leave the kitchen, I slipped my hand into his nevertheless, and he gave it a little squeeze before pulling me along after him.

Étoile had rejoined our small group in the living room, and a couple more people I didn't know were also added to the assembly. The small room was getting crowded, so, after Daniel made room for me on the armchair, with him perching on the arm, Evan stood by the door, arms folded.

"I circled the perimeter first," Evan told us when all eyes were on him. "I found three of Rachel's group. As some of you know, they were supposed to watch the area around the entrance after we entered the secret tunnels into Hawkscroft. I'm sorry, I don't have good news. Two were dead, one was unconscious."

"Who?" asked Anders, his fingers digging into his palms, the only sign that he was worried about his girlfriend.

"I don't know. Three men."

Étoile and I exchanged a look as Anders asked, "But not Rachel?"

"No. I found the one who shot Stella," Evan added, but he didn't elaborate on that, beyond, "He won't be troubling anyone again."

"What about the Brotherhood?" asked Gage, looking brighter and more alert now. Unlike the rest of us, the moonlit run seemed to have invigorated him, despite everything else. I'd never seen him change back so quickly after a full moon, though, come to think of it. He and Annalise always slept in late after the moon's cycle ended. "What's the damage?"

"It's chaos there, right now. The fire is under control but they're scattering. I saw a convoy of around six cars leave, but there's plenty of other people there."

"What about the police or fire engines?" I asked.

"Yes to the fire trucks, no to the police," Evan replied. "I heard one of the fire officers say there was a gas explosion, so I guess that's the official cause."

I asked the question everyone else wanted to ask. "What about Auberon Morgan?" Beside me, Daniel stiffened and I wondered if he'd told anyone in the room about his parentage yet.

"I'm sorry, I couldn't find out. He might have left with the convoy or he might be one of the dead."

"How many died?" I pressed.

"A few. Most of the Brotherhood's patrols were

drawn out of the house through Anders' interference, so when the fire went up, there weren't many inside."

Someone muttered, "Pity." Several people echoed the sentiment.

"What about the tunnels?" Daniel asked, clearing his throat slightly. I knew he was wondering what happened to the men who were waiting to ambush us there.

Evan shrugged. "Some of the stable yard area caved in. I don't know if anyone was still down there, or if they got out that way. I couldn't hear anything."

"What are the chances any of them are going to come here?" I asked, thinking about the traitor in our midst and the conclusion Étoile and I had come to: we were still targets. It was hard not to look at any of Anders' coven without suspicion. Bree was still here, the only face known to me, and a few others had drifted in while we were talking, but not Rachel. Not yet.

"This house is protected, and we have their witch." Anders darted a glance at Daniel who seemed to try to shrink a little lower, except I was occupying the chair and he was in full view of everyone. I gave his arm a quick squeeze and he flashed a small smile at me. "My guess is if Morgan is alive, he's made a break for it. He'll go somewhere he feels safe."

Daniel's voice was small now. "You think he'll ever come back?"

"Hope not. Hawkscroft will be a safer place without that bastard," said Anders firmly and there was a chorus of agreement.

"Not so great for the rest of the world," pointed out Étoile, spoiling the brief moment of victory. "At least, by knowing where he was, we could have kept an eye on him."

"What do you think we've been doing these past months?" said Anders, his voice growing hard. "While your precious Council have been flapping around doing nothing? We're the ones who've been risking our lives to keep track of them, to get intelligence, to try and get the police to take us seriously."

"Okay, okay, guys." I raised my hands, waving at them to calm down, wincing as the movement pulled at my side. Étoile and Anders glowered at each other, but not with any real anger, seeing as they both had a point. We were all tense. It had been a long, dramatic night and it still wasn't over. The clock on the bookcase behind Anders signalled it was six in the morning and the sun would rise soon. "We can figure all this stuff out later," I finished and, after a moment or two, where it looked like an argument might erupt, both Étoile and Anders shrugged.

Once conversations had started up in smaller groups, and some people left, fanning out through the house, I crossed to the window and looked out. It was still dark, but there were the faint fingers of light now signalling the sun was ready to rise. I could see a few people sitting around in the garden, the occasional beam of a flashlight illuminating one of them. Whether they were wolves or witches, I didn't know; but it seemed comforting that there were so many people here, on our side.

Far in the distance, I saw smoke rising as Hawkscroft smouldered. Looking back at Daniel, he looked completely beaten and I felt a rush of sympathy for him. I wondered if we would ever interact like we were family; maybe we'd call each other and email and he would come stay with me? I'd seen how my foster families interacted with their wide arrays of children, siblings, as well as past foster children and extended families, but I had no idea if that would work for me. Perhaps it took practice and I was just at a disadvantage? I could learn the family stuff, especially as Daniel was now alone. Perhaps he'd always been alone, just like I had.

"Stella?"

I realised someone had repeated my name a couple of times, and I looked around. "Yes?"

It was Étoile, beckoning me away from the window. I followed her into the small hallway where Anders was waiting. For once, Étoile looked nervous. Then Evan and Daniel joined us, and Anders signalled us to follow him into another room, some kind of study where he could shut the door and face us. "What is it you're not telling me?" he asked astutely.

"Anders, we think there..." Étoile started again, picking her words carefully. "We think there is a traitor, someone who is double-crossing us."

"What makes you think that?" Anders frowned.

"Because someone knew we were going to take that tunnel out, and they made sure the Brotherhood were waiting for us," replied Evan.

"There were patrols everywhere," Anders said cautiously. "They were on alert."

Daniel looked from Evan to me, then to Anders, as he thought about it. "Not in the tunnels," he said, his voice strong and clear, more assured now there were only five of us. "No one goes in them. Only me. I'm not even sure Morgan knew about them; not all of them anyway."

"Maybe he just never used them?" Anders suggested.

"I've been using them for over ten years. I swear, I never once saw Morgan use them, or saw any sign that he or anyone else had. I used to leave markers, pieces of string stretched across the passages, things that would have been broken or moved if anyone else passed through, and they were never broken."

"That's not all though," interjected Étoile. "What about the group supposed to be watching the tunnels, ready for when we came out? They should have been ready for us if anything happened. Instead, we were forced out the wrong exit, right into the Brotherhood's hands again."

"I don't need to point out that I only found three of them," added Evan.

"They were ambushed," said Anders, but his voice betrayed a lack of conviction. "The others will turn up."

"And what if one of them is a traitor?" I asked, studiously avoiding mentioning any names. "I know it's horrible, but we've got to consider that possibility."

Anders turned on me, his face drawn with tiredness. "Why would any of our witches help a member of the Brotherhood? That's not just being a traitor; that's tantamount to murder."

"Anders, we can go in circles talking about this for ages, or we could perform a spell." Étoile looked around the room, at the nodding heads. Sure, none of us liked the idea that someone here would betray us, but if a simple spell provided an answer, that seemed preferable.

Anders thought about it. Finally he said, "Do it."

"Wait," I said, as they turned, starting to leave. I grabbed Daniel's arm, pulling him to stand next to me and, for a moment, he looked panic-stricken. "I need to tell you something. Daniel and I need to tell you something." And I spilled. I told Anders and Evan what Étoile already knew, that Daniel was my cousin and that Auberon had wanted to recruit me too. I told them about Auberon and my mother being siblings and of the rift that had sprang between them, of the magic that had apparently skipped Auberon but was strong and clear in the rest of our family line.

When I finished, Daniel chipped in his version, telling us of Auberon's growing dissatisfaction with magic, of his conviction that witches needed to be eradicated. In a cool voice, he told us about the punishments he'd received for performing magic, for the times he'd been punished when he'd done nothing. But there was something that could not be explained. He told us about losing his mother, and how Auberon's madness got worse after that, and he began recruiting. The Brotherhood seemed like a cult to him at times. He told us what happened the day Auberon realised he could harness Daniel's magic and use it against us. Finally, exhausted, he collapsed into the chair by Anders' desk, his head in his hands and I stroked his back softly, the way a mother would a child.

Étoile was, surprisingly the most sympathetic, but then I remembered that she understood what it was like to have a family member targeted and exploited. "We'll help you, Daniel," she said, patting him awkwardly on the head. "And no, you're not homeless. Let's think of this as more of a homecoming."

He raised his head out of his hands to look up at her and I could feel the fizzling, nervous energy contained within him.

"Any more family members we need to know about?" Evan asked.

"That's it from the Morgans," said Daniel. "Just me and Auberon. And if he's dead, then... just me."

"And me," I said. "You're not alone." And neither was I now; I had a relative.

"If there is a traitor, we need to find him or her fast," interrupted Anders. "Let's call everyone to the barn. We won't all fit in the house. You can head out the kitchen door, the barn's unlocked."

Anders made his way past us, sticking his head in and out of rooms, passing on his instructions.

"Let's go," said Evan, herding us on. As we passed into the hallway, Bree joined us.

"Bree, this is Daniel, my cousin. You haven't met properly yet," I said to her.

Bree smiled at him. "Hello," she said, her voice like a whisper.

"Daniel likes plants," I told her. "He's very good at growing things." She smiled a little more brightly at Daniel and turned to walk alongside him, asking him about what he grew. If nothing else, at least I'd gotten Daniel a friend, another person to reassure him as we followed the line of people making their way to the barn.

"Uncle Auberon, eh?" said Evan, softly so no one else could hear us.

"Don't remind me," I muttered back. "All my life, I wondered if I had a family, and this is what I get?"

"I don't get any sense of malice from Daniel." Evan pulled me to one side, and I saw we were in what appeared to be a garden, bordered by a stone wall. A little further was the barn, the lights flickering on, briefly lighting up the courtyard and the fields beyond. Étoile walked past, frowning at us but I waved her on. "But keep your head together. If his father lives, and he appeals to him, it might be hard for Daniel to resist. People do all kinds of stupid things."

"You really think Auberon would reach out to Daniel?"

"I think he'd do anything to destroy every last one of you, including Daniel. He'd mourn him, but he'd think he'd done the right thing. That's his twisted reality. I don't want you to be a casualty of that."

"Ditto," I said, because there wasn't much else to say after that. "Let's go hear what Anders has to say."

CHAPTER SEVENTEEN

People seemed to emerge from everywhere, far more than could have been in the house or garden. By the time Evan and I walked in, making our way behind the assembling crowd, to Étoile and Daniel, it struck me that there were close to fifty people and still more streaming in. The barn easily held us all; it seemed to be a storage facility for animal feed and farming equipment of some variety, everything stacked in orderly piles. I perched on a hay bale, my side aching and my legs heavy while I tried to stifle a yawn.

Some of Bree's folk had arrived. None were quite as pale as she, but they had the same ethereal quality she possessed and some were barefoot, despite the cold. She moved away from us to stand with them.

I spotted Beau, searching the small crowd, before he saw us and waved him over. When he saw Annalise, he grasped her in a bear hug, completely oblivious to the people around us and kissed her full and hard on the lips. "I'm never letting you out of my sight," he told her.

"No one ever greets me like that," muttered Étoile, trying not to smile.

I nudged her in the ribs. "Don't look at me. I'm not that into you, but Jay wouldn't take any persuading." I reminded her of the Wilding wolf she had been out with a few times and she smiled happily.

"Knew you liked him," I teased.

"Yes, I do, and hush," replied Étoile. "I'm not going to tell you a thing."

"Spoilsport."

"Friends," Anders called and we all turned to him. He spun slowly in a circle, spreading his arms out, including everyone. "I thank you for your help in assisting us with retrieving our sister witch, Stella Mayweather. The Brotherhood lies in ruins." A solitary cheer went up and there was some clapping. "That does not mean we have defeated them," he continued, more ominously. "We must continue our fight for freedom from their persecution. It's time for us to rise up!"

"He'd make a great politician," whispered Étoile in my ear. It was my turn to shush her.

Anders turned again, silently this time, and the whispers that sprang up around the barn fell silent. His next words pealed out across the barn. "But we suspect there is a traitor in our midst. Someone has sold out to the Brotherhood. Someone has betrayed us."

A low rumble travelled around the assembled crowd as they darted looks at us. I glanced up at Evan, stock still, staring them down, slightly reassured when he squeezed my hand. Anders' people seemed slightly less welcoming now, though I might have imagined it. Maybe it wasn't that they thought we were traitors, but that we were the accusers. They were right, we were the ones disturbing their relative peace and I knew exactly how it felt to find out that someone close to you was working against you. Though I hoped we were wrong, I knew we weren't. I took my cue from Evan and Étoile and didn't flinch or fidget. Instead, I stared straight back and refused to be intimidated.

"We ask that person to step forward." Anders looked about him. Not a single person moved. He nodded, like he'd expected that. "Again, I ask that the person step forward so that they can explain themselves." He waited a few seconds, then glanced towards me, then Étoile. She inclined her head and something imperceptible passed between them.

Drawing a canister from his pocket, Anders shook it briefly then walked in a tight circle, spraying a larger circle on the floor around him. As he walked around twice more, Étoile and I linked hands, waiting as the spell fell from Anders' lips.

"They're the traitors," shouted a voice. "Or their daemon is!"

Anders repeated the spell, enunciating every word carefully and, this time, Étoile and I joined him, lending what power we could. After a moment, I heard Daniel, too.

I could feel the magic in the air; I could feel it searching. One more time, and the traitor would be pulled forward. We were close to finishing our second round when Evan leapt at us, pushing us to the ground. Overhead, the air parted as something sailed past to lodge in the wooden strut holding up the upper level of the barn. When I looked up, I grimaced. Wedged there was an axe. "Whoever it is, they are telekinetic," Evan whispered. "Anders would know who amongst his coven has that sort of power."

"And they're in this room," said Étoile. "You were right, Stella."

"I wish I wasn't."

We scrambled to our feet. Most of the witches remained still, even though they didn't look too happy about the turn of events. The nymphs looked startled and they huddled together, slightly away from all the witches. Anders was unmoving in the middle of us, his eyes searching the crowd. Then he started to glow. No, it wasn't a glow; magic was pouring from him, filtering into the air. I could feel its power and purity. The barn doors slammed shut, bolts shot into place from the outside. Anders had us all trapped.

"Stella, I don't think Anders is just any witch."

I looked at Étoile sharply. "What do you mean?"

"I mean, he's not just coven master of this region, I think he's the head of the UK. Possibly more by default than design, given that so many are dead," she added. "But he's powerful. I wasn't sure before but I am now. Can you feel it?"

I nodded. Magic rolled in waves from him. "We're teamed up with the head honcho without knowing it?" I asked and waited while Étoile nodded. "Yay for us!"

"Not so 'yay' right now. He's angry. Let's finish the spell." We stayed low. Gage and Annalise moved over to us, then they and Evan surrounded us as we completed the chant. The magic reached out, rolling around us and reaching back for Anders. At first, it seemed like nothing was happening and I wondered if our magic conflicted with Anders. Or if his powerful spellcraft had weakened ours in some way. Or if I were simply too weak to boost the power that the spell needed.

A shuffling and a shout went up and I searched for where it came from, finally finding it. A fight had erupted on the far side of the barn. A couple of people were pushing and shoving and one of them went down, rolling into a ball to avoid being trampled. Climbing back up on the hay bale, I stood carefully, straining to get a better view. No, they weren't fighting; they seemed to be defending themselves as a person was dragged through them by invisible hands. She was kicking and fighting and grabbing at people, trying to keep from being dragged to the circle Anders drew. Momentarily shocked, the people were trying to help her. Then, as they realised what was going on, they started hitting back, trying to free themselves from her grasping hands.

The woman fell to her knees, the power of the spell still yanking her to the circle, despite how hard she dug her nails into the floor and scrabbled for some kind of hold. The magic was too strong and it pulled her to the circle where she lay, panting. She pushed onto hands and knees, kneeling for a moment, then got to her feet. Pushing her hair back, she searched for Anders and it all seemed to click into place. There was only one person who knew all the details of the plan, of every step where we had been foiled. Then there was the phone call Auberon had curtly dismissed in front of me. It wasn't something he missed, but a woman calling.

Rachel Kelly.

Anders stared back at her, his face completely blank but for a brief flicker of pain. He folded his arms, waiting for something.

"It's a trick!" Rachel's shout rang loud and clear across the barn. "They've tricked you. They're tricking all of you!"

"You're the traitor." Anders' words echoed in the sudden silence and I couldn't tell if he were angry, disappointed, or sad. Probably all three.

"They're working for the Brotherhood." Rachel flung a hand towards us, pointing and the crowd seemed to break, leaving a clear path towards us. Suddenly aware of how vulnerable I was, I stood high up above the others. I bent over, placing my hands on Evan's shoulders and he lifted me down, tucking me into his side as Rachel ranted. "This has been their plan all along. To lure you all out to the same location, then kill you all."

The crowd murmured again, looking from each other, to us, and then to Rachel.

"Seriously," whispered Étoile. "This is her defence?"

"There's no one here but us, Rachel," said Anders, silencing everyone again. It grew so quiet, it was like they were the only two in the room. Gradually, all attention turned to them and the silence became unnerving. "And they're not traitors. Why? Why betray us?" He grasped her by the arms, looking down at her. "Tell us and we can help you. You don't have to be afraid."

"I'm not afraid." She laughed, mocking him.

"But you are a traitor."

"I'm an entrepreneur."

"They killed my sister, and you're working with

them?" Anders was incredulous. "What the hell do they have over you that would make you help them?"

"I would never have hurt you. I only told them about the tunnel. They wouldn't have hurt you, I promise. That was part of the deal."

"Are you fucking stupid? They shot Stella. They would have killed all of us if they'd had the chance."

"No, no, that wasn't the deal."

"What was the deal? Do they have someone of yours? Is it blackmail? What is it, Rachel? What prompted you make a deal with the devil?"

"Money. Enough to get me away from here forever. I hate this place."

"Money?" Anders spat the word back at her, his face darkening.

"Everyone has a price, Anders."

"Not I."

Étoile pinched my arm and I looked at her quickly. "How much?" she said.

"Fifty pence?" I guessed, shushing her.

Anders stepped away from Rachel, striding several paces before wheeling around, staring at her like he couldn't believe what he was hearing. She reached for him, her toe scuffing the circle as she stepped out of it.

"Why isn't the circle holding her?" I asked.

"It's not supposed to," Étoile replied. We were still talking in whispers, careful not to draw attention away from Anders and Rachel. I had the feeling combustion was imminent and it would take very little to ignite the match. All we could hope for now was that Anders was very, very careful. After all, these were Rachel's people as much as they were his, and we were just the unfortunate outsiders. "All it had to do was draw her out."

"Then she can escape?" Looking about me, at the soft hum of the magic navigating the barn, I realised Anders had already thought of that. He trapped us all here until it ended, one way or the other. We only thought of the spell to lure her out, but he'd gone further. He left nothing to chance.

Étoile didn't have time to reply, not that I needed her confirmation now, because Anders was speaking again, loud enough for everyone else to hear. "You have betrayed us. You put every single person in this room at risk. You cannot be trusted." He stopped, waiting while everyone absorbed his words. "I vote to bind and banish Rachel. You will no longer have power. You will no longer be welcome in this coven or in our community. You will be dead to us." He raised his hand, his palm flat towards us, unwavering. "All those in favour, raise your right hand."

There was a long pause in which Rachel started to smile. Then it faded as one by one, the hands went up through the crowd, every face hostile, but this time it was directed squarely at her. Anders stared at her too, like he had never truly seen her before.

"You can't bind me," she hissed, fury bubbling from her. "You can't make that decision."

"You betrayed the coven," Anders emphasised. The coven began to link hands, spreading in a circle around them both. "You sold us out. Turning you out with your magic would be like throwing a bomb up in the air and just standing there, waiting, while it lands. You're dangerous."

"You can't turn me out. The Brotherhood will kill me." Rachel reached for Anders' hands, drawing him to her, but he shrugged her away, stepping back as her hands fell to her sides.

"But it's okay to give them Stella?" he asked.

"She's not even one of us," Rachel hissed. "What is she to you? What are any of them to you? Come away with me, Anders, please. We've talked about this. Hawksley is a dead end. There's no future for us here. I don't know why you've waited so long."

Anders stepped back, just another pace, enough to put distance between them. "Bind her," he commanded. "Bind her magic."

She flew at him, her fists flailing. Anders didn't even have to touch her to push her back; the force of his magic was enough. She pleaded, then screamed as the coven worked together to bind her. They weren't just trapping her magic inside, but suppressing it completely, binding it and leaving no way out. I'd bound a witch once, and saw what happened when another witch's magic was restored after the binding was broken, but Anders' coven left nothing to chance. They gave her no escape clause. Within minutes, her magic was gone, leaving her crumpled on the floor, screaming, then crying, finally, just a puddle of weak little sobs.

Anders took one last look at Rachel. "Get rid of her," he told someone to his right. "I don't want to see her in Hawksley ever again." He walked away, the barn doors flying open in front of him. Behind him, a man and a woman hauled her up and walked quickly towards the doors. Rachel, at last, was silent. She looked stunned, too stunned to speak, like she could hardly believe what had just happened.

"I hope it was worth it," muttered Étoile, turning her back.

"If this was pack, she wouldn't have walked out

alive," said Gage, ignoring Annalise when she shushed him. "She should be grateful Anders showed her mercy."

"I'm going to see if he's okay," I said, sliding out from under Evan's arm, starting to make my way through the still crowd. Turning back, I said, "Give me five minutes, okay?" and waited just long enough to see Evan nod.

No one seemed to know what to do once Anders strode out and Rachel had been taken away. I had to make my way past the milling people to get outside. The sun was just beginning to rise far away over the fields and somewhere a rooster crowed. As I scanned the yard, trying to find Anders, a pair of headlights flicked on and a car pulled out. I could just make out Rachel in the back seat. She stared straight ahead, not even bothering to struggle as the car approached the gates then swung out onto the road. I didn't wait to watch it go; instead, I turned back to the yard.

For the first time, I got to see Anders' home properly and, although the light wasn't great, it was chocolate box pretty farmhouse with small windows and a slate roof. Someone had planted bushes in beds all around the garden. Now they were dusted slightly with the early morning frost. A long gravel driveway swept around the side of the house and I could just see my rental car parked in the shade of the barn. A long road stretched past the house from both directions at the front. I couldn't see Anders, so I walked further around the back, observing everything. The driveway ended in a big courtyard with fields beyond, stretching far into the half-light. It was rural and very peaceful. I couldn't imagine an odder place for magic to exist.

Spotting Anders sitting on a low wall at the junction of the house and garden, I crossed over to him, passing through the small garden gate and crossing the lawn. He was sitting slightly hunched over, hands folded under his arms for warmth and staring off into the distance.

"Are you all right?" I asked, stepping over the wall and settling down next to him.

"Three bloody years I've been with that woman and she would have sold us all out."

I didn't quite know what to say to that. We sat in silence for a while until I said, "I'm sorry."

"You've nothing to be sorry for." A sudden noise behind us made him glance back. Checking over my shoulder, I noticed people filing from the barn, some getting into cars and leaving, some aiming for the house. Anders hopped down from the wall, holding his hand out to me. "Come on. Let's walk a while."

Anders led us along a path by the side of the house and down to another field where he rested his hands over the top of a wall. I propped myself up against him, wincing at the exercise. My wound might look healed, but it was going to take a few days for it to feel right inside. "You okay?" he asked.

"I'll live." We stood there, thinking about that before I said, "If I hadn't come here, you could have kept your eye on the Brotherhood. We might have had the opportunity to find out more." I trailed off when Anders made a sceptical noise.

"Maybe it's a good thing that you're here. Perhaps it's time we made the Council listen."

"Étoile is the right person to talk to about that."

"Do you know anything about this?" Anders reached into his pocket and pulled out an envelope.

He studied it for a moment before passing it to me. When I opened it, a familiar card slid out. A summons.

"I got one a week ago. Étoile, too," I told him.

"Do you know who's running for the Council?"

I shook my head. "Don't know. I'm not exactly at the top of the Council's secret phone tree."

Anders huffed. When he turned to me, he was sober as a judge when I asked, "You ever thought of running?"

"For the Council or away?"

"Away."

I thought of Georgia Thomas' face the last time I saw her. Having her as Council leader didn't even bear thinking about. I doubted there was much I could do to change that, but I could, at least, make my vote count in a different direction, assuming the summons meant I got one. "You have got to be kidding," I said. "Running away does no good for anyone." I gulped when I realised Anders might take that as a huge criticism of Rachel's actions. A decision to run hadn't helped her either, or anyone else.

"How did they know to send you a summons?" I asked.

"Perhaps they're not as ignorant as I thought," mused Anders. "Or maybe it's just magic."

"Just magic." I smiled. Anders turned to me and surprised me by smiling too, repeating my words with a laugh. "Never thought I'd say that."

"So this summit... You are going?" Anders pressed.

"Yes."

"Then I suppose I'll see you there."

"I suppose you will."

"It's cold, Stella, and I don't like to keep you out when you've been hurt. Wouldn't want you to get ill."

"I don't mind sitting with you, if you want the company." I knew a dismissal when I heard one, but I offered anyway.

"Thanks, but I'll take some alone time. I like the early mornings, the sunsets. Rachel never did, she never really liked the life here." He stared out at the dawn.

"You'll be okay," I whispered.

He didn't turn his head. "I know."

I left Anders there to enjoy watching the sun rise, hoping that it would help ease his first steps towards putting Rachel behind him, not that things are ever easy. But seeing the beauty in something natural, after something so ugly, was always a good start.

The nymphs were the first to go, disappearing into the woods just as the dawn broke and the birds started to sing. They'd been a quiet sort, able to calm the agitated witches. I noticed that Bree and Daniel talked quietly a lot and she waved cheerfully to him as she went, following her kinfolk.

Next went the wolves, who had taken to setting up a camp of sorts in the garden. Some of them left in cars, some of them melting into the woods. I guessed that they must have been helping run interference as per Anders' plan and that was why I hadn't seen many of them until now. Gage and Annalise had been sorry to see the local wolves go. Then Annalise and Beau slunk off to the barn to talk in peace and I decided it wasn't worth losing a limb to interrupt and ask how they found their brethren.

"Hey."

I spun around and smiled when I saw Gage. "Hey

yourself."

"Can we talk for a moment? Alone."

"Yes, of course."

We walked away from where Anders sat, still silently staring at the fields, and around to the small parking area, now empty.

"I wanted to say thank you for everything you did for Annalise," he started.

"I only did what any friend would do."

"Not many friends would put themselves in danger. You got shot, Stella." He leant against my car, his face shadowed.

"Everyone came to help, not just me," I pointed out, uncomfortable with any kind of hero status. "Étoile told me Evan came to see you in Wilding, to help."

"Yeah, he really came through. His demon friend, Micah, helped coordinate the search in Wilding. We even flew over together; Evan, Beau, and me. He helped us negotiate with the local wolves to come help us. He and Beau came up with new tactics for Anders' plan to draw the guards out front, away from the house."

I smiled. Evan's business clearly put him in good stead for organising getaways. "Good."

Gage's next words stopped me still. "It came with a price."

"Wha... What do you mean?" I stuttered, puzzled by the stiff line of his jaw and the dark look that flashed across his face.

"You sure you wanna know?"

I took a deep breath. Did I want to know? Did I want to know what condition Evan had stipulated in return for helping save my friend? What could Gage possibly give him in return for his assistance? "Out with it, Gage," I said, bracing myself.

"For his support, for his help in getting Annalise out of there, he made me promise that I would stay away from you."

"But we're neighbours," I protested, realising immediately I was being way too literal. Gage was clearly talking about something that concerned Evan far more: our very brief past when we kissed, and more than once. "Oh," I said, flatly.

"I swore," Gage continued, his voice laced with anger and resentment. "I swore to Evan, I wouldn't pursue you, that I wouldn't do anything to make you doubt your relationship with him. No matter how much you got under my skin, I swore that I would never make a move on you even though you and I both know that I want to."

I was quiet for a moment, absorbing that. "You have a girlfriend," I said, at last, like that solved everything. "Michelle."

"Michelle isn't my girlfriend. We've been on a few dates, that's all. It's nothing serious."

I shook my head, looking away, unable to look at him. The short distance between us could be a chasm now and I had no idea how to breach it, to keep our friendship. "Evan shouldn't have said anything like that to you," I said, after I thought about it for a moment. "That was wrong. He should never have put any kind of condition on helping Annalise."

"Yeah, well, he did. Look, I respect Evan. He's a good guy and he said something stupid because he loves you. I get that, I do. Do I think he's the right guy for you? Maybe not, but that's because I'm me and he's him. Do I hope that you'll give me a chance some day? Yeah, I do." Gage looked at me, his eyes burning bright. "I'm glad I, we, got Annalise back. My sister's safety was the most important thing and we got her back. I'm grateful. But I thought you should know what he said. Whether that's because I'm looking out for you, or because I want you mad at him... I don't know. Maybe both."

Gage went inside the house without a backwards glance and, a few minutes later, when I could put one foot in front of the other, I found him stretched out on the sofa, fast asleep. I covered him with a blanket and figured any more questions I had would wait for another time.

I found Étoile and Evan in the kitchen. "Daniel's taken the spare room upstairs," she said. "I'm going to find somewhere to sleep too."

"Gage is on the sofa."

"Not for long," Étoile said, and winked as she left the room. I suspected Gage would hit the floor within the next few minutes.

"What about you? Tired?" asked Evan.

"Worn out," I confessed. The day's events, my injuries, Gage's bombshell were all speeding up on me. "It feels like the world's longest day. I can't remember the last time I slept properly. I want a warm bed, a soft pillow and fluffy covers."

"Will you take the study floor, a pile of blankets and me?"

I stood on tiptoes, kissed him, and pulled him in the direction of the study. He didn't need to ask me twice. "Absolutely." I could wait for his explanation, for his side of the story because I owed him that. After all, I had been the one who charged here, and Evan had come, condition or not, to help. I refused to believe he wouldn't have come. If Gage had said no, I doubted Evan would have even considered walking away. I yawned, slapping a hand over my mouth as Evan pushed the door shut behind us. We had plenty of time to talk this through. Right now, all I wanted was pure sleep.

CHAPTER EIGHTEEN

"Go away," I said, pushing at the hands that were shaking me awake. A pair of lips landed on mine, kissing me into the land of awake. "Much better," I murmured, forcing my eyes open. For a moment, I didn't have a clue where I was, then the past few hours came rushing back to me all at once. The escape, the collapsing tunnel, being shot, Rachel Kelly's exile and Anders' surprise summons.

"Hey, sleepyhead. Time to wake up." Evan's voice had just a note of amusement as his hands reached my sides, just above my wound, tickling until I pushed him away.

"I haven't been asleep nearly long enough," I complained, burrowing back under the blankets we'd scavenged and arranged on the floor. It didn't have a hope of being as good as a bed, but we curled up together and I'd fallen asleep quickly. Speaking of beds, I missed mine.

"They're waiting for us."

"Tell them you couldn't wake me up," I mumbled,

307

pulling Evan to me, but it was half hearted because my stomach ached... hell, everything ached. I was definitely taking it easy for a couple of weeks when I got home. "Let's have 'I missed you' sex."

"On the floor of Anders' study?" asked Evan.

"With us watching?" asked Étoile. I cranked open an eye, looking up to see Étoile and behind her Annalise standing in the open doorway. I saw Beau walk past, pausing to kiss Annalise's cheek. Étoile looked amused, perky even; Annalise meanwhile was sporting several unattractive shades of black and blue.

"You could leave," I suggested hopefully.

"I'll make her coffee double strength," offered Annalise, edging out with a wave of her lightly bandaged hand. "You've got five minutes, guys."

"You could do it twice in that time," Étoile teased and followed Annalise out, closing the door behind her.

Evan lay down next to me. "I think she just insulted me."

"You must have really grown on her."

"Lucky me. Time to get up, Stella. We've got things to do and time waits for no witch."

I got ready in the bathroom seeing as Anders wanted his study back and it was there that I realised the source of my stomachache, and that I wasn't pregnant. Sitting on the floor for a moment, I counted to ten slowly, waiting for relief, or disappointment, or something to hit me. While I had no doubt that I would probably enjoy being a mother someday, enjoy having a family of my own, it wasn't going to be soon, and that was okay by me. I wasn't in a hurry. I had a lot to do first, things to see, college to organise, several days of work to catch up on for sure. I hadn't even discussed the subject with Evan, nor the surprise of thinking I was pregnant. That would be something to add on to that talk we're going to have very soon.

After I got over the idea that it was really rude to go through someone else's cabinets, I scrabbled in Anders' bathroom cabinet and found some things Rachel had left behind which would do until I went to a shop. With the worry of motherhood now off my mind, I went downstairs with a spring in my step.

I found Evan and drew him outside, seeing as it was the only place we could talk alone. Evan made a coat appear and slid it around my shoulders, though he seemed impervious to the cold. We had some talking to do and we needed to do it quickly. "I know what you said to Gage," I told him. "I know that you put a condition on helping him."

Evan rolled his eyes.

"So, it's true then?" I persisted.

"Yes, I told him to back off but you've got to understand this, Stella. Even if he had told me to go to hell, I would still have come. I would still have helped both of you. There was never any question of that."

"So what was the point?" I asked. I guessed, but I wanted to hear it nevertheless.

"I knew when I found you that things happened with Gage. I knew that he kissed you when I walked out and I know that if I had never found you, maybe you would have loved him instead. I'm not blind. I see how he looks at you. I just wanted him to know that you were off limits." He ran a hand through his short crop of hair, and I think I saw a touch of chagrin. "I wanted him to be clear that you are with me."

"You couldn't just have trusted me? I'm with you. I want you. I love *you*," I reminded him as I poked his chest lightly, smiling at him. I could have gotten mad, I could have shouted, but where would that have gotten us? So, he did something stupid. For all his power, he wasn't infallible.

"You're not mad at me?" he asked cautiously.

I stepped closer, sliding into his arms. "I should be, but I'm not. Just trust me in the future, okay? I know there are some issues there so I don't expect you to like him, or trust him, but I do and I hope you will. Gage is my friend and nothing is going to happen between us, I promise."

"Okay," Evan said at last and I felt his chest rise and fall as he held me lightly, like I was fragile. Given how sore my whole body felt, he wasn't far from the truth. "Okay," he said again. Then Étoile was at the door beckoning us inside and we were pulled into the warmth of Anders' home.

An hour later, after two cups of coffee, three slices of thickly buttered toast, and my attempt to make myself look vaguely presentable, Anders suggested we go to see what was left of Hawkscroft.

We piled into Anders' car, a huge Land Rover Defender that had seen better days, and drove the short way to Hawkscroft. I half expected him to drive right up to the house, a thought that made a cold shiver run through me, but instead of taking the country roads that led that way, Anders swung the Land Rover away, finally parking on the side of a road. We followed him along a country track, worn by thousands of feet, over a stile dissecting the fence, and up a hill where we stopped, gazing down at the house, close enough to have a bird's eye view, far enough that we wouldn't get in anyone's way.

"The first floor took most of the damage," said Étoile, pointing to where windows had blown out.

"We call it the ground floor here," I murmured, but semantics aside, she was right. The fire damage was extensive. Piles of smouldering debris lay on the charred lawn, curtains, furnishings and other things all contributed to the mess. Some windows gaped, their glass spattering the gravel and lawns, including what looked like the windows to the library where I sat with Auberon Morgan. The ground floor seemed to have borne the brunt of the damage while the upper floor appeared to be largely unscathed.

"Look over there," said Annalise. Beau stood next to her, his arms crossed as looked over the scene. He hadn't left her side since they were reunited, not hovering, but always there if she needed anything. It would probably take a long time before he didn't worry every minute that he wasn't with her. "Is that... was that the tunnel?"

I followed the line of her hand, taking in the sunken strip of earth that ran away from the house. After two hundred yards or so, it abruptly stopped, the rest of the grounds shaky but intact. Two police officers stood back while their sniffer dogs circled the area, pausing to smell the grass and racing back whenever some of the ground crumbled away.

"Doesn't look like they found anyone down there," Annalise continued. "Maybe they all ran back to the house."

Looking around, at the one solitary police car and the two fire engines, bright red under the cool morning sun, I said, "It doesn't look like anyone is

311

too interested in investigating. I mean, there would be more police, wouldn't there?"

"If a gas explosion is the official cause, they wouldn't look further," replied Evan.

"What about the bodies you found last night?" I asked, when I remembered that I hadn't asked when he first told us. "Wouldn't they show foul play?"

"Their necks were snapped. It could be passed off as a fall, or, given the number of them, from being thrown back by the explosion," said Evan.

"So Auberon is just going to get off?" I couldn't keep the disappointment out of my voice. It seemed so wrong that all this had happened, and he wouldn't be punished.

"Unless he's over there." Evan pointed to the gravel driveway. Laid out on the ground were several bundles wrapped in thick plastic, long zippers up the front. It took me a moment to realise they weren't more debris, but body bags, with bodies. I looked away quickly.

Hawkscroft had looked like such an impressive, imposing house but in the cold daylight, with its windows hanging open, trails of water seeping out the front doors and over the steps, it only looked sad and depressed. People moved in and around the house like worker ants, busily scurrying here and there. Occasionally, a call or an order would carry on the wind, reaching our viewing spot. I wondered what would happen if anyone turned to look up at us. Would they think we were morbid onlookers? Perhaps we were.

I was vaguely aware of Daniel moving around Anders and coming to stand next to me. He found a scarf and wrapped it up around his chin, his shoulders hunched. I squeezed his hand. "Sorry."

He shrugged but didn't let go. "It had to happen."

"I'm sorry anyway. This was your home."

"This was a prison." He took one last look at Hawkscroft, damaged and unable to hold him anymore, and turned away, starting the steady descent down the grassy slope.

"What happens to Daniel now?" I asked no one in particular when I was sure he was out of earshot.

Anders looked at Daniel's retreating figure. "We'll look after him. Train him to use his magic. He can live at the farm with me. Bree said she might like him as an apprentice so he'll have work if he wants it."

"Is that wise?" asked Evan. He was still suspicious, I could tell. Daniel had been an intricate part of the Brotherhood for his whole life, and their way to find and track witches, as well as their protection. Daniel was a valuable asset and they'd lost him. Even I could see they wouldn't be willing to give him up so easily. Plus, Morgan was Daniel's father. There was no telling what sort of scars, or blood-loyalty, lay there, though I suspected there was none, but my word might not be enough to secure Daniel's tenuous position in the community.

"We have to give him the benefit of the doubt. He's one of our own." Anders' voice was firm. "Plus, we can show him a different life as a witch, a more natural life. It will be part of his rehabilitation."

"Before you put him back into the wild?"

"Yep." Anders and I shared a smile before he added, "And his intel, whatever he is, will mean a lot." *Ah, witches. Always an ulterior motive and may I never forget it.*

"The Council will be interested to hear," mused

Étoile. "If Morgan survived this, we need to know where to find him, not just the identities of the members of this organisation. Someone has protected them from prosecution all these years. We need to know who. If things change with the Council soon, we'll be better prepared."

"You really think he survived?" I couldn't bring myself to mutter Morgan's name. Calling him uncle was even more unlikely. I was having a hard time accepting that we were related, that he was my mother's brother. For years, I wondered about my parents, finally laying them to rest a year ago. After that, I found out a little about my father's family and nothing about my mother's until these past few days. I should have prepared myself for the worst, but I didn't think anything could be as bad as the truth I now knew.

Gage took a long sniff of the air. "He isn't among the bodies."

"Maybe he's still inside the house?" I was glad Daniel couldn't hear the almost hopeful note in my voice. Perhaps I was a cruel person to wish someone dead, especially when his son would have to bear the memory and the loss harder than I, but I couldn't help it. Having Morgan gone would be a huge relief.

"I don't think so," said Annalise. "But there are other bodies in there. That man who hurt us, the one missing teeth, he's one of the dead but they haven't found him yet."

"May he rot in hell," added Beau.

I didn't say anything to that. To confess relief would feel wrong, but I felt it, felt glad even that the world was rid such an awful excuse for a human being.

"Even if Morgan were dead, the Brotherhood is a large organisation. There will be someone to take his place." Evan was solemn. He hadn't spoken to me much last night about everything that happened and I sensed he was worried more than angry. I put everyone in danger by coming here. Was it worth it to ensure Annalise's life? Did the one matter more than the many? In this moment, for me, it did. Still, it was too late for regrets now. Perhaps some things were best left unspoken. I slipped my hand into Evan's, holding my breath as his fingers closed over mine. He looked down at me and smiled slightly as I leaned into him.

It was over.

We might not have won the war yet, but we'd won a battle. For now.

"I'll go check on Daniel. Make sure he's okay," offered Étoile, striding off after him. "Meet you back at the car."

"You're all welcome to stay," Anders said, but he was looking at me. Offering me the chance to come home. One glance told me everything he wanted me to know: that I could return home to my country, the one I'd fled, and start again. If he'd asked me on one of summer's blazing hot days, instead of on this windswept hill overlooking the place I'd been held captive, and a party to destroying, I might have been more open to the idea.

"Thanks for the offer," I said, because I was polite, at least. "I appreciate it."

"No problem. You're welcome any time." Anders moved off to talk to Gage, Annalise and Beau but I saw Gage glancing at me and knew he heard Anders' offer and hoped I wasn't going to take it. But it wasn't his choice to make, even if he wished it were.

I turned away as Evan gave my hand a little tug and we walked off, just far enough to talk without being overheard. I was looking forward to some real alone time with him, and some time to heal too, but waiting at home was Kitty, probably worried out of her mind. Étoile would be coming home with us too. Perhaps some time at Evan's home might be the cure. I was pretty sure I could put up with Micah for a couple of weeks, if I tried.

"Do you want to stay, Stella?" Evan's voice, for once, was unsure. Looking up at him, I wondered how much it cost him to say that. He made a lot of sacrifices for me, living where I wanted, managing his business from afar. Now he was giving me the option to stay in my home country. I couldn't help wonder what it would mean for him, for us, if I chose to stay. He pressed on, "This is your home, your country."

"No," I said, with absolute certainty. Slipping my hand from his, I moved in closer, wrapping my arms around his waist. After a moment, Evan's arm slid around me, hugging me into his warm body as I thought about how my life had changed. I had a home to call my own, a boyfriend I loved and cherished who made me happy, friends I cared about, a job I enjoyed. My life shone with potential. I had none of those things in my own country, the soil on which I now stood. I didn't want to lose any of it. One day, I would come back, but it wouldn't be today and it wouldn't be forever. Though I was open to visiting, now I knew I had someone to come back for and maybe even friends to see.

The wind rose around us, sending leaves scattering into the air in a colourful dance and I watched them for a moment before I spoke again. "No, I want to go home."

*Continue the Stella Mayweather series with Magic Rising,
out now in ebook and paperback!*

For Stella, the Witches' Council Summit is supposed to be about getting to know her fellow witches but instead she finds herself on trial for murder. The accusations may be evidence of a sinister plot at work or they may be a ruse to draw attention away from the mounting tensions as the witches vie for supremacy. Reaching out to her boyfriend Evan for help would be reassuring… if he wasn't oddly unreachable, working a case even his closest friend doesn't know anything about.

As the ominous reasons behind the trial come to light, an assassin unleashes a terrifying campaign against the Council candidates. With tensions running high and accusations flying faster than a backfiring spell, the witches are forced to gather together for safety, but that might just lead to an implosion as the culprit is sought.

Plus there's the small matter of an ancient talisman the werewolves want, a talisman that they say was stolen, but the more she investigates, the more it appears that it isn't the simple artefact they claim it to be.

With Evan still missing and her world more complicated than ever, the choices Stella must make might confirm her place as a formidable witch in her new world or leave her excommunicated… forever.

www.ingramcontent.com/pod-product-compliance
Lightning Source LLC
Chambersburg PA
CBHW020249200626
46816CB00001BA/196